T

DEATH OF A SUPERHERO

DEATH OF A SUPERHERO

ANTHONY MCCARTEN

ALMA BOOKS

ALMA BOOKS LTD
London House
243–253 Lower Mortlake Road
Richmond
Surrey TW9 2LL
United Kingdom
www.almabooks.com

Death of a Superhero first published by Random House Inc. NZ in 2005
This revised edition first published by Alma Books Limited in 2006
This paperback edition first published by Alma Books in 2007
Copyright © Anthony McCarten, 2006. Reprinted 2008
This new edition first printed by Alma Books Ltd in 2012

Printed in Great Britain by CPI Group (UK) Ltd, Croydon CR0 4YY

ISBN: 978-1-84688-287-6

FOR MY SONS

CONTENTS

DEATH OF A SUPERHERO

ACT ONE

Fade in... DONALD DELPE. Fourteen years old. A skinny kid, shoulders as meatless as coat-hangers. Odd-looking. No eyebrows, no hair. Face like a peeled potato. Walks paddle-footed down the streets of Watford into a stiff northerly umbrella-buster straight out of Siberia, a beanie pulled low on his head, music full-throttle via his earbuds wired to an iPod as he crosses the cloud-banked town. Anger is his default setting. Melancholy too. He looks at the ground most of the time. A sunflower in the rain.

His big problem? Sex is on his mind, as usual. Been this way for a couple of years now. Acid-tripping on testosterone, lonesome as hell, his every second thought X-rated. Were these mind movies ever to go out on general release, the film censors would have to cut them to ribbons for family audiences, bleeping and blanking and pixelating all the reality out them, until they became the 12A-rated sleeper which is all the world ever sees of Donald F. Delpe.

Flap, flap, flap go his size-elevens as he makes his way moodily across this town north of London, so familiar he can close his eyes at any moment and know just when to raise his step to avoid a misaligned slab of paving, or when to wheel left-right-left so as to place himself at his favourite table at the local KFC, the red plastic booth with arse-moulded chairs facing the window and the huge billboard across the road filled all four seasons with a magnificent example of womanhood writ large: a lingerie model ten metres wide, a vixen (his favourite word), whose man-high breasts are hammocked in a monster brassiere, a sling to string between trees, inside which he could happily while away his long life (if a long life had been an option for him): her elongated body reclines on its side, her football fields of flesh stippled by goose bumps as she stares across the road at Donald F. Delpe with a sultry, love-ready expression that for him bespeaks an ardent longing.

Is he sick in the head? Does the fact that this super-sized poster girl gives him a semi make him disturbed? Not at all. He's fourteen. A fourteen-year-old virgin. That a billboard should give him a semi is one of nature's brightest wonders.

But today he blows right by his gargantuan girl. He barely shoots her a hi-ya glance, for today he's busy, as busy as the streets around him, this town he often thinks he defends and protects – a once-sedate backwater that now is crazy-eyed and unblinking in the amphetamine rush of an overnight film industry, as the locals work overtime to make the most of the financial spin-offs to have arisen from the global box-office successes of the *Wizard's Apprentice* films, a rolling phenomenon that puts this satellite town on the map and makes A-list stars of its hitherto unknown B-rate actors.

The most visible impact of these films is that whole neighbourhoods of Watford and Leavesden parish have been turned into movie-studio back lots. Huge latex monsters menace the old arrivals hall at the tiny aerodrome; posters of malefic ghouls with bloodshot eyes and fang-cluttered gobs leer out from the windows of shops selling toasters and gas barbecues; a dragon twenty metres across has its talons sunk into the roof of the local picture house as if, with a flap of horny wings, it will carry the whole place away to hell.

It's high summer, 2006: the summer when nearly everyone feels they have tentative links with Hollywood, that land of fantasias so far away across the roiling sea; the summer when nearly everybody fancies themselves in show business and has begun to think in frames per second, dream in Panavision, see the world in montage, as scenes either brilliantly or poorly directed, as a series of smash-cuts and slow-fades to black, of lives as hits or flops, of relationships as comedies with cliché endings, of the Past as prequel and the Future as a franchise whose film rights are unencumbered – making all life, all of it, behave in the glorious nowness of the present tense common to film scripts, so that even the rubbish man is insomniac waiting for a call from his agent, and all the local barbers and bars display photos of staff with their arms wrapped around a star. It is the first summer in memory when an ordinary, hard-working, God-fearing life looks like an awfully dim choice compared with the brilliant projections of white light through celluloid. Donald walks through this population of extras, stand-ins, shortlisted body doubles, under-understudies, near-auditionees, relatives twice removed of bit-part players, wannabes of all kinds so excruciatingly close to the Big Time. But Don is happy just to keep his head down. Tracked by the sweep of a CCTV camera (for everyone is on film these days more or less), he is listening to his own jungle beat when, in the jargon of his beloved comic books, **DISASTER STRIKES!**

A child on foot. A speeding Toyota Corolla. Two incompatibles. Donald looks up from his shoes for the first time. His eyes narrow. Think laser vision, think telemetric lenses, think Clark Kent. From an impossible distance this funny kid foresees all that will unfold, and he starts to run, to run fast as a car, as the Corolla closes in on a child strayed into the road, a child too young to comprehend the peril she faces, having become detached from her father (who is babbling real-estate jargon on the kerb: "Well, Bruce, it all depends on whether it's indexed, whether it's pegged to the base rate..."), whilst the driver of the Corolla is also lost in a world of her own, thanks to the kids in the back just then fighting for control of the rear-seat entertainment system and turning an otherwise competent parent into the equivalent of a drunk in the throes of epilepsy, her eyes everywhere but on the child in her path. Sadly for everyone, Donald, our hero, even though he is running now, is surely too far away to be of help – there is no way on earth he can assist – and yet, with a reaction time that would allow you to survive *Grand Theft Auto* without recourse to a Bulletproof Vest and with a perfect "health" rating, he flips a skateboard from under the arm of a slack-jawed kid, kick-launches himself towards the emergency with extraordinary thrust, board-jumps the legs of a homeless man splayed crosswise on the footpath, even adds a competition-winning board-flip combination of vertical and horizontal spins just *because he can*, then banks into the road with zero concern for himself and scoops up the tyke in one arm, lifting her above the height of the oncoming bumper just as the death-delivering chrome careens to a halt

(**Screeeeeeeee!...**) five and a half centimetres from his Adidas sweatpants.

Freeze frame. Hold for five seconds. Awesome. MEGA-CLOSE!

By the time the clouds of blue tyre smoke dissipate, Donald has niftily back-flicked the board to its owner and reunited the nipper with her dickwit father, and is now strolling on as if nothing of consequence has occurred. The fact that four more vehicles then career into the back of the stopped Corolla (in slo-mo: **KRUNCH**, **DOOSH**, **KRANCH**, **KA-BOOM!!!**), creating the most God-awful pile of metallic origami, is of small import. It doesn't register with Don. He has to be somewhere.

The crowd is left to wonder only who the hell that kid is.

What is important to Donald right now is getting to the appointment for which his parents said he must not be late. He is on the move again, and does not look back as his brand-new iPod earbuds pound out a song at atom-splitting volume. It's his current favourite:

> I know you think I'm so uncouth
> It's just the pornography of youth,
> So don't be blamin' me, girl, cos it's the truth
> It's just the P.O.R.N.O. of youth
> Break it down.

Our hero reaches into his pocket to adjust the volume: upwards. The beat becomes life-threatening. Mind-altering. Lobotomizing. *Ooontz... Ooontz... Ooontz... Ooontz... Ooontz...* Then he stops. Is this the appointed place? An odd place to halt. He looks about him. Why is he standing midway across a railway track on a cross tie, his feet astride a rail? What kind of appointment would this be?

The sound of a goods train grows in magnitude, shaking the general environs. But instead of hurrying to safety, Donald glances down at his threadbare Vans on the oily sleeper and sees that a lace has come undone and needs attention at once. The left one has escaped the nest of his triple knotting and demands that he bend down onto one knee in slow genuflection, even as a hurtling locomotive rounds the corner. Slowly Don reties the lace from scratch, taking his time, undoing first the snarl of what remains until he has two straight threads to deal with and, beginning with the crossover, pressing his index finger down on the new junction (the way a doctor monitors a pulsing veinlet), then making two bows of equal size in the lace-tying style favoured by kids everywhere, before making a granny of the final result. Geronimo. His left lace is restored: a nice bow. And only then does he stand up and, with a sigh, step off the tracks the second – the very second! – 10,000 tonnes of metal hurtle by at his back, missing him by millimetres, so close that the train guillotines Donald's shadow at the neck.

MEGA-CLOSE!

Without looking back, insulated against the scream of the train's whistle by his earbuds, he continues on his way with nothing of what has happened showing in his general comportment. He notes only that he is now running a little late, and picks up speed. He jaywalks, takes short cuts, shuttles through traffic and people. He even turns into a blind alley off the High Street's café quarter and walks up to where it terminates in a solid brick wall four metres high. Where to from here? He looks at the wall, turns briefly to look over his shoulder, then sets his right trainer up on the brickwork, at ninety degrees to his body. Next, and with a concerted heave and swinging his hips up and forwards, he stabs his left trainer beside the first! Now in general defiance of Newtonian physics, he is horizontal, standing there. He sure hopes no one is watching.

Walking up the wall, then, as he would negotiate a slightly slippery pavement – a little gingerly, making sure of each step – a mere six paces takes him to the top, whereupon he throws his weight forwards again, expertly flipping vertical. *Voilà*. He is now standing on top of the wall, balanced, masterful, the late-morning sun on his face, his eyes closed for a second as he enjoys a moment's serenity before he opens them wide and looks down – looks down, down the sickening miles of the abysmal drop at his feet. For what should be a four-metre drop to the ground on the other side has become a vertiginous eighty-floor dive down the face of a skyscraper to a teeming city street not quite real, not entirely credible. What is going on here? What kind of wall is this, one side a low Watford abutment, the other the view down from an Empire State Building? Clearly, he is standing within a portal of some kind, a portal to a bustling megalopolis to which he has secret and unrestricted access. In a capitulation of consciousness, he doesn't baulk or turn back, but instead adjusts his backpack, takes a deep breath and, in command of his destiny, jumps...

He jumps. Geronimo. From the banal vantage of the Watford alleyway he is just a kid jumping over a wall. Nothing suicidal in this at all. But... but... if you know what Donald knows, then... then...

Sometimes all is not as it seems – eyes do not bear infallible witness, mystery and fact play tag and take turns at being *It* – because a mere fifteen minutes later this same young man is spotted in another part of Watford, safe, unhurt, unharmed in…

Cut to…

…A hospital wing, the appointed place and right on time, walking into the building just as expected, just as instructed by his parents, entering on foot and not via the electronic revolving doors out front but via a discreet side door known only to regular visitors.

One Doctor Fred Sipetka is there to meet him. Donald reaches into the well of his pocket to find, Braille-like, the indented Stop button on the iPod. The music dies in his ears, and the doctor smiles and sees that it is now possible to talk to him.

DOCTOR: Hello, Donald. All set then?

Don nods, and Sipetka leads him to an elevator. Together they rise, rise, rise eight floors in a whoosh to the top. When they emerge they bear right and pass through a swing door with a faded two-word sign overhead. Donald doesn't glance up as he passes under it. His eyes are on his shoes. Anyway, he knows what it says. It says "Cancer Wing".

Interior. Vestibule. Day.

JIM DELPE: How do you feel, son?

DONALD: Like puking.

The Delpes would call themselves disobedient Christians. While they ought to come to church to hear about rectitude and transcendence and the evangelizing spirit, this is not what they seek any more. Their needs are much more human, urgent and grounded. They come here looking for comfort.

This four-strong family arrives late. The Sunday Mass is already in progress.

The cast (in order of appearance):

RENATA DELPE, Don's mother, thin-lipped (late forties), the careful type. Values: hard work, diligence, love. This is her default setting. Trusts in life insurance, crosses her sevens, heeds precautionary advice wherever she can find it, and is forever looking for wood to touch just so she can say "Touch wood". She hopes by this to be spared the worst that life can deal out, but the news is coming in fast that she is not to be spared. She is, however, still youthful, with the wellspring of a woman who is well-loved. This is not simply a matter of good fortune. This has been planned for too, laid in like supplies. She insists on affection and does not permit her husband, Jim, to succumb to any dereliction of duty in this area – and because he likes it that way, for her to crack the whip, to chivvy him along, then her marriage is one thing she doesn't need to worry about. As for her kids, they're another matter.

JIM DELPE (early fifties), six foot three, thinning hair, thickening girth, softly spoken. With quiet industry he has hauled himself to a position of respect both at home and at large. He is that rare thing: a selfless lawyer. Specializes in cases over Crown Land disputes but tacks on a little pro bono and Legal Aid work when he can. Jim S. Delpe, BCM, LLM (Bristol), is also available as coach for junior basketball. Used to play himself, could even jam it in his twenties, until his left knee gave out. Now, this quiet man is merely the most knowledgeable father in the stands when his boys play. When excited, he can show a different side – witness him, cupped hands around a shouting mouth: "Go to the hoop, go to the hoop, Donny!" – but it's rare. He is a determined, stubborn, persevering force. If he were a boat, he'd be a bulky old triple-huller, reliable, lumbering, good for punching through floe ice in the Northwest Passage.

JEFF DELPE (eighteen), Don's older brother. For most of his life an unremarkable kid, lately a mutant gene has kicked in, altering his course: this now defines him. Call it the Bullshit gene. He is suddenly incapable of honesty. Renouncing Truth in all its forms, he is interested only in inspiring incredulity. He has had sixty-five girlfriends, will be a multi-millionaire by the time he is thirty, and could run a sub-four-minute mile should he ever feel compelled. This one rogue gene makes him unbearable. His parents are not like this, and you have to go back to Renata's father – a two-timer, kept a fancy woman on the side for twenty years – to find a progenitor, but perhaps genes can jump like chess knights. His parents have lately given up on correctional strategies, and now can only hope Jeff changes his name by deed poll until he calms down. If not, they can only wait for God to intercede.

In the vestibule, while his father waits to open the main doors, Don reaches back and unties his mask, a sterile surgical item worn on his doctor's advice to ward against cross-infection. Chemotherapy has done this to him. He is susceptible to everything. But he leaves the beanie on. He needs the beanie. The beanie stays. He's now ready, against his will, to go inside. He folds the cotton purdah and puts it in his pocket, then takes his first unfiltered intake of air in an hour.

JIM: Ready?

Donald nods. He's ready. The family enters the church proper.

Int. Church. Day.

How do priests find so much to talk about? This is Donald's thought bubble as he sits there on the hard, cold wooden seat listening to a celibate (or pseudo-celibate) man: a virgin listening to a virgin, the blind leading the blind. What certainties are there that can be so certainly dispatched on a Sunday morning to a packed and uncertain congregation other than the confirmation, uttered afresh since the dawn of faith and never losing its sheen for those with an ear for consolations, that God loves you?

This is the long form of what Donald thinks. The short form is: So what? These two words float above him, are circumscribed by a line as drawn by an artist's-quality fine-ball felt pen, while a trail of lesser-and-lesser-sized bubbles, all empty, extends back to the side of his head, the point of departure.

He listens glumly, completely unconsoled, and inspects the church designed in-the-round so that the faithful might look as much upon each other as the celebrant. And then his eyes light upon...

...upon a certain girl. Distant. The far side of the church. A stunner. Hallelujah, chants his choirboy heart. Hosanna in the Highest. *Gloria in Excelsis Deo*. What a honey. Brunette, brown as a berry, near his own age. An Eve with centre-parted hair, a radiant babe, a babeatron, a looker to send his heart tom-tomming. Saved, he thought-bubbles. Now *this* is more like Salvation! This is what heaven on earth should look like. This at last is an object worthy of worship, something he could really fall to his knees and plead for, make a pact with the devil for, if he had to. At the very least this girl is destined for a starring role in his latest romantic comedy, a starlet whom he will cast (without her consent) in a lurid scenario (his latest mental project) whose storyline charts a red-hot first-date grope-fest followed by a year's elastic-snapping romance, climaxing on their sixteenth birthdays with a decision to move in together to cement their filthy liaison, to move into some pitiful little shoebox, animated by their animal love for each other, dirty dishes in the sink, but not giving a damn, devoted to each other, this girl wrapping her legs around him four, five, six times a day, binding him tight, her feet fluttering on his back like angel's wings, she the one who holds all the erotic secrets while he is the happy student, his health perfect for ever and nothing ever to come to an end.

The film is obviously a turkey, shot for his own amusement, and repetitive in its obsessions, but he will not touch a frame of it. He needs only to stare at her across the church for the unravelling scenes to enthrall him and deliver what every movie should: complete absorption and giddy identification. But then he gets an itch. An unscripted itch. Under his beanie. A monster scalp tickle that will be cured only by removing the woolen disguise, by real fingers digging into actual skin. Oh God, oh God, he prays. Where art thou?

He pulls off his beanie.

And what a moment for her to look over at him, this girl who should've / could've / would've worn his ring. Their eyes meet, lock. Donald's fingers freeze mid-scratch. He dips his chin, tugs his hat back on, and in self-disgust lowers his head to the hymnal, which bears a lyric: *Tho' Death may conquer all, we shall have no fear, for God is near*. It's bad enough, bubbles Don, that he barely has any eyebrows left, but without his beanie he looks like one of those bald subalterns on the bridge of the *Enterprise* whom Captain Picard asks for star coordinates. Dear God, reads his new prayer bubble, may Death conquer me now.

This is all that Donald Delpe can pray for this morning: his own demise. But he makes his request with more conviction than anyone else in the whole place. Next to him, these other petitioners are amateurs.

Some time later, towards the end of the Mass, when the end is nigh, he dares glance over at his golden girl again. (*Organ music dominates the soundtrack.*) Like the rest of the faithful she is singing aloud another ode to death and redemption, red-lipped and lovely. She looks up at the priest but never again at Donald, never again at fucking Yoda in the back row; not once does she give him the sign that will ignite their courtship. Instead, she lets the casting opportunity of a lifetime dwindle, as it so often does, into heartbreak and loss.

"Cut!" a disgusted director (perhaps God) somewhere calls. The Heads of Department all confer and agree. This film is wrapped. It's history. It's dusted. Title: *Loser Strikes Again*.

Int. Bathroom / Delpe House. Day.
Freak, the kid thinks as his vomit splashes into the toilet bowl, and *freak* again with every heave, *freak*, *freak*, *freak*, coughing into that sewer-connected hole, his insides aching with every gastric concertina, every type of

17

nastiness floating before him in the hand-mirror of water in the bottom of the bowl – sickness, phlegm, food, blood too, he thinks. *I want to die* are the words now crystallized in the ultimate bubble that streams up over his head on a thermal of putridity. His stomach can't discharge anything else, and he stands up and looks at himself in the real mirror on the wall. *I want to die.* And so he takes off his T-shirt to reveal a clear plastic tube sticking out of his chest near the shoulder and terminating in a plastic spigot: a "Port-a-Cath" catheter for the administering of chemotherapy. *Freak.* The suture where the pipe breaks the skin and enters his body is as red and raw as the skin inside your bottom lip. Don, not liking what he sees, punches the mirror on the medicine chest. He hits it hard. It breaks. **KIIIISH!** He has a good right hand. He was designed to be strong, ought to be getting his father's muscles by now, slam-dunking the basketball too. Little chance of that. He is heading in the other direction. Withering. Flightless. Thin and pale among the broken scimitars of glass that turn what's left of his reflection into collage.

He looks down at his fist. Amazingly, there is no blood, not a drop – a strange time to be inviolate. But his hand is sore and so he rubs it. A comfort. These are his consolations. The gentle rubbing of his own body.

His family's beating on the locked door seems like it's coming from a whole other movie.

Int. Don's Bedroom. Day.

It is hard for Renata to talk to her son while a portable Travenol pump on the floor beside his bed delivers chemicals into his body via a tube connected to the Port-a-Cath implanted in his shoulder. It is unbelievably hard, but not because the pump is too noisy: it emits only a regular click and an almost sub-aural hum. What makes talking so difficult, indeed what makes it almost impossibly tough, is the knowledge that the Travenol pump is metering into her beloved son, right now as she prattles on, some of the most noxious poisons a body can withstand, a regime of chemotherapy targeting healthy and rogue cells alike, killing indiscriminately, reducing him to zero, figuring that the last bit to die will be a healthy bit. Some gamble, but this is the rocket science of chemotherapy, so it's pretty damn hard to sit beside your son and talk in a calm, upbeat, controlled and maternal manner when a tragedy is unfurling before your eyes.

In an effort to manage her own pain better, she ordered all the best-selling death books; she surfed Amazon, one-click-purchased in bulk to avoid shipping fees. It proved a mixed blessing: the info-overload gave her pain a graphic new intensity, merely schooling her in T-cells and white blood counts, in X-rays and tumour necrosis factors. She knows all about MRIs and ECGs and CEAs, metastasizing cells and monoclonal therapies, enzyme therapies, Simonton visualization, Burzynski's antineoplastin therapy, Hoxsey, Revici, Burton, the Janker Klinik where Bob Marley died. She has marked up the margins of Lance Armstrong's autobiography, has hopes for the Gerson diet, and knows about comparative survival rates across the spectrum of treatments – who boasts what and why and for how long. So she knows full well that her boy, right now, is being killed in microcosm, cell by cell, in the hope of preserving the whole: medicine by way of Stalin, whole populations dying so that the idea of the State endures.

Don is sitting up on his bed, staring balefully towards

the window while his mother, at the foot of the bed, regards him with her own maternal X-ray eyes, eyes that can virtually see through to the poisons on their internal journey from organ to organ, see inside him to his arteries running yellow like a putrid Yangtze, watch his organs within flinch and clench and withdraw as the river reaches them, infiltrates them, makes them gag and wither, seeing all of this as if his skin were removed, vivisected. This is what it's like to visit a son receiving cancer treatment.

RENATA (*a thin tired smile*): Three more days, honey. That's it. You'll be off this stuff. Hopefully for good, touch wood. (*Her left hand reaches for the desk just beyond her reach.*) You had an anxiety attack, a reaction to the Reglan, the doctor said. It's lucky you weren't hurt, that's all. It happens to a lot of people. Anxiety. It's often even worse than that. Okay? (*No reply*) Shall I read to you? I brought a book. (*Holds it up.*) There was a bit I wanted to read you. Here: "In the summer" – this is the bit – "in the summer we long for winter, but with winter's frosty advance – with winter's frosty advance…"

But Donald has heard enough already and puts in his earbuds, rejecting his mother's striving, faith-healing, mind-over-matter, crystal-carrying, eastern-mystical, self-help-book-plundering approach.

Renata stops, looks at him. This too is hard for her, this emotional foreclosure. But what can she do? She is exhausted from trying to midwife his awareness of his illness, from trying to coax him into joining her in the supreme battle. He has a magnificent chance of beating this but will not try to help himself. She is fit to drop. Exasperated, she tries another tack, something from her own childhood (the last redoubt), and tugs out his earbuds.

RENATA (*loudly*): Donald! You will bloody listen to me! Just listen to me, okay? (*Takes a deep breath.*) We! Have! To help! Each! Other here!

But Donald just picks up an artist's fine-ball felt pen and an exercise book from his bedside table, and starts to draw with rapid, expert strokes. He is unreachable.

Renata gives up, feels tears slide down her cheeks. She wipes them away before he can see them. Be strong, be strong, be... anything other than a blubberer. In her hands the music leaks sickly from the dangling earbuds. Her work is impossibly cut out for her: a woodworm in a cathedral. But what can she do?

She hands him back his earbuds. He takes them without looking up, and seals his ears with them once more. She rises, exhausted in body and mind, and it's only eleven o'clock. She glances at the softly whirring Travenol pump and leaves the room.

Int. Dining Room / Delpe House. Night.
Renata, Jim and Jeff eat dinner. Don's place is set but his chair remains empty. Chiming of cutlery on plates. Long silences. Jeff eats fastest, and seems the least affected by the events of the day. In fact, he appears wholly unaffected. He's the picture of a hungry young man trying to impale the whole of life on the tines of his fork.

RENATA (*very worried*): All he wants to do is draw those... those hideous comic pictures of his.

JIM: So let's invite his friends over. Michael and the other one. (*To* JEFF) Who's the other one?

JEFF: Raff.

JIM: Why can't they come over? Let's get 'em over.

RENATA: We need help. Don needs help. We all do.

JIM: Let's get some friends over for him. (*Heavy pause*)
We can do that at least, right?

Int. Master Bedroom. Night.

The Delpe parents haven't had sex in five months. Stress,
strain, squabbles, a pent-up sense of injustice have all taken
their toll. They've taken a toll in many areas of their lives
but it's quantifiable in the bedroom where the number zero
hovers like a halo of shame over the queen-size bed. But
they have appointed tonight as the night in which they will
end the drought. Tonight is rumpy-pumpy night. Neither
would have thought it would come to this, scheduling sex
days ahead of time (it's Friday, and they made the decision
on Monday over cereal), but that's just how it is.

Jim has put Springsteen on. He remains keen.
Surprisingly so. In fact, he has even enjoyed the pre-
arranged nature of it, finding in the tick-tick-tick of the
clock something teasing and anticipatory and sexy. But
the waiting has proved too much for Renata. The build-
up has been crippling. When the time comes for her to
slip into bed beside her lover (naked, ready for her), she
delays for twenty minutes, abluting, brushing her teeth,
flossing, taking her make-up off, exfoliating, masking
up, de-masking, applying overnight cream to her cheeks,
wrinkle-reducing serum under her eyes, before she climbs
into bed – only to want, right away, to slow things down.
When Jim slides into position above her, adopting a
posture similar to that of a sprinter in the starting blocks,
she asks him not to rush.

RENATA: It's been such a long time, hon.

They've always been like this: Jim keen, urgent when the
time arrives, now or never; Renata stalling, taking her time,

complicating things, shiny with her unguents. As it is for many men and women, for the Delpes sex is like shopping. Men want to go in quick, get what they want, and then get out. Women like to browse, try things on, fancy one thing then change their mind, try on something else instead: no rush at all. But tonight Renata has promised him she knows exactly what she wants and so on this basis Jim has agreed to go shopping with her once more, trusting her. As usual he finds himself waiting impatiently while she aimlessly peruses the entire store. Fury builds in him, while she is oblivious to the time she is taking, unconcerned that, for him, they are parked on a double yellow line and that every minute sees another ticket inserted under the wiper blade. Finally, he calls it off. This is crazy, passionless. His pride is wounded now. She has broken her promises. And when she doesn't protest, is perhaps even relieved, they drift asleep, worse off than ever.

But when they awake next morning, remembering the previous night's plan and their failure, by then too sleepy to launch another shopping spree or blame each other for yesterday's fiasco, they visit the corner store instead. It's simple. It's quick. There's only one item on one rack in this store and Renata knows suddenly that she wants it. She gets it. And so does he. It's so easy. Why isn't it always so easy? The deed is done. They both sigh. They actually bought something. Together! They sigh again, still only half-awake. Chalk it up: one.

Exterior. Delpe House. Day.
Jim has put the sprinkler out today. It's shaping up to be a hot dry season. You can almost hear the grass sighing with relief as the water hits it with a hiss. Donald sits there on

the steps of his house watching the three revolving arms chuck out the droplets like corn to chickens, the sprinkler making its soothing *Ssshh – Sssshh – Ssshh*, reminding him of a mother pacifying a child. Soon the birds will be down, the birds that are keeping their distance on the power line. When the lawn's good and soft, he thought-bubbles, they'll come down for worms. Don's been waiting for an hour for this to happen. Even when he had to go inside to vomit, he came back out and there'd still been no action. They seem to be waiting for him to go and not come back, just as he is waiting for them to come and feed, just as they must be aching to do. It's a game. So who can wait longest, man or beast? No contest. Every beast is waiting for death. Ours. He awards the birds their own collective thought bubble. It reads: "Yeah, we're still here, arsehole. 150 million years and counting, buddy. And we'll wait another 150 million if we have to, until you noisy, selfish, all-consuming murderous bastards shit so badly in your own nests you expire and let us real animals pick up where we left off. No pollution, no forest destruction, no menus with our names on them. A level playing field. Paradise. Remember?" No wonder beasts are tops in the waiting game. They've had epochs of practice. A beast understands that waiting is what life is almost entirely about.

Jim's car turns into the drive, left-hand indicator blinking, though there's no other car for miles around. Typical law-abiding Jim. Doesn't want to make a turn without indicating properly because sloppiness begets sloppiness and before you know it you're in jail for axe-murder. Out of the back of the parked car alight Michael and Raff. **DISASTER STRIKES!**

MICHAEL REEVES and RAFF BENNETT (both just turned fifteen), friends of Donald's since primary school. At ten they form a gang, a clique, a posse of outlaws, whose early purpose is to flaunt convention and foment acts of civil disobedience. They build a clubhouse in the middle of a run of gorse on empty land, make walls out of apple boxes, the roof out of pilfered corrugated iron. The rules of the club are simple but they are iron-cast: whenever two or more members are meeting in the clubhouse, then, under pain of death, they have to say the word *Fuck* at least once in every sentence they speak. It's not as easy to do as it sounds, and failure to do so risks instant expulsion from the gang. Ten years old. Voices still to break. Boys playing men. A knock on the clubhouse door: "Who's fucken there?" "It's fucking me. Raffy fuck. Let me fucken in." "Okay, fuck you. But what's the fucking password?" Pause to think. "*Fuck*. Now let me fucking in." Locks unlock. This is their first infantile intifada. The hardest part of all this is going home afterwards. (MOTHER: Where have you been, dear? SON: Fuck knows.) Bang. Grounded. One week. But despite this, the club stays together, progresses in infamy to the present day, when its members run a small but lucrative racket in bootleg CDs, operating a £100-a-week business out of their schoolbags. But with Donald's illness and withdrawal from the scene – he owns the high-quality CD-burner (with 7800 KB/sec. Sustained Transfer Rate) – they're no longer hitting their strict sales targets. Bummer.

Cut to Don...

...His face conveys horror as Mike and Raff get out of the car. Here are the last people he wants to see. Friends to visit? He doesn't *have* any friends. Not any more. Doesn't want any, either. Not looking like this anyway, not while he's unfit for public exhibition: hairless, eyebrowless, pale, rake-thin, a condom on legs. He can only imagine the deadly reports going back to school now: that Donald looks like a cotton bud, that he looks like a Durex, a drumstick, a thermometer, a human hard-on. It's been almost six months since he's seen these old buddies and it's taken a lot of orchestrated work on his part to keep it this way. Unanswered phone calls. Skipped meetings. Skilful avoidance. And now his stupid fucking jerk-off father goes and transports them here! Don feels violated, busted, nabbed red-handed, like Michael Jackson being telephotoed playing naked Twister with some under-tens. What the hell is his father thinking?

Don gets up and rushes straight inside. The front door bangs.

On the drive Michael and Raff turn and look ques-tioningly at Jim Delpe, still standing within the gauge of the driver's door and looking as if he's decided already that the idea is dead in the water. It is dead. Dead as a doornail...

Int. Don's Bedroom. Day.

Hearing his father's car start up, Donald goes to the window of his upstairs bedroom and parts the micromesh curtains to see his father slow-reversing down the drive, arm over the seat back, hazard lights flashing – good old Dad – rearing into the road and giving Don a brief glimpse of his mates in the back before they disappear.

Donald stands at the window for a while, his eyes shifting to the birds on the wires, but they're gone now, scared away. Then he goes and gets his wind-cheater, pulls on his Vans, triple-knots the laces for perhaps the last time, says goodbye with a cool look to his bedroom, steps over the Travenol pump and exits.

Ext. Bridge. Day.
Donald stands on the edge of a pedestrian footbridge. He has climbed over the handrail. Below is a motorway streaming with a rush-hour mayhem of cars and trucks. The tips of his good old Vans overhang the abyss, producing something of a frame for his view of his destination. Well, the picture doesn't lie. It's a leap into the human machine.

How far down to the road? Far enough to make him unrecognizable, that's for sure. Having to identify his jellified features from dental records will be hard on his family. But should he let this sway him? No open casket for Donald F. Delpe if he goes ahead. His injuries will oblige his folks to cremate, but this in itself may be no bad thing. Yes, his earthly passing will contribute slightly to the build up of greenhouse gases – he backs Kyoto – but he prefers the thought of flames to worms in his eyeholes and mites tucking into his cerebellum and testicles.

Every death is ugly. Even the stars, burning up their gases and terminating via supernova, pollute such an area of space afterwards you couldn't even give that real estate away. Yes, the boy on the bridge likens himself to cooling stars as he waits upon the various elements of his death wish – disgust, anger, pain, nausea, frailty, frustration, injustice, envy, loneliness, regret – to fuse together into a force sufficient to cast him outwards. He releases one hand, feeling it time to get serious. Halfway there. Halfway to not existing. No pussyfooting around now. Say goodbye, world, to a freak, to someone who didn't even have his shit together enough to reach his 16th birthday, to a loser in every department but who's going out in style, saying *au revoir* and *sayonara* and *seeya 'round* to all the untrod pathways and unseen futures, to all the un-unfastened bras and unkissed girls, farewell to all the unlearnt lessons and unperformed mistakes and a hearty *fuck off* to all the torturous medical practices and humiliations, and finally *so long* to the entire human jamboree that will barely register the absence of one more hundred-pound of flesh wrapped around a soul.

Then, in a late flourish, he takes out his pen and decides to leave something behind, a last message to the world. Probably no one will ever find it, but that's okay too. The world is full of unrecognized epitaphs, unknown initials left on trees, scratched onto bus shelters, lonely places. Well, here's one more. With his expert hand he scrawls on the painted ironwork a parting thought, a final analysis. When he is done he signs it, like the good cartoonist he is. He is ready to go now. Ready to explode and shower his particles throughout the universe. He faces the concrete river below. *Dive*, he thinks. Dive, Don. The cars stream on and on in the gap between his parted Vans. He inserts his earbuds, pushes Play in his pocket, then steadies himself to bury the Olympic competition in one spectacular dive whose degree of difficulty has never before been remotely approached.

His epitaph behind him, the one he leaves for posterity reads: "I want my money back. I didn't understand a thing." © **DD Comix**

Ext. Delpe House. Day.
Renata opens her front door to see a policeman standing beside her son. Her adrenal glands begin to pump as if she's hooked up to Don's portable Travenol.

RENATA (*shakily*): What's happened? Oh Lord, what's happened? Donald? What's going on? What is it?

POLICEMAN: Mrs Delpe?

RENATA (*face draining of blood*): Yes?

Int. Hallway / Hospital. Day.
The sign on the door reads: "Clinical Psychologist".

Int. Adrian's Office. Day.
Jim and Renata sit across the desk of:

DOCTOR ADRIAN KING, early fifties, revered, published, brilliant. Speaks in a mellow voice that he rarely raises. Strong, firm in his opinions, but with mild manners. Looks at clients over an imaginary pair of spectacles. Dresses disastrously, old tweeds and corduroy. Although he is calm, benign, and patient – every gesture gilded, life in adagio – there is something pinched about him also, something too systematic and corseted and correct. Still, he is liked, respected, even adored at a distance. ("Oh, we all looove Adrian.") People don't imagine he has any trouble being himself.

His résumé: born in Portsmouth to waterfront publicans. He ghosts through his childhood surrounded by drunkards and failed fathers of many nationalities – debauched railwaymen, horny cod fishermen, oyster-farmers, merchant seamen, local flotsam as well – soon determining he will be another breed of man entirely. Not better, just different. Studying in the corner of the pub while men five times his age joke, swear, roar, blast, rage and fall into drunken fights, Adrian takes his cue from the overhead ceiling fan slowly stirring a dozen warring dialects into a single smooth Esperanto. Leafing the pages on his O-level books, then a year later his

A-level papers, he zeroes in on Freud, Jung, Reich, J.B. Watson, B.F. Skinner, Max Wertheimer in his senior year – when he isn't swilling out the gents' with Jeyes Fluid until his nostrils sting as Filipinos sing 'Hey Jude' through the wall. Graduates baby-faced in '77, first in his class, an erudite man, fully briefed in the art world as well, the complete package: Amnesty supporter, a nascent wine connoisseur. People have him pinned as a socialite and possible womanizer. But the impression is mistaken. Never a sexy man (he has gained weight around the middle and under the chin by the time he's thirty), he has a redeeming elegance that makes him uplifting company among people who wish to contemplate higher-order things. He has high hopes for love and is patient in its absence, feeling his day must come. Finally meets a French woman while wine-tasting in the Loire. Delicious. She is delicious. She shadows him back to England. They marry quickly, their cultural differences a spur. Choosing public service over an affluent private practice, he enters the asylums of the troubled, the half-mad and the totally barking, working his spells on brilliant freaks and human luncheon sausage alike, talking up his remedies, rising to his current position as Head of Clinical Psychology at Watford General, where he now sits, unopposed and lauded, before two new petitioners for his talents.

ADRIAN: My specialist area? Grief.

JIM: Well then, looks like we've come to the right place.

RENATA (*scrummaging her fingers in her lap*): Donald's an extremely bright, creative boy, and the doctors say he's got a great chance of beating this – a great chance, if only…

JIM: Eighty per cent. Eighty per cent.

RENATA: But… (*Sighs.*)

JIM: He won't fight. There's no will to fight.

(*Long silence*)

RENATA: All he does is… is draw a comic strip. About some superhero who never dies. (*To* JIM) Show him.

ADRIAN: Well, it's common for people with serious illnesses to construct immortality symbols.

RENATA: Okay, but this is disgusting. (*To* JIM) Show – (*to* ADRIAN) It's disturbed, grotesque.

Jim hands over a large notebook.

RENATA: And with these anxiety attacks from the chemo…

JIM: We're worried that he might do something… terrible. I dunno.

ADRIAN (*scratching his temple slowly with his index finger*): Okay, but you need to be aware that therapy is proven to have no impact on cancer survival rates.

RENATA: I don't believe that. People fight.

ADRIAN: Well, I was about to say – the only thing that seems to save lives, to make a difference – is joy, simple enjoyment of life. (*The parents stare at him.*) So I think you should look at ways to help Donald find this. That's one way you could help him.

Int. Adrian's Apartment. Night.

Adrian enters his apartment, his body heavy tonight. He drops his bags the way a scuba-diver dumps weight belts on a dock. He chooses a CD from his alphabetized collection. Soothing opera becomes the score. He takes off his jacket as a knock comes on the door. It's SYLVIA, a woman in her sixties, hair like sofa batting, five different kinds of colours. She is holding a cat that looks over-loved, and she's in a bad mood today. Passes the cat to him. She lives alone and looks after his cat in the flat below. But with a few soothing words from Adrian she changes, opens up, can't stop talking suddenly. Oh, this and that, and did Adrian know, and oh by the way etc., and Adrian doesn't cut her short. Not ever. This is how he *really* pays for her help, by listening, nodding his head to this lonely woman, giving her the time of day, polite to all things (women, men, beasts, fauna, flora, even azoic matter). He shuts the door only as she clumps down the stairs. An immaculately tidy apartment. Original art on the walls. Yards of books, floor to ceiling, most of them dissections of why people do what they do. Long answers. What do we really want? What do we *think* we want? Why do we *want* what we think we want? Inconclusive always. Leading back to the original mysteries. Still, a simplified, ordered, intelligent life on show, evidence only of someone working hard to put back the gold in the teeth of those whom society has robbed. The broken, the faulty, the unrepaired, they are his clients. Taxing work, this, a draining vocation that would take him down but for his secret antidotes. Classical learning, art, balance, reason, the golden mean, upholding beauty, these are his pick-me-ups. His means of getting up in the morning, his means of curing himself at the end of a day. He brings the cat over to the couch. Rufus. Rufus was his wife's idea, before her interest in pets spread, became equine. He has inherited care of the critter, and his early revulsion for it has settled into a comfortable and reciprocal tolerance. In fact, "Roof" has become something of his wife's representative, he thinks, now that Sophie's unwillingness to spend time in town has become more pronounced with each passing year. Some compensation, huh? A musty fluff ball with a love for herring. He reaches for a steel comb and begins to run it through the fur, quietly singing snatches of opera to himself. Music lilts. *Maudite à jamais soit la race.* Fleas? Not one. Good boy. *Amour! Viens aider ma faiblesse.* Adrian keeps combing anyway.

Int. Adrian's Kitchen. Night.
Before he allows himself to go to bed, there is something Adrian must attend to. It is the small matter of the mouse.

He has been subject to this one-rodent pestilence for three weeks now and he is sick of finding pellets on his benchtop and toothmarks in the butter. The last straw is finding a small butternut pumpkin dragged halfway across the kitchen floor since this morning, leading him to believe that this mouse is mightier than he first thought. And so, he gets on his knees in his Japanese robe: ah, the robe! A little fey, this item, a gift from his wife. How he had hated it at first. But now it is the only après-shower apparel he wears: and he has to admit that he secretly likes its silky caress on his hairy thighs, the closest thing he has to a human touch at present. Did Sophie guess this? Could she have foreseen his sensory needs and known long before he did about the growing separation that was to develop? No, he is being stupid. *Maudite à jamais soit la race.* He baits a trap with cheese and, careful not to set it off and so bark his fingers, opens the spring-hinged cupboard under the sink which the mouse has made its base of operations. He peeks inside, real slow. He closes the door again quickly. Yes, he has seen it! Oh my God, the little guy is sitting there waiting for him. Two tiny reflective eyes peering back at him, twin jewels in the dark. And not very big either, this Hercules in hiding. A baby. How can he think about killing it? But if you give succour to one vermin, you end up with hundreds. The liberal's dilemma: principles or realpolitik? So Adrian rotates at the hip and picks up the trap set with cheese, and is about to arch back the killing lever with his thumb when his cat meows behind him.

Rufus, the old campaigner, ambles forwards, sleepy, postprandial, fart-smelling, to check out what his master is up to. Seeing him, Adrian has a whole new idea. He puts down the trap and picks up Rufus. A superior plan, Darwinism at work. He is *living* with a killer, the mouse's mortal enemy: so why does he need a trap? He tilts open the cupboard door and, after a small struggle with Rufus, who is more than a little reluctant to be shoved into that dark place, shuts the door and waits for the old boy to do his work. A scrap breaks out inside at once, an unholy rumpus. Go, Rufus, he thinks. Go, boy! Claws, teeth, night vision, blood, the mouse's head in the cat's jaws – all of this Adrian imagines. Bodies bang on the door from the inside. The door reverberates with attacks, retreats, offensives, counter-offensives, so that Adrian has to keep the door weighted shut with his hand, until it dawns on him that the bangs belong solely to Rufus and that his cat is trying to get out. As its keening cries rise to serious levels of distress, Adrian takes his hand away from the door – Rufus bursts out of the cupboard, a meteor of fur, and is gone.

ADRIAN (*sighs*): Coward.

Down on his knees in his Japanese robe he once more sets the trap.

Int. Adrian's Office. Day.

Donald is staring back at the psychologist. He looks infuriated to be here. Heavy dragooning has taken place chez Delpe to get him this far.

ADRIAN: So... why don't you tell me something about yourself. (*Silence*) Okay, so what do you like doing, for example? (*Silence*) Football? Rugby? (*Silence*)

Adrian isn't used to this. Most of his clients want to be here, crave his insights, his soaring words, snatching them out of the air like home-run baseballs. But this kid wants to take nothing home from the game.

ADRIAN: Well how about this then? (*He produces* DON's *comic book.*)

DONALD (*annoyed*): Where'd you get that?

ADRIAN: Your parents dropped it off. (*Hands it over,* DON *grabs it.*) I'm sorry. I thought you must have okayed it. (*Silence*) You're very, very talented. I know a little about art.

DONALD: You wanna star on the back of your hand?

ADRIAN: I was wondering how it's going to end. Sorry, I read it.

DONALD: Who cares how it ends.

ADRIAN: Well, my answer to that would be that in every situation in which we find ourselves... sooner or later...

Donald has stopped listening. This old guy holds about as much interest for him as do cinema ads for Coruba rum, Renault cars, the perks of flying Singapore Airlines. And where usually he would insert his earbuds and escape stereophonically from people trying to tell him what to do and how to feel, pumping up his own soundtrack to drown out all the jerks and dry-sacks and boring do-gooders the world seems intent on lobbing at him lately, he now chooses to lower the volume of the shrink instead, turning *him* down, as if the dimple on his iPod is hardwired to this doctor's voice box. Soon, all that Don can see in front of him is a mute therapist, a moving mouth but nothing coming out. Bull's-eye. Suddenly, this session is a whole lot more interesting.

How idiotic talking people look when you rob them of volume. Even a low-key guy like this is suddenly a clownish mime artist, hands pressing on absent walls, then kneading invisible dough, then, next, seeming to play a single piano chord in the air, accompanied by dancing eyebrows and rolling eyes. Don can't resist his own next move. Mentally, he takes out one of his finest pens – the one his imagination always wields, and starts to...

...starts to doodle on the shrink's twitching face. He visualizes a scribbled moustache over the bare upper lip, deep wrinkles between the brows, aging him thirty years, giving the guy a set of satanic horns for good measure, an arrow right through his head, defacing him in the casual way you do a magazine cover in a doctor's waiting room (the way he'd just done in this one, actually), even adding a quick-pic dominatrix in bondage gear, her giant melons lolling over the shrink's left shoulder while she lashes a serpent's tongue into his left ear-hole, then finishing off the whole despoilment with a cluster of effervescing speech bubbles above the guy's head that all read the same thing: "Blah – blah – blah – blah – blah".

Donald is snapped back to reality only by the mention of a name.

ADRIAN: MiracleMan – it's a good name.

DONALD: Uh…

ADRIAN: A superhero. He's interesting.

Donald refuses to be drawn into conversation.

ADRIAN: He farts. (*Pause*) Interesting.

DONALD: He's real. People do that. Well, you probably don't.

ADRIAN: He's real – but he's indestructible. (*Silence*) So who does MiracleMan triumph over?

DONALD (*staring hard at* ADRIAN): Arseholes. (*Silence*)

ADRIAN: And… he can't be killed?

DONALD: Yeah. That's sort of what indestructible means.

ADRIAN: I noticed that he sometimes digs up a dead body and has sex with it. Why is that?

DONALD: He has no choice. Girls don't like him.

ADRIAN: Why?

DONALD: He farts.

ADRIAN: Why do you give MiracleMan an aspect like that?

DONALD: Like I said, I want him to be real. I'm sick of phoney superheroes.

ADRIAN: But superheroes aren't real.

DONALD (*a level gaze*): This has just occurred to you?

ADRIAN (*handing back the comic*): His nemesis – The Glove? A surgeon who is forever snapping on surgical gloves?

DONALD: Yeah. Cool.

ADRIAN: You don't like doctors?

DONALD: Go figure. Can I go now? I'm gonna be nuked this afternoon.

Int. Radiotherapy Unit. Day.

Life's soundtrack rises (or ought to) to give us the glorious strains of the intermezzo from Mascagni's *Cavalleria Rusticana*. Donald's body floats slo-mo into the huge white conch shell that is the radiotherapy apparatus. His eyes are goggled. He is in another world now, victim to a battery of X-rays, particles (electrons, neutrons, pi-mesons), gamma rays, of cobalt-60, carbon-12, neon-20 and argon-40, all these forces passing invisibly through the layers of his body, cooking his insides like a TV dinner, chowing down on his maw.

For Donald, this serves as inspiration. He gets a great new idea for where to take his work in progress, his graphic novel, *The Adventures of MiracleMan*, now nearing its climax. And so, while rays and photons rip through him, he transcends his predicament and enters the world of his alter ego, MiracleMan, inanimate frames flickering to life, becoming animate. The first thing he sees is the title for this new episode:

THE GLOVE RETURNS

by DONALD DELPE, adapted from his self-penned comic book, in which MiracleMan (© DD Comix) is trapped by his nemesis, THE GLOVE.

THE GLOVE, a masked surgeon, snaps on new surgical gloves. ENTIRE SCREEN FILLS with the word **SNAP!!!** encased by a zag-edged bubble. His NURSE, a busty vixen (her bitty dress so short that her black-pantied crotch shows beneath), asks him:

NURSE: Another internal probe, Glover Boy?

THE GLOVE: Not this time, nursey-wursey. Something more final for our indestructible friend.

MIRACLEMAN is strapped to an operating table, where a DEATH RAY is pointed at him, a contraption that looks like a huge whipped-cream piping bag. THE GLOVE smirks malevolently and throws the switch. MIRACLEMAN arches in pain, the small of his back rises a good twenty centimetres off the table, and he suffers greatly before he collapses, finally to DIE.

THE GLOVE: There. There.

The NURSE goes to release MIRACLEMAN, looking down on him with a tear in her eye. A thought bubble appears over her. We read it:

NURSE (*bubble*): "...What a beautiful corpse."

THE GLOVE: Hey, did you just THINK something?

NURSE (*embarrassed*): Er... uh...

THE GLOVE then checks MIRACLEMAN's pulse.

THE GLOVE: We appear to have lost him. Terrific. (*Smiles malevolently.*) Nurse, is the injection ready?

NURSE: Naturally.

THE GLOVE: Good. Excellent. This should do the trick.

THE GLOVE takes the HYPODERMIC, squirts a small jet into the air and then injects the NEEDLE – INTO HIS OWN ARM – with an ORGIASTIC SIGH.

THE GLOVE: At this rate I may need to repledge the Hypocrite's Oath.

As he injects himself, the NURSE rubs herself against him like a cat.

NURSE: Please, please, pretty please, purrrrrr...

THE GLOVE: Of course. How selfish of me.

He now slides the same HYPODERMIC into her willingly proffered arm, bruised already with the track marks of an addict. She sighs with sensuous delight as the remaining drugs enter her vein. They KISS then, their TONGUES entwining like vipers in a basket, as THE GLOVE undresses the NURSE from behind. MIRACLEMAN is forgotten.

Meanwhile, as the DEAD HAND of MIRACLEMAN lies on the operating table, we go into EXTREME CLOSE-UP on a LONG BLUE VEIN in MIRACLEMAN's arm. Suddenly we hear a magnified HEARTBEAT SOUND and a second later see A BULGE OF BLOOD speeding along the vein – we follow the fourth or fifth bulge down the arm to the dead hand, whereupon the FINGERS spasm and clench. When no one suspects it – and just as THE GLOVE and THE NURSE go at it on the next table like dogs – MIRACLEMAN leaps miraculously up.

MIRACLEMAN: Not so fast, butcher-boy! Didn't anyone tell you pathetic junkies that grime shouldn't play?

THE GLOVE: Whah... How???...

MIRACLEMAN: Sorry. Longevity runs in my family.

Whereupon MIRACLEMAN pummels his foe and uses the DEATH RAY as a LASER CANNON to destroy the place. As the machinery explodes...

Int. Oncology Ward / Hospital. Day.

Nobody refers to this place as a cancer ward any more, thinks Dr Adrian King. The term went out in the mid-'80s, about the time a whore became an Affection Surrogate. And it wasn't just the whores who were terminologically terminated. A garbage collector became a Refuse Executive, a housewife a Domestic Engineer, the criminal a Private Legislator. It seemed that only the glockenspiel-maker escaped the insult of euphemism.

Why was the term Cancer Ward retired? Adrian could cite two reasons. Firstly, it was considered poor taste to remind sufferers that they had cancer. Secondly, the term was associated with too many years of hopeless suffering, a one-way ticket to the boneyard. The Latinate term, oncology, was meant to fix all this, to convey science, Swiss breakthroughs, lifelong remissions, Pfizer research grants, an industry of hope when – incredibly – neither time nor science nor terminology had actually made a lot of difference to survival rates. The disease has proved immune to semantics, resistant to hype, deaf to technology. One hundred years on, it's still the same lethal little curse. Cancer, in the end, is still cancer. A ward, in the end, is a ward.

Such thoughts roam through Adrian King's head as he surveys the bedridden from the door: the change in nomenclature seems to him about as pointless as giving a corpse a facelift. Indeed, the ward even recalls the opening to Edgar Allan Poe's *Fall of the House of Usher*. How does the passage run? He remembers it verbatim from American Lit. "During the whole of a dull, dark and soundless day in the autumn of the year, when the clouds hung oppressively low in the heavens, I had been passing alone, on horseback, through a singularly dreary tract of country; and at length found myself, as the shades of evening drew on, within view of the melancholy House of Usher. I know not how it was – but, with the first glimpse of the building, a sense of insufferable gloom pervaded my spirit." *Insufferable gloom*. This is the phrase he wants. And it strikes him now – he knows not why it is – that it's this exact gloom, insufferable and dreary and oppressive, that it is his job to address. And yet, as he looks down the ward of semi-curtained beds, six on each side, occupied by an assortment of cases from every walk of life, the high and the low, as many winners as losers (such distinctions are meaningless here), he also feels that the job is beyond him.

After all, what do you tell people facing a horrible death? You paraphrase their misery in pretty language, but how much relief does this provide? "Psychologist" is the wrong term for what he does. Quite useless. He is a Salaried Echo. This is more like it. An echo, throwing back what they know already.

Then again, perhaps all he needs is a holiday. He has been collecting the glossy brochures, begun to crave a tan. Somewhere quiet. An unincorporated country. Standing there, going over all this, he notices Roy, the orderly, moving between the beds at the far end of the ward as if he were the spirit of the place, doing the rounds, up to something, flitting from one pillow to the next like Tinkerbell and whispering sweet nothings into each sufferer's ear, which, as Adrian watches, causes each of them to guffaw suddenly! To roar! Lazarine, the half-dead join him in a conspiratorial chit-chat! What the hell? What is the guy up to this time? Roy, Roy, Roy, Roy, Roy.

ROY JESSONS, thirty-two years old, peerless energy for a big man – thirty-two per cent body fat. A pig is only twenty-four per cent body fat, so to call him a fat pig is to insult the pig. "Hell, I'd have to work out for a year to be a fat pig. I *dream* of being a fat pig." That's Roy, a comedian, a law unto himself. Detests authority whenever he feels it originates from dickheads. Lives alone in a hygienist's hell. Rides to work on a 50 cc scooter that will not convey his bulk up hills. Still, he appears to enjoy life indecently, even though he possesses few of the established pre-requisites: looks, money, property, possessions, a woman. Because none of society's nets have snarled his propellers, he goes where others cannot. He finds fun in dark places. Folks with no axe to grind any more, such as the dying, adore him. They see heaven in his sparkling eyes, mirth in his multiple chins, so many chins that were he a violinist he'd be pressed to know under which to set the instrument.

Roy Jessons finds nursing tangentially. Leaves school, unemployed for three years, one day a mix-up on the Welfare Computer. He comes up 4D, a quadriplegic. Papers even arrive. Open arms to destiny, he signs 'em all, qualifies for the full treatment: Meals on Wheels, home visits, even an all-over handwash three times a week from a tidy young half-Jamaican nurse. He fakes debility. Procures a wheelchair from the airport, plays the part for six months. Soon reacts like Pavlov's dog with an erection whenever he hears Nurse Barbara ring his doorbell. Learns an enormous amount about nursing as well, acquires massive respect for the profession, at least until his pretty helper quits and a six-foot-six rugby player turns up to take over with the sponge. A miracle: his disability ends. But figuring to find more Jamaican girls with genial hands like Nurse Barbara, he joins a nursing trainee scheme. He wants to be surrounded by angels with warm hands. But apart from the occasional act of selfless sacrifice on the part of some big-hearted girl, he remains single. The nurses treat him like a mascot. Make him run the hostel halls in his underwear on Halloween. He soon drops out of the nursing training but becomes an orderly. Winds up in Oncology. Dying people worship him.

As Roy works his way closer to the door, zigzagging from bed to bed, Adrian slips back out of sight and watches.

ROY (*to* PATIENT 7, *pancreatic*): Odessa in the third? Nice. Nice. Good bet. Like it. (*To* ALL) We could have a winner here, people! (*To* PATIENT 8, *non-Hodgkin's lymphoma*) And how about you, Gunga Din?

GUNGA DIN (*holding cash*): I'll take Mother of Compassion.

ROY (*whistles*): Not afraid of long odds. Good man. Just because it's never won a race in its considerably long life doesn't mean it can't start now, right? Got to believe in eleventh-hour miracles round here, right? Am I right? Bring it on. Okay. (*To* ALL) Well, I shall hence away to the makers of books and thereafter your bedpans shall be my highest priority. (*He makes a courtly bow, spins around and bumps into* ADRIAN.) Race Three at Ascot is almost fully subscribed, but speak now and I'll see what I can do.

Int. Outer Corridor / Hospital. Contin.

ADRIAN (*lowered voice, disapproving, hierarchical*): You gave me your word. Listen, you know the drill – part of dying involves…

ADRIAN AND ROY (*together*): …preparation for the end…

ROY: You told me.

Adrian tosses Roy's notebook full of bets in the trash bin of a passing janitor. The janitor stops his cart a little further down the corridor.

ADRIAN: I know what you're trying to do. The principle's fine but… you know what I mean. Gambling? We can do better.

ROY: Hey, I'm old school. We're different. And my feeling is: for as long as these people have four wheels on the road, why not let 'em burn some rubber. You say banana, I say potato. But hey, you're the professional.

ADRIAN (*proffers hand*): Deal?

ROY (*shaking it reluctantly*): You're killing me.

Roy starts to walk off then stops, cheekily retrieving his notebook from the trash bin, waves it wantonly over his head, taunting Adrian, at least until a senior member of staff comes out of an office down the corridor, at which Roy snaps the book behind his back, nodding professionally to the senior member, who nods back. Adrian, watching, shakes his head, amused despite himself.

At this moment, an attractive nurse walks past. Astonishingly, she gives Adrian a talk-to-me smile. Adrian, no longer used to such attention, is baffled in that instant, and forgets to return the smile.

NURSE: Doctor.

She even pauses in front of him, giving him a last opportunity.

ADRIAN: Uh… hello.

But instead of pursuing the conversation even cordially and without overtones, he turns and acts busy and walks off down the corridor with almost a jog in his gait. The woman, behind him, looks disappointed, but Adrian, as usual, doesn't see it.

Int. Examination Room / Hospital. Day.

Donald is sitting bare-chested on an examination table as Dr Sipetka takes down two X-rays from the light-board: *snap, snap.* Jim and Renata wait on tenterhooks as the doctor turns and at last irradiates them with his movie-star smile.

DR SIPETKA: Therefore, I'm feeling optimistic enough about these results to suggest we take out the Port-a-Cath. (*He taps the tube embedded in* DON's *shoulder.*)

JIM: You mean… it may not be needed any more?

DR SIPETKA: Let's see. The radiation has helped us a

lot. We're not out of the woods, but I'm liking this. I'm liking it a lot.

RENATA: Oh my God! OH MY GOD! She throws a hand over her mouth and, as realization crosses every synapse, throws her arms around Jim. They celebrate. The first relief in six months. The remission of their own pain. Revealed by its retreat is joy. But they almost forget to include the person for whom this news is the real lifeline. They turn and look at Donald, sitting there against the wall.

RENATA: Oh my God. (*She and* JIM *smother* DON *in a blanket hug.* RENATA *is blubbing.* JIM *halfway there too.*) I'd almost stopped thinking there was any such thing as good news.

DR SIPETKA (*smiling, to* DONALD): Good job. We're not finished yet. The fight goes on, right? We're still fighting, right? But good job, Don.

DONALD (*looking almost nonplussed*): I didn't *do* anything.

Int. Life-drawing Class. Night.
The life-drawing class is painting a female nude tonight. Adrian, in the back row, glances around the side of his canvas to study the model, and only then adds another touch of flesh-tone to his canvas. Satisfied, he looks around at his fellow artists. All of them are hard at work. He looks back at the model, lowers his brush and studies her with a less artistic eye. Thirty-something. A fine specimen. He wonders who she is. Look at her, reclined like that on pillows in her birthday suit, not a pixel of shame in her whole body – and deservedly so. *Nuditas virtualis*. The nakedness enjoyed by Adam and Eve but by

few since then. What a piece of work is a man! Beauty. It's everywhere! He has always been in thrall to it. His heart is often like this: bursting. But bursting privately, unseen, hidden. He feels like crying but cannot allow it. Beauty, beauty everywhere, nor any drop to drink. What relief is there for the thirsting soul of Dr Adrian King?

Int. Movie Theatre. Night.
Don chooses the movie tonight. Jim says it's up to him, and Renata and Jeff agree to abide by his choice. And so here they are, a regular British family out together for a night at the flicks, passing around the popcorn, craning for a clear view between heads in front, and watching a movie about three deviant American teenagers who are superheroes, each possessing eccentric but overwhelming powers that perfectly complement those of their crime-busting pals. The irony is that the only Delpe *not* enjoying the blockbuster is Donald, who keeps shaking his head in the darkness, disgusted by every new implausibility in the plot and muttering "Such horseshit" over and over and so loudly that at least six other people in the theatre have had cause to tell him to shut the hell up. That three of these should be members of his own family only makes it all the more galling.

Int. Car. Night.
Renata's mistake is to ask Donald, on the drive back home, what he thinks of the movie. Terrible move. Jeff groans, anticipating the flood: he has heard it all before. It was a kind of rhetorical question anyway, intended by Renata as a joke, but it gives Donald the chance he needs to unload – and boy how he unloads, beginning right away to talk

more than he has done in the last six months, raving, in fact. He is outraged. He has never seen such horseshit. Call that a movie? He wants his money back. Hype, deep-fried in special effects, served up in a nutrition-free fluffy-white plot. He is incensed by the stupidity of *the last-second rescue*. He wants this idiot cliché exterminated. He's done some research too. The Greeks never needed it for their fables. It never occurred to those German dudes, the Brothers Grimm. Shakespeare, the ultimate dude, from what Don's been forced to read, never resorted to it. But every superhero movie you see nowadays (and every action movie as well) uses it. Where's the entertainment value when the 150-metre rooftop plummet of the sweet old granny is allowed to end not in road pizza but in a perfect last-second rescue, Gran arrested centimetres above the footpath by some superheroic effort, as if the superhero were toying with her, smooching his girl (or boy in the case of all these new spandex-coated über-vixens) while Gran goes **Aaaaaahhhhhhh** until, from two miles away the hero(ine) picks up the scream and in the tradition of all these crowd-pleasers takes his/her leave of their lover with a last dazzling line sufficient to make their sweetheart swoon and then dives, swings, vaults or catapults to the rescue, making up a two-mile shortfall in 0.75 seconds so that we're thinking, Ooo ooo ooo there's no way, there's no way, then... Way! Amazing! Good ol' superhero. Gran saved, cradled like a babe in arms, even her false teeth in place. Roll credits. Don pledges to never again see one of these overblown, moralistic pocket-drainers as long as he lives. Fuck them. ("Language," his mother reprimands.) Why can't it be lifelike *just once*? Why can't the hero feel cheated, abused, cheap and empty? Gran should strawberry-jam herself straight onto a cop car. Life. The superhero's lover should start banging someone else. Regular cruelties. He'd bust his boycott for that.

His family wait for him to slow down. It's Donald's night. They let him run and run on this pet subject. But it is only when Jim Delpe begins to indicate for a left turn 150,000 miles ahead of time that Donald is jerked from his theme.

Int. Shoe Shop. Day.

Man does not walk in Vans alone. Upon this premise Don has agreed to let his mother take him shopping. It's a celebratory buy-up. Anything he wants. At least, that's what she says at first. He even gets excited. But as they make their way into town in the Saab she piles on the caveats: so long as it's practical. Oh, and just so long as it's worn on the feet. The feet? Yes, anything in Footlocker, basically. The field has been narrowed down to shoes. This is his reward for not dying. Fucking mothers.

In the store he has found a pair of Chinese-made Vans lookalikes that he prefers to the new Vans. A modern perversion. And anyway there's nothing else in the store he needs. He hardly has a call for Italian winkle-pickers or a gentleman's brogues, and he'll be damned if he'll make his mother's day by trying on some new black school shoes. What a difference a day makes. School is back on the menu again. Whoop-de-shit, he bubbles: ritual abuse, mind-sapping boredom, daily confirmation of your shortcomings, and the ancient Chinese water torture and systematic brutality of watching the clock creak and groan towards three o'clock and only getting there, finally, when you've lost all concept of freedom, all reason to live. Chemo and radiation are starting to sound pretty good after all.

RENATA: You like these? (DON *nods at the Vans lookalikes.*) Okay. (*To* SHOP GIRL) These'll be great, thanks. But have you got them one size bigger?

SHOP GIRL: Are they too small?

RENATA: No. Perfect fit, but... you know how they grow at this age.

What a difference a day makes, is Donald's thought bubble at that moment. His mother doesn't even say "Touch wood".

Ext. Delpe House. Day.

Donald, the undead, opens up the garage and takes out his old pushbike. The thing is pretty banged up, a veteran of too many kamikaze downhill assaults that terminated in tree trunks and fence lines and parking meters, but it still looks worthy. He gets on it gingerly, points it at the street, then rides down to the end of the drive, turns around and rides back again. End of adventure.

He's knackered. Fucking exhausted. Sitting there, recovering, he rings the rusty old bell on the handlebar. It works, in a dingly sort of way. One ring is almost all he can manage. His stamina is gone. He gets off, puts the bike away and shuts the garage doors.

Standing there, feeling a little nauseous, he surveys the upmarket neighbourhood, one of the best in Watford, a row of mortgage-free houses under heavy DIY fire this morning. He grew up here. The only street he's ever really known. Lucky town. The Tuesday-morning soundtrack is a compressed scream of mowers, circular saws, hammers and revved engines, all conveyed on a steady 15 mph

Gulf Stream wind. Hopeful people, he bubbles, long-range forecasters preparing for the future. Safe and snug strivers all working their foreseeable lives. Pearl Harbor complacency, the day before. That's what this place really is, behind the scenes. Pearl Harbor, December 6. Or else, business as usual on September 10 in a certain two-tower complex in Uptown Manhattan. Don knows that nothing is safe. Nothing can be taken for granted. Nothing is ever out of harm's way.

He breathes deeply. The mid-morning light peeps through the trees and prints lace patterns on his face. "I'm alive." A pretty self-evident thought bubble, this one, but a novelty for Donald. Although he feels something akin to shit warmed up in a microwave right now, he's alive. He has to admit it. His body is performing. His head is clear. It's good. Good enough. But still, his spirits can only manage to ring a feeble dingle of joy.

The reason? It's probably because last night he looked up cobalt-60 on the Internet. The radiologists use a lot of this stuff. How much of it they have already fired into him he will never know, no one will ever tell him, but the Internet site said that cobalt-60 had a half-life of 5.6 years. He then googled "half-life". Well, half-life turns out to be the time a substance takes to lose *half* its radioactivity. Spectacular. By this calculation he'll be a walking Chernobyl until his twenty-first birthday, feeling pretty much as he does now. He will be a semi-Chernobyl until his twenty-sixth.

Bring on the kamikazes, is his next thought bubble. Bring the little bastards on, those echelons of Japanese Zeroes streaming out of the rising sun, targeting him right where he's standing, on the drive in front of his house on a normal Tuesday morning in God's own country, where grass is being mowed, lawns are being watered and unbuilt barbecue decks are being staked out with peg and string. Bring 'em on.

Int. Backyard / Delpe House. Day.

Don sits in the backyard tree-swing, drawing his epic cartoon. He is not wearing his beanie. His hair appears to be growing back. A little girl from next door calls over the fence.

LITTLE GIRL: Why aren't you in school?

DONALD: Why aren't you?

LITTLE GIRL: I'm sick.

DONALD: Makes two of us.

LITTLE GIRL: What have you got?

DONALD: Leprosy.

LITTLE GIRL: What's that?

DONALD: Look it up.

LITTLE GIRL: I've got asthma.

DONALD: I win. Want some morphine?

LITTLE GIRL: What's morphine?

Donald doesn't answer and resumes drawing. He's on a roll. Maybe his annoyance over the previous night's movie has fired him up. He is completing so many single frames so quickly right now that although they only move when he turns the page they feel to him to be flashing by at forty frames a second, sliding through his consciousness like cinema. The story is alive today. Alive.

UP WITH CAPTION (*full frame*): A SECOND TER-RORIST BOMB ROCKS THE ALREADY DEVASTATED BUILDING.

From behind the security cordon a night-time crowd gasps in horror. And then a figure appears through the smoke. It's MIRACLEMAN, carrying an OLD MAN who he places in the arms of TWO POLICEMEN. MIRACLEMAN looks hurt, and is bleeding from several wounds.

POLICEWOMAN: Wait! Who are you? Are you hurt?

MIRACLEMAN: Hurt? I just walked into a blazing inferno. Hello? Sixty per cent of my body is covered in third-degree burns. Of course I'm fucking hurt.

POLICEWOMAN: Language.

MIRACLEMAN: But don't sweat it. It'll heal. Believe me.

MIRACLEMAN wanders off into the night as the CROWD applauds him. Later, in the GRAVEYARD, MIRACLEMAN sinks a SHOVEL into the soil over a GRAVE. But he is spotted. Torchlight finds him.

CEMETERY WORKER: Hey there… what are you doing?

MIRACLEMAN (*embarrassed*): Ah… er… I was just… He drops the shovel and runs away into the night. The CEMETERY WORKER scratches his head.

Later, in a LONELY CITY PARK, MIRACLEMAN sits on a bench, bereft, alone, despairing. His thought bubble reads: "I am depraved…" Suddenly a VOICE behind him startles him.

RACHEL (*O.C.*): So this is where you're hiding.

RACHEL sits beside him. She's prim, brunette, respectable but a knockout.

MIRACLEMAN: I guess I owe you an explanation.

RACHEL: Uh huh.

MIRACLEMAN: Okay, well, here goes. (*Pause*) It was a few years ago. I was working in the city sewers as an engineer.

SWIRLING '70s *flashback transition to…*

...the SEWERS. MIRACLEMAN in a HARD HAT with CLIPBOARD. Suddenly, the bulwark he stands on collapses. He is plunged into the RIVER of SHIT and VILE TOXINS and TOILET PAPER and RATS. He must swim through this HELL to save himself.

RACHEL (*O.S.*): Uggghhh! Disgusting!

MIRACLEMAN (*O.S.*): I know. I know. But at least I got to see what sort of shit was going down.

Cut to...

...MIRACLEMAN in a HOSPITAL BED.

MIRACLEMAN (*O.S.*): Surprise, surprise, I got sick. Some kinda super-virus and bacteria no one has ever seen before. Mystery disease. The doctors were sure I was finished. In fact, for a few seconds...

A HEART-RATE MONITOR FLATLINES...

BURRRRRRRRRRRR!!!

MIRACLEMAN: I was. I was gone. But then...

HEART RATE returns – Blip – blip – blip...

MIRACLEMAN: As they say, what doesn't kill you makes you stronger, right?

Cut to...

...MIRACLEMAN RISES from a WHEELCHAIR and feels his strength return.

Cut to...

...A DOCTOR in his office addresses MIRACLEMAN.

DOCTOR: I've never seen anything like these results! Your immune system is... well, it's off the charts!

MIRACLEMAN: Off-the-charts good, I hope.

DOCTOR: A normal white blood count is around 2000. Yours is... well, yours is...

MIRACLEMAN: What? Spit it out, Doc! I'm getting piles waiting.

DOCTOR: 140,000!

MIRACLEMAN: 140,000? But how?...

DOCTOR: These figures... er... gotta run these figures again. They can't be right. It's IMPOSSIBLE!

Flash forwards: PARK BENCH...

MIRACLEMAN: So ever since, no matter what happens to me, nothing can touch me. Nothing.

RACHEL: Nothing? Not even love?

MIRACLEMAN stares deeply into this beauty's eyes.

MIRACLEMAN (*ruefully*): I wouldn't know.

At this most romantic of moments MIRACLEMAN FARTS.

MIRACLEMAN: Sorry. I hate it when I do that.

RACHEL: Know what? I hate it too. Can you stop it?

MIRACLEMAN: I'll try. I'm only human. That's the best I can do. I'll try.

Ext. High School. Day.

Donald wanders up the snaking front drive in his school clothes (plus shiny new school shoes from Footlocker – yes, he succumbed), while most of the other boys look like they've just survived a battle, though it's only 9 a.m. – an army trudging in defeat back to their lines. The school bell peals. Donald joins their ranks and his feet scrape the ground as he walks. His beanie is condom-tight on his head, pulled down over his eyebrows, and it is breached only by the earbuds of his iPod, thumping into his wool-warm skull a cyclotron of self-inflicted sound while his thumbs jog the + control on a Gameboy, bringing his "man" into battle again and again, both in and out of the line of fire. School daze. The best daze of your life.

Int. High School. Day.

In the hallways he talks to no one, as usual. And no one talks to him. Where is the banner in the hallway: Welcome Back Donald? The spontaneous valedictory chant? He is not sure if anyone is staring at him. He expects they are staring, but he would have to look up from his Gameboy to be sure and he's not looking up, not for all the G-strings in Rio de Janeiro. The Mario Brothers are extremely helpful at times like this. They may lack a dimension, as well as any conversational faculties (so they fall short of being actual friends), but they can sure get you through a tough social moment.

When the bell rings he takes his old desk in his class near the window and then, after being embarrassingly welcomed back (from the dead) – a mortifying moment of exposure, greeted with an actual *booo*, a low, almost sub-aural *booo* from his peers (bless them all) – his eye-line veers between the teacher, the grimy collar of the boy in front of him, the wall clock (senile in its progress) and the window where he psychologically evaluates himself by doing ink-blot tests with the clouds: he sees cleavage in the cirrocumulus, arse in the altocumulus, yet more cleavage in the high-flying cirrostratus, yet more arse in the low-drifting cumulonimbus, and tits almost everywhere, forming and unforming in a tangled orgy of suggestion – in short, one horny flesh fest of a cloudbank. Time lags. Seconds extrapolate into aeons. He dreams, returns, dreams, returns, makes compulsory notes in his exercise books and finally, mercifully, it's 12.20. Time for lunch.

Ext. Lower Field / High School. Day.

What will it be? Pant, pant. A hot dog and fries? Pant, pant. A Kit Kat and Coke? Pizza and Jack Daniels? No, as Donald opens his lunchbox – packed by Chef Renata of *Restaurant Cancer Foundation* – he ought to be more surprised than he is to find inside a salad garnished with rye grass. The latest experiment. A little chopped tomato, yes, boiled broccoli, sure, but liberally sprinkled with the same matter that surrounds him as he sits under this tree, the same flora upon which he will later watch his classmates hit fours during the sports break, the same staple that presently sustains the nation's rain-lashed sheep, or that when raised into a knoll once supported one of the three teams of shooters in Dallas's Dealey Plaza, to JFK's ruin. Turf. Fucking mothers. She's feeding him turf. He doesn't know what to do. Should he pick up the useful plastic fork his mother has supplied him with, or place the box on the ground, assume the proportions of a field animal and advance upon the box on all fours? Fucking mothers.

RAFF: Hey!

MICHAEL: So... this is where you're hiding.

DONALD: Hey.

MICHAEL: Hey.

RAFF: So, what? You don't want to be seen with us, or what?

DONALD: No. I just...

RAFF: Looked like you'd seen a ghost when we showed up at your house.

DONALD: Yeah well... I had a puke coming. That's all. I saw you guys and it just came over me.

Donald gets to his feet, closes his Tupperware box of veg and pasture, shakes hands with his old cohorts.

MICHAEL: Anyway, enough of this shit. You're back now, so let's get down to business like before, 'kay?

DONALD: So... you've still been selling, then?

MICHAEL: Selling? You kidding? What do you think is in this fucking bag?

Michael has a heavy-looking Nike sports bag over his shoulder. Donald stares at his friends, at the fateful bag, then back at them, until it is just assumed they are all listening to the same song.

Int. Principal's Office. Day.
PRINCIPAL: You were seen *selling* these in the gymnasium. You were *observed*. Okay. Is there anyone else involved with you in this? (*Holds up a pirated CD.*) You have nothing to say? You were alone. You acted at no one's *behest*. Then I'll tell you what I'm going to do. First, I'll address the school tomorrow morning about music piracy and I shall make it grounds for expulsion. Then, as to you. As to you, young man. I *could* phone the police. I *could*. But because of your medical situation I have decided against this. I have, however, spoken with your father – yes – and he assures me that he will take away your ability to make such recordings in the future. He will remove your CD-burner permanently. It will then be expected that you and your... collaborators – yes, collaborators – don't underestimate me, will not make or try to sell another one of these... these... productions. Do you understand me? Do you? Donald? Don?

Int. Adrian's Office. Day.
Adrian waits for Donald to answer him, but the boy has withdrawn again. It is impossible to tell what he is thinking.

ADRIAN: Your parents thought we should have another talk. (*Silence*) Do you like liquorice? (*When* DON *doesn't reply,* ADRIAN *eats some liquorice on his own.*) So – do you know any jokes?

DONALD: What? (*A sign of life.*)

ADRIAN: This man was once asked… this man was once asked how he wanted to die. He thought for a moment. He thought for a moment and said that he probably wanted to go just like his father did, quietly in his sleep – quietly in his sleep – not screaming like his passengers. (DON *is a statue.*) Look, why don't we have an outing? Would you like that?

DONALD: An outing?

ADRIAN: A little outing, yes.

DONALD: Do I look eighty-five years old? An outing?

ADRIAN: Say whatever you think. Please. You can say anything you want here.

DONALD: Fuck you. How's that?

ADRIAN: Okay. Good.

DONALD (*loudly*): FUCK!!! YOU!!!!!

(*Pause*)

ADRIAN (*calmly*): Excellent.

Int. Adrian's Office. Day.

RENATA: An outing?

Adrian picks up his gold-tip Mont Blanc fountain pen and rolls it back and forth between his fingers, as if he's making a roll-up: a gesture both spontaneous and practised, a pose seemingly schooled into psychologists.

ADRIAN: He doesn't seem to want to talk with me. Despite the good news on the physical front, he is still extremely angry, pessimistic, withdrawn and trying to shock me. So the idea came to me. It came from you showing me his journal – his graphic novel, as he calls it. I began to think he's an artist. I know a little about art. I paint in my spare time. There are a couple of things I could show him. Re-interest him in something. See, I've become interested in art's ability to move, to inspire, perhaps even to heal. Sort of a sideline of mine at the moment.

RENATA: Art therapy?

ADRIAN: Well, not exactly. I suppose it revolves around the concept of beauty — exposure to beauty, its curative powers. Tell me if you think it's a bad idea.

JIM: No, it sounds... Yeah. Anything. Anything like that you can think of.

RENATA: So you'd?... What? Take him?...

ADRIAN: I don't know yet. I'd have to think about it. But first I wanted to run the idea by you to see if you... because none of this...

RENATA: Whatever you can do.

ADRIAN: ...is... it's really...

RENATA: Yes.

JIM: I think it's a great idea.

RENATA: Actually I'm so relieved. I thought you wanted to tell us you couldn't do anything with him. (*Nervous laugh*)

ADRIAN: This might be another approach.

Int. Lobby / London Art Gallery. Day.
The sign reads: "For Exhibitions Follow Signage". Adrian and Don follow the arrows until they pass under a portico draped with a billowing silk advertising *Lovers in Art*. A regular father-and-son team. The father leading the son towards some edifying experience, the son lagging behind and wanting to turn left and join the long queue waiting to get into *The Making of The Wizard's Apprentice* exhibition which is guarded by a life-size effigy of its teen star, David Sutcliffe. There is no queue for *Lovers in Art*.

Don's new stand-in Vans are making a terrible racket on the flagged marble. With every extension of his leading leg, the ball of the trailing foot shrieks **"SQUEEEEE!"**, its echo turning heads previously intent on contemplating 400 years' artistic expression of human passion.

Adrian is excited. The exhibition has come as part of a world tour direct from Frankfurt. It's a superb assemblage and he likes the thematic presentation: so much better to see what twenty people make of one subject than what one artist makes of twenty. Among the works: Hugh Goldwin Riviere's *The Garden of Eden* in which a woman in Kensington Gardens on a grey London day studies her fiancé's face as if it's a map and she's lost: simple adoration; Evelyn de Morgan's gorgeous *Boreas and Orithyia*, in which a winged suitor, bored of a damsel's refusals, simply grabs the broad and hijacks her heavenwards; Renoir's *Dance in the Country*, a simple scene straight out of Flaubert, an older man and a young beauty, pure provincial sunshine shining out of the canvas. But perhaps most poignant of all (at least for Adrian, who stops at length in front of it) is Jean-Léon Gérôme's *Pygmalion and Galatea* in which a puritanical sculptor, bachelorized by the appalling morals of the women of his time, chisels a nude to his own design and mounts the plinth to deliver kisses to her cold, cold lips: the rank foolishness of the pious.

Donald joins Adrian, casts a dull glance at the canvas and walks on. Adrian catches him up. Donald is bored, bored, bored.

DONALD: What are we doing here?

ADRIAN: Well… in art we can sometimes find the essence of life. "It is through Art, and Art alone, that we can realize perfection." Oscar Wilde.

DONALD: Friend of yours?

ADRIAN: I wanted you to see this.

DONALD: You mean, before I die?

ADRIAN: Who says you're going to die? You're responding very well. There's every reason for hope. Every reason. And… and I thought this might inspire you. You're an artist. It inspires me. But if you're not enjoying it, we can go.

They pass on to some new paintings, also female nudes. Donald stops and appears to take an interest at last. Adrian approaches.

DONALD: They're all fat. All these chicks. This is one big booty right here.

ADRIAN: Well, this is pre-Pilates classes remember, pre-aerobics. And only the poor were slim and brown in those days.

DONALD: Then they need a few more paintings of poor people if you ask me.

They leave the exhibition and step into another room, the Vanettes chirping on the marble floor. Another touring piece stands on a low podium: an icon of twentieth-century art.

ADRIAN: What do you think of that?

DON: Looks like a cycling accident.

A velvet rope separates them from an upended wheel whose forks are set into a wooden stool.

ADRIAN: Marcel Duchamp's *Bicycle Wheel*. You know, when this work was originally displayed, in 1913, it was the artist's intention that the viewer touch the piece. He wanted people to spin it, to experience art with all five senses.

Don nods and then, before Adrian can stop him, he climbs over the velvet rope.

ADRIAN (*under his breath, suffering cardiac arrest*): Donald – Donald – Donald – Don – Don – Don…

Donald gives the ancient bicycle wheel an almighty spin and nods approvingly as it flies into life, as if once again speeding down the boulevards of Paris. He returns to stand beside Adrian as the wheel rattles on and only finally slows – but much too slowly for Adrian, for whom the next minute seems to take about as long to elapse as the Ch'ing dynasty.

And it is while the most famous bicycle wheel in the history of art is still turning that the security guard strolls back into the gallery and comes their way, ambling, arms behind his back, eyes as yet on the multi-million-pound paintings and their viewers. Adrian hopes for a second that they might just have got away with it – until Duchamp abruptly starts to squeak. *Squeak – squeak – squeak*, says Duchamp, finding his voice again after eighty silent years. It's a faint twitter, but in a huge hall like this it's amplified into a head-turner.

The guard stops, turns on his heels, his face flushing red – it takes a moment for him to recognize the source of the noise. It's just enough time for Adrian to grab Donald and drag the grinning kid out by the sleeve before the guard can do anything more than fumble for his walkie-talkie.

DONALD (*To* GUARD *as they pass*): All five senses!

Squeee, squeee, squeee go the Van-clones. *Squeak – squeak – squeak – squeak*, replies Duchamp, in a conversation befitting budgerigars.

Ext. Gallery. Contin.
Hurrying down the steps, fleeing, a laughing Don surprises once again by sliding down the long banister – sailing,

feet up, leaning back, hands behind controlling the rate of descent, and gathering quite a speed so that when he jumps off just before hitting the crotch-busting newel the ground comes at him so fast he's forced to run, head first now, arms windmilling to keep him upright but, in the end, failing. He crashes in a heap, hard. Adrian chases down the steps two at a time but when he arrives Donald is already back on his feet, pretending nothing has happened.

DONALD (*dusting himself off*): Don't sweat it.

ADRIAN: Sure you're okay?

DONALD: I'm titanium. (*Pause*) I'm hungry.

Int. Upmarket Restaurant. Day.

Donald, still pleased with himself, looks through the fancy menu. For a few seconds Adrian stops monitoring the boy and looks around. This is his first visit here, and he's impressed. Bright, well-mannered staff, tasteful decor, and three wine glasses set at each place. His eye stops on a salmanazar of champagne (twelve bottles' worth) displayed near the entrance in a keg of ice.

ADRIAN: Have you ever had champagne?

DONALD: Champagne? Course I have. Well, kinda. A few sips.

ADRIAN: Would you like some now? Just this once?

DONALD (*smiles, shrugs and looks around*): Swish place.

WAITER (*arriving*): Are you ready to order?

ADRIAN: Donald?

DONALD (*studying the menu*): Uh… um… just give me… like some bread, gotta be white, fluffy, and some butter, and I want some French fries with ketchup and mustard. (*The waiter is a statue.*) Got that?

The statue looks at Adrian who nods.

WAITER (*To* ADRIAN): And you, sir?

ADRIAN: The same. But I'll have brown bread. And a bottle of Cristal '98. Thank you. Excellent.

He smiles at Don.

DONALD: So. You're gay, right?

ADRIAN (*his jaw dropping*): Why do you say that?

DONALD: I dunno. There's just something a little foofy about you. But that's cool. Just admit it.

ADRIAN: I'm not gay. (*Pause*) Would you like to know about my private life?

DONALD: Definitely not.

Two flutes arrive. A bottle of champagne. Don watches closely as the waiter tears open the foil and unwinds the wire brace.

Ext. Upmarket Restaurant. Day.

At a puddle, Don walks straight through, while Adrian, a little giddy from drinking the bulk of the champagne, kind of hitches up his pants and bounds over it. It's an accidentally effete gesture, unfortunate because Don sees it and fires him a told-you-so look right away.

DONALD (*sotto voce*): Well done, Adrian.

Adrian has to smile and shake his head. Smart kid. Precocious. And so much more worldly than he was at the same age; in some ways, more worldly than he'll ever be, at least in an understanding of the current global pop culture. But then, he was cynical about all these whirling trends, the whole tyranny of what is cool or uncool. Let Don's generation worship that exhaustive game of Now-you-see-'em Now-you-don't. The drone of trouble coming was a roar in Adrian's ears. Psyches were darkening. He saw it daily on the wards. Following the prozac-gulping crowd wouldn't help you. Let the man of intellect, with a heart, find his own way. He will back classic values, the Culture of Permanence. And this grand classification he divides, like God, into a trinity: Lasting Works of Beauty, Enduring Mysteries and Timeless Principles. But he suspects all this would simply make a kid like Don laugh. Loser, would be Don's verdict. Gay loser.

He tries to imagine himself, at fourteen, asking a man some forty years his senior – and an authority figure to boot – if he was gay. Impossible.

They reach the car. Adrian starts the engine without a word.

Int. Don's Bedroom / Delpe House. Night.

On the computer screen: the word "Downloading", beneath it a bar in which a blue band is slowly being displaced by white, like mercury climbing in a thermometer, serum flooding a syringe, drugs filling a vein. Below this: the icon of a demon.

Donald unpacks from his rucksack a portable CD-burner (it took barely an hour to replace the one his Dad had confiscated), plugs it in, then takes the mouse and clicks on a screen icon. Then he gets up, unlocks the door and exits his bedroom, leaving behind his 20-gigaflop hard drive whirring at cyclonic speed under the table: the near equal of the human-memory-storage capacity of a small country, all in a single box. His screen flicks to a screensaver, ushering in from all sides little red she-devils riding writhing pythons.

Int. Jeff's Bedroom / Delpe House. Night.

Don creeps into this off-limits area and reaches for a book, *Introduction to Macroeconomics*, in whose pages he locates a sandwiched plastic bag of grass. About twenty-five grams of it, most of it quality heads. He puts the book back on the shelf, reuniting once more a chapter on Keynes and another on Friedman, two divided theories which can agree on one at least: no matter how precise the mathematical forecasts, everybody is guessing. More or less just picking numbers from hats. Our supposedly secure futures are always out there on the bidding table, our possessions never safe no matter how well-hidden or protected, outcomes to be decided by a spin of the irksome and ever-spinning wheel of diminishing returns. That's just how it is. Nobody can foretell anything. Randomness rules. No true havens or hedges or sure bets. It's dog-eat-dog to the power of ten – and Don, an instrument of laissez-faire, closes the door carefully on his way out. The market has spoken.

Int. Don's Bedroom / Delpe House. Night.

Don lights up, takes a puff and nods as if his head is on a spring, back and forth, back and forth.

DONALD: Rock the house.

With the joint streaming smoke in his right hand, he checks on the progress of the download with his left. The demons vanish in a puff. The download bar is seventy-five per cent flooded with white. The files are coming down the pike slowly. He snaps back to the screensaver, which is much more soothing on the eye, and then, to introduce even more atmosphere, he stands and reverses his favourite poster – a leaping, airborne youth, an exponent of Free

Running, or *Le Parkour*, hanging in the deadly blue between tall buildings – to reveal…

…to reveal, on the back, a topless double-D vixen straddling a Harley. Dope always gives Don a semi. He has a semi most of the time anyway but dope really gets him horny. Lucky he always has his vixen on stand-by.

After gazing at his motorcycle chick for a couple of puffs, Don takes out his pens, opens his cartoon book and begins to colour in a few plates he has outlined earlier, pausing only to take further drags of the joint as… as… as… the room around him saturates with ambient light, a magic-hour gloaming, the kind of light seen on Day One in the Garden of Eden when God was the Key Grip and lit everything like a motherfucker and Saw That It Was Good – heavenly tones to everything, divine interplay of light and shadow at first, until, like a sunrise, the colours deepen and become bolder as Don takes further tokes and feels evermore at one with his maker, that master cartoonist, pinks and primrose and turquoise seeping into block reds, greens and vivid blues until Donald's room transfigures utterly and becomes… becomes… becomes…

MIRACLEMAN reaches over to the ashtray beside his mouldy single bed and taps ash from his doobie when he hears – a KNOCK on his rat-trap motel door. A knock isn't good. Paradise Lost. He rises from his damp bare mattress, rapidly hides the dope behind Roy Wiston's excellent compendium *Comic Book Planet*, the only book in the room. He then fans the air pointlessly. The odour of dope is unmistakable. He goes over to a 2-D door handle (which miraculously supports his hand nonetheless) and nervously pulls open the Toontown pane to reveal...

...RACHEL (15), his heart's desire, a girl-band singer and dancer, but dressed primly tonight, smiling at him two-dimensionally, one arm behind her back: FLOWERS? A nice girl, this, a hand-reared, hothouse variety girl, but with a little devil inside her somewhere, he can sense it, a side never before unloosed in his presence. He smiles back at her, but then, from behind her back, she produces a gun, a high-calibre side arm, which she aims between his eyes from point-blank range.

MIRACLEMAN: What the?...

BOOM!!!!

The HIGH-CALIBRE DUM-DUM blasts a HUGE and GAPING HOLE clear through MIRACLEMAN's head, then slams into the window frame across the room, **KRAANCH!!!**, there disturbing a FLY, a household *musca domestica*, on the windowsill, who takes flight, crosses in panic the now BLOOD- & BONE-SPATTERED ROOM, retracing more or less the bullet's trajectory and zigzagging towards our miraculously still standing and breathing hero, at last entering (**UGGGHH!**) MiracleMan's skull by the rear portal, disappearing for a few seconds into that GRIM PASSAGE where we CUT TO... FLY-CAM, heading for the LIGHT AT THE END OF THE TUNNEL and final purchase on the warm unwavering tip of RACHEL's smoking gun. Behind that gun, still taking aim, is RACHEL's sweet face. Her mouth opens. She speaks – but with a detestably MALE VOICE:

RACHEL: What are you up to, dog breath?

With this, the dream collapses.

JEFF: I said… what are you up to?

Donald blinks. His brother is standing before him in the doorway, showing anger in three vivid dimensions. Jeff's nostrils flare, sniffing, determining smells. He barges in, pushing Don aside.

JEFF: So where is it? What have you done with it? Just cos you've got cancer doesn't mean you can do anything you want, okay.

DONALD: Yes it does.

JEFF: You little… Just give it to me, all right? That shit's expensive. You know how long it took me to steal money from Dad to buy that? Fucking ages, that's how long. So give it up.

DONALD: What are you gonna do?

JEFF: I'll make your life hell.

DONALD: Too late. What else you gonna do?

JEFF: I dunno. I'll tear this room apart till I find it and then… (*Grabs the computer keyboard, jerks the stretch cable out.*) …then I'll tell Mum and Dad about all the illegal MP3s you've been burning and selling.

DONALD: Too late. They know already.

JEFF: Bullshit. Give me the fucken dope.

DONALD: Wanna hear something? (DONALD *plugs in his iPod to the computer's speakers.*) Cos Mum and Dad might like to hear this too.

Donald hits Play. There is the noise of Jeff and a girlfriend giggling and moaning and sighing to the sound of bed springs going crazy.

GIRLFRIEND (O.S.): *Is this okay? Oh God. Mmmmm. Mmwahh. Ohhhhh.*

JEFF (O.S.): *Yeah. It's sexy. This… this is where I was made.* (SMASH OF A VASE!) Jesus!

GIRLFRIEND (O.S.): *Yeah. You're right. This is sexy. In your parents' bed. Hey, hey. Ha! Ha! Come on. No, not like that. Here. No, silly. Don't you know? Stop. Tse! Dummy. Don't you know…*

Jeff, with a sudden bad case of facial sunburn, slams off the volume and stares at Donald.

JEFF: You wouldn't. Dad'd… Dad'd… he'd kill me.

DONALD: Ooohhh. Aahhhhhh.

JEFF: Wow. You're pretty hard-arse these days.

DONALD: Titanium.

The she-devils have by now defaulted back onto the screen all by themselves.

Int. Adrian's Office. Day.
Session Three.

ADRIAN: What are you feeling right now?

DONALD: Horny. Any more questions?

ADRIAN: Are you depressed?

DONALD: No.

ADRIAN: What are you afraid of? Dying?

DONALD: No.

ADRIAN: Why not? Don't you want to live?
(*Silence, then…*)

DONALD: Life is a sexually transmitted disease. It's spread by people having sex, and in the end it kills you.

ADRIAN: Who said that?

DONALD: MiracleMan. When The Glove drives over him with a steamroller.

ADRIAN: You tried to kill yourself. Let's talk about that.

DONALD: Better to go out in a blaze of glory.

ADRIAN: Are you afraid of hurting your parents?

DONALD: No.

ADRIAN: So you're not afraid of anything?

DONALD: No.

ADRIAN: No?

DONALD: Nothing can touch me.

ADRIAN: You have nothing to lose, right?

DONALD: Go figure.

Int. Adrian's Apartment. Day.

Adrian shows Donald round his apartment. Opera is playing. The place smells faintly of fruit-scented cleaning products and coffee.

DONALD: Nice place. Lush.

In the hallway he stops and looks at a painting of a bare-breasted woman slumped as if after a tragedy, grief-stricken, holding a dead man in her arms. The man's head is thrown back, the eyes closed – he's dead all right. The background has not been attempted. There is no context to this suffering.

ADRIAN: It's a pietà.

DONALD: It's pretty good.

ADRIAN: Thanks. I did a better one over there, I think. More balance to the colours.

DONALD: *You* did this?

ADRIAN: Don't sound so surprised.

Donald moves into the living room, looking at the other pietà, nodding with approval.

DONALD: Wow. Not bad. So… so what's it about?

ADRIAN: It's about… form, I guess.

DONALD: Okay, that means a lot. What's it about? Tell me what it's about.

ADRIAN (*a little taken aback*): Okay. It's about… I

suppose it's about... what I see, almost every day, on the ward. This is a kind of... well, a symbolic representation of what I see. I suppose.

DONALD: On the ward? The cancer ward?

ADRIAN: Yes. The cancer ward. This is one of the principal motifs used in art to represent human suffering. Every great artist has contributed to this tradition. Even the moderns try to, after a fashion.

DONALD: No shit?

ADRIAN: No shit.

Donald is finally happy with this answer and he moves on, going to the CD collection. His index and second fingers do a walk down the titles.

ADRIAN: Can I get you a drink? A Coke?

DONALD (*pulling out CDs*): Sure. So what's this then? That you're playing now?

ADRIAN (*calling*): You're listening to an aria from *Samson et Dalila*.

DONALD: Oh yeah?

ADRIAN: It's called... 'My Heart Trembles at the Sound of Your Voice'.

DONALD: Corny.

ADRIAN (*returning with the Coke*): All opera is corny. Fundamentally. But somehow it works. If you let it.

Donald picks up the cat, which has been winding figure eights around his legs, then plonks himself down on the couch, puts his feet up and begins to stroke the life out of the animal.

DONALD: So... (*taking in the whole apartment now, and ready to give his assessment*) so you're still trying to tell me you're not gay? (*Pause*) Come on. You probably like working with young boys, right?

ADRIAN: What's gay about what you see? I'm curious.

DONALD: Come on. I mean, you own a cat. I rest my case. Time to be honest with yourself, guy. So what's your lover's name? Oh, I just got it. Oscar, right?! Bull's-eye! So how is Oscar in the sack, then? Who's the bitch?

ADRIAN: Where do you learn this stuff? I'm married. And Oscar Wilde died in 1900.

DONALD: So how old's that make you?

ADRIAN: My wife simply prefers to spend her time in the country. I see her on weekends.

DONALD: Wife in the country? Yeah? I get it. Nice one.

ADRIAN: The cat is hers.

DONALD: Yeah. Right.

Ext. City Street. Day.
Adrian's car drives out of Watford, enters a dark underpass on the M1 and reappears, somewhat magically…

Ext. Countryside. Day.
…in idyllic Warwickshire countryside, eighty miles further up the road. Around his car rolling slopes shimmer under an overhead sun that makes them glow fluorescent. Beyond the dotted cow sheds stretch grassy tracts as perfect in their way as fitted carpet.

Ext. Country House. Day.
Adrian's Audi 900 pulls into a gravel drive leading to a smart Tudor-style cottage with conservatories fore and aft. As he comes to a stop he notices a stranger's car parked in the drive beside the house. Adrian gets out, presses his face to the passenger window of the car – sees a notepad

inside, a mobile phone, remnants of a takeaway, a ball of twine, a Tom Clancy novel – then rises and walks towards the house, stooping to pick up a garden trowel dropped on the path. The trowel head is caked in fresh mud. A worm has yet to forsake the sod, the tail showing – tail or head, hard to tell. He goes to the gatepost and taps the trowel. After a moment's thought, he proceeds to the house.

Int. Country House. Day.

No one is in the living room. Adrian hears voices from the kitchen. He goes through, still carrying the trowel. In the kitchen he finds his wife, his beautiful wife, the beautiful French-born Sophie, talking quietly to CONRAD MORGAN, the local vet. Only one in the area. Stand-out handsome. Thirty-six. Married. Two children.

CONRAD (*animated*): Adrian! Fantastic.

SOPHIE (*surprised*): Adrian! I thought I heard a car.

ADRIAN (*unanimated*): Conrad. (*He kisses SOPHIE on the cheek.*) Dear.

He shakes Conrad's already extended hand, then turns again to look at Sophie. Ah, Sophie, Sophie, Sophie, Sophie.

SOPHIE, thirty-five, restless, hot, impatient. Hair seacoal black, tied back. Hourglass figure, skin unfaultable. An oven of a body, a degree over normal her whole life. Wide eyes. A huge mouth. A beauty. She views life as a search for a secret door, one operated by a hidden spring that must be sought and pressured to work. Behind the secret door, she feels, is her True Fate. Her search for the spring has been excruciating and lifelong. She often thinks she has found it, only to discover that the void behind the removed library book is just an architect's accident, and that the head of the magnificent bust – which turns! – simply grinds plaster dust onto the floor at her feet... Born in the resort town of Le Touquet. Her father closes their ancestral hotel when Holiday Inn opens next door. Develops early a taste for protest. Leaves school and later a secretarial position in a Paris car dealership to be a human shield in Palestine, linking arms around a *Médecins Sans Frontières* hospital. Falls in love with a medic. Meets Adrian two years later, at twenty-five, while still involved with her French doctor. A clandestine affair, which she propels, fuels long-shot plans. When Adrian returns to England she cannot live without him. He picks her up from the airport. They marry within days of her arrival. She delights in him, talks of children, is dovetailed to his needs. He can think of nothing but her. A devoted year. Bliss. But it does not last. Soon she is bored. Not of him, she assures him, just bored. A lifelong susceptibility. She cannot help it. And despite his qualifications, he has no remedy except love. Now when he comes home she is silent, stern, reprimanding and cold. She is hopelessly at odds with the locals. She wants out, out of the city. Horses. A solution. She has always loved them. She wants to be surrounded by horses. She finds a farmlet near Coventry with stables. Adrian cannot leave his post in the city, and the rush-hour drive is two hours each way. But she is adamant. The mortgage is ridiculous, but he straps this on his back too. For the next two years she lets him commute, grow fatter, lose his hair, driving the four hours each day to be with her. But when he reaches her, after all the twisting miles, with his skin mealy, his shirt sucked to his back, she increasingly doesn't want him to touch her. Finally she persuades him to rent a flat in town during the week. He complies, lovesick. She would visit him more often in the city, she explains, but for the horses, who need her. At last she is almost satisfied.

And so, on Mondays, before birdsong, his tyres spit gravel in the drive. And on Fridays his car returns. He loves her. That is all he reports each time. If she loves him then they will be just fine. If they can only have weekends, he will take that. And if she doesn't wish to sleep with him, then he will tolerate this too. And if all this is no guarantee of happiness, then so be it. When is happiness ever guaranteed anyway?

CONRAD (*very warmly*): Great to see you again. Just up for the weekend then?

ADRIAN (*looking at his wife*): Yes. Just up for the weekend.

SOPHIE: I was just… gardening… when Conrad called in… to tell us about Regency.

ADRIAN (*offering* SOPHIE *the fallen trowel*): I see. I see. And how is the old nag doing?

SOPHIE: On his last legs, looks like. Conrad says – don't you – that it's just old age.

ADRIAN: Right. Well. Every horse has its day. I dare say the time will come to put him out of his misery. (*Smiles at* SOPHIE, *then back to* CONRAD.) Will you stay for dinner, Conrad?

CONRAD (*ill at ease*): Dinner? Well I… actually, I don't think I can. Damn. More rounds to make. Got another mare in foal to deal with, y'see.

ADRIAN: Quite the stud. Old Regency. In his heyday. Quite the stud. Wouldn't you say, Sophie? That he was quite a stud?

SOPHIE: Yes. I suppose so.

CONRAD (*awkwardly*): Right then. Great to see you again, Adrian.

Conrad somehow fashions a smile out of nothing and goes out of the front door. Adrian turns to his wife, who says nothing and then turns and goes out of the back door with her trowel, leaving Adrian standing there, alone.

Int. Dining Room / Country House. Night.
At supper, after a lengthy silence...

ADRIAN: I'm seeing a boy. An interesting, very smart boy – with leukaemia. Fourteen years old. An extraordinary kid. Totally resigned to dying. Or at least, that's what he'd have people believe. Refuses to fight. I've started to write my paper again. About art...

SOPHIE (*suddenly*): There must be something else we can talk about.

Cut to ADRIAN...

He stares at her, angry, his fists bunched.

ADRIAN: Why? Why must there be?

An insufferable gloom pervades the room. They resume eating. Husband and wife. There is only one more verbal exchange before dessert.

SOPHIE: Have you ever cried, Adrian? Don't you ever cry?

ADRIAN. Sometimes. During a cricket match. (*Later*) Like most men, I cry when it doesn't count.

Int. Master Bedroom/ Country House. Night.
Adrian tries to make love to his Sophie. She complains that he makes the bed too hot. He moves down onto the carpet beside the bed, and under a sheet and staring at the ceiling listens to her childlike breathing in the night.

Int. Master Bedroom / Country House. Night.

The next night he tries to make love to her again. She turns her face away. He feels elephantine next to her and releases her. She rolls away from him, a mouse. He rises, hurting, paces the house. Looks out of the bay windows on the fallow vineyard, a mass of weeds. He'll wait for sun-up. Then he'll drive back early while the roads over the ranges to the city are empty.

His eyes fill with tears. He sobs. Unseen. Useless tears.

Ext. Fairground. Day.

A windless Watford day. Hung washing doesn't flap. Hair isn't disturbed. Weather vanes have no bearing.

Donald is setting the agenda today. The fairground is his idea. Quid pro quo. So Donald smiles when he sees Adrian looking squeamishly at the roller-coaster carriages crashing by overhead, at the vomit-inducing centrifuges and human slingshots that keep people sucked back into their seats like astronauts at take-off.

DONALD: Come on!

Donald is up for everything, Adrian nothing. They wait in line at the ticket booth for a ride that should be cited in the Geneva Convention: the Cyclotron.

ADRIAN: Sounds like a device to split atoms, to drive electrons from the gravitation field of the nuclei.

DONALD: Close. Very close. Come on, this queue is horseshit. This is gonna take for ever. Come on. (*He grabs ADRIAN's sleeve and pulls him forwards, announcing, at megaphone strength.*) Excuse me, sorry, cancer, I'm dying, sorry, cancer, thanks. Only got a short time to live, thanksalot.

At the ticket window (the ploy works brilliantly, for nobody wants to wrangle with death):

DONALD (*To* SELLER): Two for the Cyclotron and two for the Death Express.

ADRIAN: Woah, woah... now hold on... I'm a spectator here.

DONALD: Two.

SELLER (*ignoring* ADRIAN): That's sixteen pounds.

DONALD: Great. (*To* ADRIAN) Pay him.

ADRIAN (*opening his wallet*): I'm not sure this is such a good idea.

DONALD: Don't tell me what I can do. I'm screwed anyway.

ADRIAN: I'm not worried about you. I'm worried about me.

Donald laughs for the first time. They grab the tickets, move away and bump right into Michael Reeves and Raff Bennett, just coming off the Cyclotron. Don's entire demeanour shape-shifts for the worse.

MICHAEL: Hey Donny Darko!

DONALD (*awkward, suddenly fidgety*): Oh... uh... hi...

MICHAEL: Gotta try the Cyclotron, mate. Awesome. (*Eyes flick to* ADRIAN.)

RAFF: Yeah, it's hard out.

DONALD: Cool.

RAFF: No, serious. Hey, what's up? (*Eyes flick to* ADRIAN.)

DONALD: Yeah. Yeah. (*Turns to* ADRIAN.) Oh, uh... this is... this is like my... my karate teacher.

MICHAEL: Hi.

ADRIAN (*does small karate chop in the air*): Haaah!

Only Adrian thinks this is amusing.

MICHAEL: Anyway, see ya. Call you, OK? Let's talk business.

DONALD: Yeah, yeah.

(*The boys walk off.*)

ADRIAN: Karate teacher?

Later, riding the Cyclotron alone, Don is pressed back against the inner wall of the spinning cylinder. Round and round he goes, at terrible speed, but he is grinning. He looks for Adrian but the world is flashing by too fast.

Adrian, waiting below on the ground, gets a peek at Don for a split second on each revolution. It's the stuttering image of early film footage, a frame updating itself. He sees and notes a wide grin.

On the roller-coaster, Donald's next choice, Adrian timidly straps himself in beside his client. What compels him to do this Adrian will need to psychoanalyse later. It may be a reckless experiment in doctor–client relations. He may be searching for the breakthrough which he feels should have come by now. He may just wish to know what all the excitement these kids feel is about. Or he may just be committing suicide.

DONALD: Don't worry, it's gonna be a breeze. (*Grins.*) A pretty strong motherfucking breeze, but. (*Even bigger grin*)

Smash-cut to…

…Hell. A world of distortions, of subtracted consciousness, of antimatter, wormholes in space, gut-gymnastics on the outer limits of endurance that can best be likened to pulling a rubber glove inside out and then chucking it in the spin dryer. Donald is whoop, whoop, whooping throughout. Adrian needs to be helped, at its end, to unfasten his own harness. Donald points out a refreshment area where they should go and sit down for a minute. Adrian sees three such areas beckoning him.

Donald, unfazed, jumps energetically into a plastic chair at a plastic table, grabbing the plastic triangular menu listing forty types of plastic food. Adrian sits silent, bilious, wretched, feeling in his guts that he now understands the appeal of such attractions: they are a cheap and safe foretaste of death. A way of simulating a fatal accident for under ten pounds. Humans toying with self-destruction. The desire to sneak a preview of a violent end. This is his analysis.

As Adrian reflects on mortality, Donald is torn between a hamburger or a fish in a bun.

DONALD: I'm starving.

ADRIAN: I think it's time to go.

DONALD: You think it's time to *throw*?

ADRIAN: To go. I said. To go.

DONALD (*laughs*): Fuck you. I did your art galleries. Now that was real hell. And besides, I'm the one with life-threatening leukaemia here. Okay, currently in remission, but who knows for how long? So order something.

The burgers and fries soon arrive. A bottle of hot sauce too. All for Donald.

ADRIAN (*looking up from his mobile where he's been checking messages: replies to his SOS?*): Thanks.

Donald grabs the hot sauce, dumps it on his fries and starts to munch as he looks around. What his eyes light upon, with his mouth jammed to capacity, is a group of six pretty young girls speech-bubbling at a nearby table. He stares at the six-pack, imagining their boy-crazy surmising, but none of the girls repays his attention.

Adrian glances up from his phone again and takes in the scene. He looks at Don, then at the girls, then at Don, back at the girls, and can't miss the mantle of misery stealing over the teenager, the good humour draining away. In the end, Donald himself can take no more of this affliction, and angles his chair away from the gorgeous sextet.

ADRIAN: So how often do you think about sex?

Donald gives him a look…

ADRIAN: Stupid question.

Adrian reaches over and steals a single fry and also, in an act of solidarity, a reckless glob of hot sauce that Don has been splurging so liberally across his lunch. Mistake number two. This stuff peels the ceiling off Adrian's mouth and then sets to work on excoriating the bone.

ADRIAN: Oh my God! How can you… Christ, that's… (*Drinks some of the Coke in a hurry.*) How can you *eat*?

DONALD : Spicy, huh?

Don casually dips a fry in the sauce and eats it without a smidgen of difficulty. The smirk returns to his face.

ADRIAN: Spicy? How can you… oh my God… possibly eat that stuff?

DONALD: Titanium. It's one of my special powers. You didn't know I was superhuman, did ya?

Donald glances over his shoulder, showing he hasn't ever stopped thinking about the girls, even through this, polishing off the rest of the fries distractedly, giant gloops of Agent Orange dripping from each one.

Ext. School Gates. Day.

A week later – a week of medical results (no change), of T-cells holding, of brightening parents but stubbornly fatalistic son, parents trying to take an interest in getting said patient to help cure himself (request denied), of school-going and of keeping to himself after the CD incident, staying out of trouble, of occasional after-school work on his comic masterpiece (more and more of it created under the influence of marijuana now that supply has been normalized), a week of overheard conversations, Mum and Dad arguing, stress spreading out its own toxins despite the positive news, infecting others, a week without a session with Dr Adrian King who uncharacteristically reports sick (the killer chilli sauce and high-speed loop-the-loops perhaps the cause), and a week in which Donald's semi to meet a girl has now proceeded to genuine emergency status... After a week like this, he waits with his hood up over his patchwork scalp for his old pals *Homo delinquentus*, to join him at the school gates.

MICHAEL: Ready?

DONALD: Ready.

RAFF: Got any money?

DONALD: Yeah.

RAFF: Okay. Let's roll.

Ext. Movie Theatre. Day.

The billboard announces two movies: a cookie-cutter PG thriller, *Hit 'n' Run,* then, on the smaller, second screen, a steamy little number called *Gina-Town* where all the cast promisingly appear under pseudonyms. The three boys stand before the ticket-seller.

MICHAEL: *Gina-Town*. Three.

The ticket-seller stares back as if Mike has just regaled him in Vietnamese.

MICHAEL: *Gina-Town*... Thanks. *Gina-Town*... Three. Okay?

TICKET-SELLER: How old are you?

MICHAEL: Seventeen.

TICKET-SELLER: Yeah, if I added your ages together. I need to see some ID.

MICHAEL: See, I knew you were gonna say that. (*Turns to his pals.*) I fucken told you he was gonna fucken say that. Fuck. Didn't I?

DONALD: Let me… here, let me handle this. (*To* TICKET-SELLER) Hi. My name's Donald. So here's the thing. I've got cancer.

TICKET-SELLER: Cancer?

DONALD: Check it out (*Pulls aside the neck on his favourite T-shirt, bearing the statement "Chicks Dig Me (Don't Ask Me Why)", to reveal the still raw Port-a-Cath wound in his shoulder.*) This is where they pumped the chemo in. See that? I'm terminal. It didn't work. This is probably the last movie I'm ever gonna see. I'm history.

Int. Movie Theatre. Day.

The movie playing at the newest movie house in Watford, complete with Lucas THX sound and super-comfy new seats installed with Hollywood money for the cast and crew premiere of *The Wizard's Apprentice 3* a year before, has the three young men staring slack-jawed at the screen. The actress is screaming and moaning. It's not clear how much longer she can take it.

Angle on…

…Donald and Michael and Raff, slumped glumly in the stalls watching *Hit 'n' Run*, perhaps the worst thriller ever made, encircled by a smattering of ten- to twelve-year-olds.

DONALD: Normally works.

Long silence, as the B-movie plays. The actress is trapped in a car wreck. Awaiting rescue after willfully driving it into a bridge abutment. Injuries to head and arms. The electrics are sparking. Gas leaks onto the road. It looks bad. But her boyfriend appears from nowhere. Now *this* is a movie where the cast should have used pseudonyms.

RAFF (*To* MICHAEL): We should have filmed this. We should have filmed this.

MICHAEL: No point. It's already out on pirate. And it's old. You can buy it from anybody already. But *Gina-Town*, oh man, that would have been *massive*. We gotta get into that show somehow and record it. Dress up in suits or something.

He pulls out his digicam, and aims it at the screen, without turning it on.

DONALD: Glue on some facial hair or something.

MICHAEL: Woulda loved to have burned a few hundred copies of that. The big money's in porno.

He lowers his digicam, looks around to check no one saw him, then stuffs it back under his jacket.

DONALD: So... listen... wanna ask you guys something, okay? Have any of you guys, like, lost your virginity yet? Since I last seen ya?

MICHAEL: Sure.

RAFF: Oh yeah. Big time.

Silence. They all stare at the screen.

DONALD: Cool.

On screen, the hero is kicking arse improbably while performing a last-second rescue.

MICHAEL: Haven't you?

DONALD (*after pregnant pause*): Not yet.

MICHAEL: Yeah? Lost mine two years ago. To my

German au pair. Oh man. Eighteen. Beautiful. She used to wear, like, these leather dresses for me. Phew! Tits like basketballs and an arse – oh man...

DONALD: Did she... y'know... blow you?

MICHAEL: Are you kidding? This girl could suck the chrome off a towel rail. But she got too possessive – didn't like me seeing other girls – so I let her go.

DONALD (*To* RAFF): Do you believe this?

RAFF: I lost mine last month. Didn't even know her name. Crazy, man. I pulled her into the bathroom at Burger King, y'know, and just gave her one right up against the blow-dryer.

DONALD: (*laughing*): Jesus...

RAFF: Boom! (*Laughs.*)

MICHAEL: Yeah – they love that sort of thing.

Donald's eyes return to the silver screen. No one dies. And everyone in the world gets exactly what they want at the last minute, as per usual. End of story. Fade to black. There's even a smattering of cosy applause from a few parents and children. But Don has enjoyed it all less than ever, even less than his friends who'd at least laughed loudly from time to time. And he doesn't understand his disdain for these tales of human goodness. Not at all. It isn't just the phoney banality that oppresses him. It's something he can't put his finger on. When he should be happy, and be happy to watch other people being happy, having had his own fair share of good news and filmic reprieves lately, he wants his money back more than ever. Happiness seems a lie. Maybe that's it. One big fat lie, that everyone believes without thinking. And it drives him crazy, that he's the only one who sees this. Jesus Christ, everyone has bought into the happiness game now. And it makes him want to scream, or do something.

Anything. Just to show people. To show them. And also to prove it to himself anew. See! See! Fucken see!

Black. Black is the heart of Donald F. Delpe.

Ext. Cinema Rooftop. Day.

Don knows the way up. The janitor never locked the door to the rooftop. The three friends stand on the edge of the complex and look over to the next rooftop. Four hundred feet off the ground, the street perilously far below.

DONALD: It's only about twenty feet to jump.

MICHAEL: Are you kidding?

DONALD: Who wants to go first?

RAFF: No way, man. Let's get off this roof.

DONALD: This is Free Running, man. *Le Parkour.* It's the bomb. Okay, I'll do it alone. (*Pulls out their bootleg digicam whose tapes should now be full of* Gina-Town.) Here. Film me. Someone film this.

MICHAEL: Film your fucking self. This is a bad idea.

Donald hands it to Raff, and then prepares by tying his laces.

DONALD: Okay. Nice knowing you guys.

RAFF (*to* MICHAEL): We gotta stop him. Seriously. He'll do it.

DONALD: This is nothing. Turn the camera on. Turn the camera on. Turn the camera on. TURN IT ON OR I DO IT WITH MY EYES CLOSED!

MICHAEL (*to* RAFF, *scared*): He will. The guy's nuts. Turn it on.

Raff reluctantly obeys.

DONALD: Okay. Are you filming?

RAFF: Yeah.

DONALD: Here we go. Geronimo.

He goes to the edge, takes some deep breathes and then paces backwards, measuring his run-up. Finally, he's ready.

MICHAEL: This is stupid, man. This is totally insane. Don't do it Don. Please.

DONALD: No special effects. No stunt doubles – no mirrors...

Don starts to run – to run – until he hits the mark and leaps. He sails out into empty space, his arms windmilling, fear suddenly on his face, as if he's suddenly made a huge miscalculation...

Int. Delpe Kitchen. Night.

Renata is crying as she prepares dinner. She grabs a paper towel and wipes her eyes as Don enters with a large plaster on his forehead.

DONALD: I'm sorry, okay? I'll sort it out. Don't worry. It's gonna be okay.

Jim is there too. Silent. Turning an expensive-looking fountain pen in his hands. A Mont Blanc. Turning it real slow, staring at it.

JIM (*holds up the pen*): And when you're done jumping off buildings and upsetting your mother, where did this come from?

DONALD: It's mine. What are you going through my things for?

JIM: Where? (*Reads the inscribed initials.*) Where'd you get it from? "A.L.K." I'm just asking where it came from?

Jeff enters, wearing Don's iPod, which pounds with muffled music before he turns it off.

JIM: A.L.K? Is that Dr King? Is it Adrian's? You stole this? You know what a Mont Blanc is worth? Don! (*No response*) He's a close friend of ours!

JEFF (*to DONALD*): You dork. Why didn't you steal something interesting?

DONALD (*to his father*): I picked it up accidentally. I'll take it back.

JIM: You bet your life you're taking it back!

RENATA: He's gonna take it back.

Don grabs the pen from his father and the iPod from his brother and exits. Jim and Renata share a defeated look.

JEFF: You're too soft on him. Just my opinion.

Jeff is gone.

RENATA: Don't shout at him. Stop shouting at him! I've told you.

JIM: Don't shout at him? So, what? I'm gonna let him turn into a suicidal kleptomaniac and not say a word?

RENATA: Maybe if you did some reading, OK, about what he's actually going through, then you'd see that your anger might not need to be top of the family agenda right now!

Renata cries, says she's fed up with crying all the time. He tries to make it stop. But it's no good.

Int. Adrian's Office. Day.

DONALD: Feeling better?

ADRIAN: I feel fine. Thank you. How about you?

DONALD: Oh yeah.

But Donald is slumped in his seat today. He looks gloomy. Adrian is holding his "lost" Mont Blanc once again.

ADRIAN: I think I've seen this mood before actually. This is the "life is a sexually transmitted disease" mood, correct? (*Silence*) I've got a present for you. Here. Take it.

Adrian passes over a parcel wrapped in a single layer of brown paper. Donald eventually opens it. It's a painting. One of Adrian's. The pietà, from the entrance hallway.

ADRIAN: It's the painting you liked.

DONALD: I liked the other one.

ADRIAN: Really? I can change it. Here. That's fine. I'll switch it.

But Donald seems reluctant to give it up. He puts the painting down, but at his feet, resting against his legs, and the glimmer of a smile lasts only a second before his face implodes, folds inwards, into a frown and then into something altogether more defeated.

DONALD: Shit.

ADRIAN: What is it?

DONALD: I'm sick of this shit.

ADRIAN: Your illness? I know. But you're winning.

DONALD: Yeah? It can come back. What if it comes back?

ADRIAN: Well... well, that we can't control. We all need to remember, it's not the problem, it's how we cope with it.

Donald is crying: is this surreal or what? His eyes water for the first time in years (he can't put a date on the day his tears dried up but he was half the size he is now) and he barely believes he's producing them here and now. Awful fucking timing, he bubbles as he blubs. Ashamed to have let this happen, especially in front of a professional, he wipes them away quickly but it only serves to underline the fact that Donald Delpe has emotions, and that they can't be capped any longer.

DONALD: I haven't done anything yet. It's not fair.

ADRIAN: You've done a lot. Listen to me. More than you think. Most of life is just a repetition anyway. Beyond a few basic things, the rest are variations. Believe me.

DONALD: That's crap.

ADRIAN: By the age of seven there are very few things we haven't already felt. Okay, we might not have painted the Sistine Chapel or driven a Jaguar V-12 or tried crack cocaine or hit the perfect drive off the tee, but we've known what triumph feels like, what disappointment feels like, injustice, despair, love, what joy feels like. A human heart has really seen it all before we can walk.

DONALD (*his face twisting into a portrait of disgust*): What are you talking about? Jesus. Your life must really suck.

Adrian knits his fingers and gives Don the time to speak his mind.

DONALD: Jesus, you must have a sad life. I might die, okay, without... without ever even having had sex. And that's not okay. That's not... not a whatever you said – a variation. That just sucks. I've never even... I've never even seen a naked breast, okay? I might die without ever even seeing naked breasts!

(*Silence*)

ADRIAN: What are you doing tomorrow night?

Int. Life-drawing Class. Night.

Adrian tells Donald to wait in the hall while he pops into one of the institute's evening art classes. He wants to check out who tonight's nude model is – and sees that it's Jennifer, a wonderful woman, no doubt, but one who for the purposes of this evening – Donald's first ever real-life sighting of female bosoms – is probably not the right person for the job, being in her mid-fifties and five times a mother, her breasts now oven mitts, luxurious to draw but not so fetching to behold, her body a wonderful and generous study for the pen and brush, a Hindu Kush of alps and valleys, but not tonight what the doctor ordered.

Adrian closes the door quietly as crayon, charcoal and gouache begin their labours.

Int. Life-drawing Class No. 2. Night.
Adrian has never seen this model before. She's a gorgeous young woman, in her prime. She is still wearing her bathrobe, and carefully arranges the cushions on the platform as she prepares to assume the recumbent pose that she must hold for an hour and a half. In her left hand she holds a sandwich, a quick bite, a skipped meal: a detail that, were she to retain it, would be worthy of Magritte.

Adrian is in a flutter, worried firstly that the faith Don's parents have placed in him might be abused by such an outing, and secondly that Donald will not take from the experience something uplifting. But he is excited too, excited to witness such a moment in a boy's life, and excited for himself. There is a sense in which these classes also renew and expand his own reverence for the female form.

When Adrian turns to look at Donald, next to him in the front row of the class, he is not at all surprised to see that the mere promise of the young woman's nudity has turned him into stone, that Don is waiting, breathless, as if the gates of heaven are about to open, his body more still than any model's, and that perhaps he is already seeing what Michelangelo once saw in David, minus the sandwich.

Around them, not party to the import of this moment in a boy's life, a dozen other artists, mostly women, many elderly, open their sketch pads or arrange their canvases with clinical poise, and cast concerned looks in their direction – what is a kid doing in a nude life-drawing class? While the model continues to fuss with the cushions, Donald looks as if he will die from oxygen loss unless she takes off her bathrobe soon. Adrian has to smile to himself. It is beautiful to watch: not the model, but Donald. It is a life study that he would like to capture, if not on paper, then in some folio of his memory. So precious, such first-time moments, he thinks. Awaited for so long, over in a second, behind us for ever.

With her back to the class the model slips off her robe. It falls to the floor in a single cascade. A gust of air even reaches the faces of Don and his chaperone. But for Donald, with his super-sensibilities, the moment is being replayed already, happening in extreme slo-mo, the camera over-cranked, revealing her body curve by curve, inch by inch, feature by feature, limb by limb, cell by cell as the fabric falls, falls, falls until – until she is…

Nuditas virtualis, thinks Adrian.

She lies down, takes a comfortable pose, reclining on her side, propping herself on one elbow, one knee slightly higher than the other… sweet Jesus, bubbles Don, *she's his poster girl*! The goosebumped flesh, the face a dead ringer, it's all there. Could it be the same giantess? Could his billboard Brobdingnagian girl have shrunk and come to life?

The rest of the class is already sketching in a businesslike fashion as Donald (and Adrian) stare at the creature before them. Adrian is the first to realize that two males sitting in the front row of an art class before a naked young woman and drawing nothing will simply not do.

ADRIAN: Pssst.

He gets Donald's attention, and holds up his stick of charcoal. Donald finally understands and takes out his felt pens from his pockets, two, three, five, eight, ten, in myriad colours, laying them on the desk beside him. They begin to sketch.

Adrian, studying his model carefully, her classic lines, proportions, her ratios, mapping her orientation as if on a grid, the distension of limbs as they trail away, the foreshortening of those that advance, tentatively permits himself to stake out her basic geometry and draw his first nervous line. Donald, however, is in an artistic flurry. The nibs of his felt pens *squeak – squeak – squeak* as they fly, swoop, oscillate and dive. *Squeak, squeak, squeak*, goes Donald, the sound virtually his trademark. The squeak of youth.

Elsewhere around the room, in a dozen other sketchbooks, a dozen decorous pictures are taking shape. Some artists are going for verisimilitude, life as it is, and others for how it appears, life as they *want* it to be, letting themselves be informed by the twentieth-century breakthrough in thought that says that the seen object is changed by the act of seeing. And so the modernists in the group either thicken the form or emaciate it, depending on the impression they get from the model, reflecting in the end their own emotions, the mood of their own lives, revealing whether *they* feel starved or overfed.

But none comes close, not even remotely, to the liberties Donald has taken with his picture. When the tutor arrives to check progress, he looks over Donald's shoulder and beholds – beholds – beholds…

The tutor's mouth drops open. Drawn large is a super-vixen with a tail, with red leather bondage gear and wielding a pitchfork. The tutor can't take it seriously. It's perverse: the tail's arrowed end flirts with her opening, and there are knee-length boots, two horns, breasts that are simply ridiculous, pubic hair groomed into a lightning bolt! The kid has transformed the model, albeit brilliantly, into a comic-book, heavy-metal, triple-D, semi-conducting, masturbatory fantasy.

But Donald looks incredibly pleased with his effort, and regards with satisfaction his masterpiece, rating it among the best things he's ever done.

At last Adrian notices the look on the tutor's face and wonders if his charge has done something wrong. He puts down his pencil, rises, leaves behind his own still life (he has completed only the topography of one foot) and takes a look.

Int. Burger King Restaurant. Night.

ADRIAN: I'm not saying it's *bad*. It's not. Bad is not a word we use. In many ways it's brilliant. But – is that what you saw? Because I didn't see this. Why did you draw her like this?

DONALD: She was hot. (*Pause*) Right? So maybe it's not what I saw, but it's what I thought of when I looked at her.

ADRIAN: Is that what you think of when you look at all girls?

DONALD: No. Only the good-looking ones.

ADRIAN: Good-looking girls all have tails? And a pitchfork?

DONALD: Yeah. They're going to hell.

ADRIAN: Do you want to go to hell?

DONALD: If the devils look like that, yeah.

ADRIAN: Can I give you some advice? (*No invitation is forthcoming.*) Girls are as nervous as you are. They are as nervous as you are.

DONALD: What's that got to do with anything?

ADRIAN: You don't have to turn them into demons, just because you like them. Don't make them unreal. They're approachable, you know.

DONALD: I need a refill.

At the counter Donald spots, in the distance, the vixen from his church fantasy, the girl in the yellow cardigan, his future wife, rising from a table of girlfriends and heading – heading – heading his way! A nation holds its breath.

Cut to...

...her slo-mo approach: Action! shout Donald's loins, heart and soul; cue the music, cue the dry ice; freeze-frame everything else in this temple of gloom as she approaches, this radiant, vestal high priestess in the service of the great God Semi.

And as predicted, when she reaches the counter and stands beside him, he is struck mute by the same pagan gods that created her. He can hardly look at her. He could feast for a month on her smell alone.

SHELLY DRISCOLL, fifteen years old, brunette, from an unhampered upper-income family, two credit cards already in her wallet, going places. She plays the piano, can pound out the Minute Waltz in fifty-five seconds flat, toys with the idea of being a concert pianist but is unlikely to marshal the discipline. Boys feature and don't feature: they are talked about jaw-taxingly by her group (their wants, their needs, their base and lovely urges), but they seldom appear in reality. She is tired of being asked out on Friday nights by mono-browed boys with tent-like clothes and back-to-front caps when she would rather sit with her girlfriends *talking about* being asked out on Friday nights. It's the exquisite rise in romantic heat she likes, the slow build of hot text messages from suitors, the endless caress of offers, of rendezvous she will never make, until her mobile brims, maxes out and can take no more. Sated, delighted, she shows her friends the alert: Memory Full.

SHELLY: Hi.

DONALD: Oh. Hi.

SHELLY: Do you go to my school?

DONALD: No. I uh... I saw you at uh... at Mass. You go to our church. You were wearing a uh... a yellow cardigan.

SHELLY: Oh. I don't go to church often.

DONALD: Me neither. God no. My... my ah... my parents are just freaking out.

Donald is smitten. He can't help it – he drafts behind her a devil's tail, flitting in and out of sight behind her back, and a pitchfork in her left hand.

SHELLY (*pointing to* DONALD's *T-shirt which bears the word: SNIKT*): What's that mean?

DONALD: Oh, that's uh... that's just the sound Wolverine makes whenever, y'know, he gets his claws out.

SHELLY: Oh. Wolverine? Like?... Yeah, I get it. So – so how come you don't have any hair?

DONALD: I've got hair.

SHELLY: So where is it then?

DONALD: It's a karate thing.

SHELLY (*impressed*): Cool. So... who are you here with?

DONALD: I'm, ah... I'm on my own. On my own.

SHELLY: Cool.

At this, she drifts away from him with a charming smile. Is this an invitation? Should he follow? His heart is a tom-tom played by Masai warriors during a fertility rite. He glances back at Adrian, can see only the back of the man's head. He's on his own. The way forwards is uncharted. Shelly is as nervous as he is. She is not unreal. He does not need to demonize her. She is real. She is real. She is real.

He approaches her booth, his eyes targeting his girl, Shelly from church, Shelly of his dreams, but Shelly most especially from his own cartoon strip. For two months she has insinuated herself into his representation of MiracleMan's arch-lust, Rachel, whose refined ways and perfect features spring from this real-life model in front of him now – not a vixen at all, but something altogether more intimidating: the real thing. Still, if he manages to keep Shelly real, he can't manage to do the same with her three babbling friends, zapping them into a frozen 2-D cartoon Bimbo (Limbo for pubescent girls), and viewing the booth at which they sit as a Playstation graphic. He is left with the impression, as he slow-tracks in on them, that he is zooming in on a single cell from a comic strip, with Shelly the only living, breathing thing in it. Real.

He stops on the perimeter of this scene, respecting its legitimacy. Only his voice bubble intrudes. It reads: "Baby, where have you been all my life?"

Shelly responds, melts, folds, delighted to be addressed this way. Her chest heaves in response. One hand tries to quell it, five piano-fit fingers outspread, a star on her bosom.

SHELLY (*gasp*): MiracleMan!

She jumps up and out of frame.

Suddenly a second frame is required from the master cartoonist. Frame Two is up already. In it, MiracleMan

(Don's stand-in for purposes of this fantasy), in 2-D just like the Babes in Bimbo, is a picture of the mature, besuited ladykiller, certain not to screw up like Donald would, his sheer handsomeness overpowering her. A second voice bubble appears over his head: "**Sorry I was late.**" By now Shelly is enveloped in his 2-D titanium embrace, her real, animate flesh writhing in inanimate arms.

SHELLY: I need you soooo much.

MIRACLEMAN (*voice bubble*): I need you too. We have to be alone.

SHELLY: Take me somewhere. Anywhere. Now!

MIRACLEMAN (*voice bubble*): Now?

SHELLY (*blotto voce*): Now.

Frame Three, frame three, frame three. MiracleMan has Shelly up against the wall in the toilets. She has one leg wrapped around him, and is sucking the pixels off his face. Her hair is blown by the hand-dryer, whose button her right shoulder accidentally depresses, creating a self-photographic effect. What a beauty! Swirling hair like a mermaid beneath the waves.

SHELLY: Yes, yes, mmmm, whmmmm… (*She mumbles as best she can between slobbers, as…*)

…as Donald, in reality, stands before a booth occupied by three teenage girls, one of whom is his heart's desire, and finds himself utterly tongue-tied in their presence, utterly unschooled in language, a creature from another planet, one of the swamp people, at least until he remembers one rudimentary word from a lost lexicon many centuries old: "Hi."

The girls stare at him.

He stares back.

The girls stare at him.

He stares back.
Hell.

Ext. Burger King. Night.
Outside the burger bar, Adrian buttons his coat against the bronchial wind.

DONALD: Thanks.

ADRIAN: For what?

DONALD: The advice.

ADRIAN: Why?

DONALD: I got a date.

ADRIAN: With a girl? Or with a devil?

DONALD: With a girl. With a girl.

Int. Dining Room / Delpe House. Night.
Renata is reading medical research books, night by long night turning herself into an expert on oncology at the dining-room table, making notes and then adding new pages to a tower of older ones that tonight are weighed down with a bunch of rubber-banded asparagus. Donald comes in the door, more upbeat than he has been in a very long time, a skip in his step.

DONALD: Hi.

RENATA: Donny? Hello darling. How was it?

DONALD: Pretty cool, actually.

RENATA: Pretty cool? Really?

The needles on all Renata's maternal gauges jump right off the scale. She swivels in her chair, pushing her glasses up on her head, and ceases her reading, which right now concerns a German clinic that boasts an eighty per cent remission rate.

DONALD: He's quite a cool guy.

RENATA: Dr King? Well, that's great, sweetheart. That's so great.

Donald approaches her and at once notices all the cancer books on the table.

DONALD: It's gonna be okay, Ma. I'm gonna be okay.

He touches her on the shoulder, looks her in the eye and *doesn't look away*, then turns and heads up the stairs two at a time. Renata's hand moves towards her mouth but freezes just in front of it, suspended in air.

Int. Donald's Bedroom. Night.

Donald drops into his chair and waits for the computer to boot, to erect its firewalls, to configure its desktop, to defragment its memory – a cyclone of activity under his desk. In a few seconds he's surfing, but he's headed to none of the usual sites. Tonight he's giving a wide berth to the file-sharing pages on the darker edge of cyberspace, the hinter-quadrants known only to software pirates, web terrorists, child molesters, arms dealers and kooks looking for parts for nuclear reactors. Tonight he's going straight to Google, the McDonald's of the web, where he types six letters: C – A – N – C – E – R.

Instantaneously he is presented with a lifetime's reading. Two lifetimes'. But Donald isn't deterred: he's going to learn about his disease for the first time. He's going to learn about this thing that has busted through all his own firewalls, hacked into his mainframe, viciously corrupted all his files, sites and operating systems. If he's going to defeat this super-virus then he needs first to understand it. Understanding starts here: it starts tonight. The task is doable. It's got to be. Right?

Ext. Yard / Delpe House. Day.

Donald is shooting baskets. Cancer may have given him the body of a bookworm, but it hasn't given him the intellectual stamina of one. The sun pours down. He hasn't shot hoops for quite a while. And it shows.

It was a few years ago that Don put the old backboard up there, nailed it to the garage roof with a hundred nails, most of them bending over before he could drive them home, but although he did a messy job at least he struck the hoop the regulation height. Pity the hoop's diameter isn't a little bigger today, however. Nothing much is falling and he can't just blame the ball, which is only a little flat. He's draining only twenty per cent, and none of these shots have been swishes. He can't buy a swish today, and that's what he's looking for: all net, no rim. As in life, so here: the honey-sweet feeling of passing through Possibility's gates without touching the sides. But soon he is out of breath. He stops, grips his knees. He's done, or so it feels like. Cancer 1, Donald 0. Still, not a bad workout. Seven minutes.

But where he would usually break at this point and go inside, he waits to catch his breath. He ambles to the free-throw line again, regards the hoop as if it's the enemy, readies himself and goes again. The perfect buckets might not be coming, but his jump-shot has got okay form: he pledges he won't quit until he hits the perfect jumper. The balls pepper the backboard, off-ending against the rim, ricocheting everywhere but *in* for the next five minutes until finally, from four metres... perfect release, high rainbow arc... travelling, travelling, travelling...

Int. Delpe House. Day.

Jim watches through the curtains as the ball swishes perfectly through the net and then as his second-born son retires the ball in the back of the old trailer. He nods and clenches his fist as if his kid has just drained the winning basket from deep in three-point land in the provincial championships. All net. What a thrill. Don't sons make sense at times like this? They just make sense. There are times when there is nothing else like them. Yes! His fist is still clenched, he realizes. Yes!

Int. Jeff's Bedroom / Delpe House. Night.

The brothers are just hanging out tonight, as they have not done in months. Donald passes the joint back to Jeff, who lies on his bed, sermonizing. Jeff employs the voice of experience, the voice of a veteran romancer.

JEFF: I'm serious. When you get your chance, move in for the kill, but you gotta do it *fast*, before she has time to think about it, because every girl if you give 'em time'll say no. That's just how they are. So the first time's gotta be, like, at the speed of a traffic accident – *bam*! Shit, something happened, nobody knows, oh wow, she just gave it up. Understand?

Jeff sits up, excited to pass on his truths, his reality lessons, and half pulls up his T-shirt over his head so that it looks like a nun's wimple.

JEFF: Okay, lemme show ya. I'm a girl. Now lay a move on me. Come on, lay a move on me, bitch.

DONALD (*a little confused*): I thought you were the bitch?

JEFF: I am the bitch. Now get on with it, bitch. Say something to me.

DONALD: What?

JEFF: Anything. Doesn't matter. Cos it's while I'm thinking about the answer that you're gonna make your move. Understand? Ask me what six times seven is. Ask me six times seven.

DONALD: Okay. (*Prepares.*) What's six times seven?

JEFF: Forty-two. (*Pause*) You fucked up. Nothing has happened.

DONALD: I don't get it.

JEFF: You missed your chance! You blew it, mate. That's how fast you gotta be. Understand? You gotta roll before I can say forty-two. See? See how fast? Like fucking greased lightning. That's how I've got every girl I've ever had.

DONALD: What's eight times nine?

JEFF: It's...

Donald grabs Jeff and tries to kiss him.

JEFF (*pushing him off*): What are you doing? Get the fuck off me, faggot! Jesus. Just tell me you understand. I'm just painting a picture for you.

DONALD: I understand.

JEFF (*pulling his T-shirt back down*): Good. Now here. (*Opens a drawer and pulls out some condoms.*) If it all goes to plan, use these. They might not fit your little dick but it's better than nothing.

DONALD: I don't need these.

JEFF: Take them.

Donald throws them in the rubbish bin, as Jeff heads for the door.

JEFF: You're gonna blow it. I can feel it.

DONALD: No I'm not. I got it.

JEFF: You got it?

DONALD: Forty-two.

JEFF: Forty-two!

When Donald is alone, he goes to the rubbish bin and retrieves the condoms.

Int. Burger King. Night.

At the counter, hands clammy, Donald's heart is trying to pump a golf ball through his aorta. He and Shelly and four other kids (two girls and two unwelcome older boys who can piss off pronto or else it's duels at dawn, Don bubbles) are just standing around, engaged in purposeless mooching. The place is full of dorks tonight. Everybody in the world seems to be talking except Don, seems to have something really funny and cool and fundamental to say, while he, Marcel Marceau, Mr Fucking Bean, waits for Shelly, his *official date*, to give him the time of day. And he's been waiting twenty minutes now for a gesture from her, some lifeline, something to confirm that they are actually *having* a date, but so far nothing. It's not as if he isn't trying, smiling his best goofy smiles whenever she looks his way, hands plunged deep in his low-riders, being cool, hood up, sometimes doing his best wrinkled-brow Brad Pitt from *Thelma and Louise* imitation (to this day his Mum's favourite hot-patootie) and other times sneaking glances at her as she speaks with others. He views her as a series of close-ups, a montage of eyes, nape, nose in profile, ringed fingers of right hand holding a Coke, ringed belly button (exposed), three toes sprouting like truffles from the front of her slingbacks. And just as he gives up plugging in his earbuds to drown out the hell of being with a girl who you want, *badly*, but who is giving you less than nothing to go on, there comes a tap on his shoulder, the tap of an angel. He pulls off his cans.

SHELLY: Am I boring you?

Donald prepares to give this a serious answer. She waits. He prepares. She waits. Alternative reality: people in this world don't talk. Talk has been dispensed with. It is quite normal to stare into the faces of others for hours, sometimes days: it's even considered charming.

SHELLY: Are you okay?

DONALD: Sorry?

SHELLY: Are you okay? (*Further silence*) Do they make you take a vow of silence or something when you do karate? (*Silence*) You like me, don't you? (*He nods. Brad would not have.*) You don't look so good. Are you sweating?

DONALD: No.

SHELLY: It's okay. A lot of guys sweat when they talk to me. I kind of like it.

Donald has no reply to this. He's floored. Shelly looks around. The other teenagers in their group have paired off and are starting to kiss one another.

SHELLY: Do you wanna kiss me?

DONALD: Sure.

SHELLY: Come here.

Shelly leads him into a darker corner and takes out her gum.

They kiss. No rim. Semi City. But when he makes a lunge for her breasts she throws his hand away.

SHELLY: Hey! I'm only fifteen. Don't get any big ideas. (*Stares into his face, then pushes back his hood to reveal his ray-shorn head.*) You're strange. But quite cute. (*Calls to her* FRIENDS.) I'm going to the bathroom!

She hands her Coke to a girlfriend and heads for the toilets. Is this a come-on? Donald is confused. There are a thousand ways to interpret this. Only one of these says he should stay where he is.

Shelly's girlfriends look at Donald, and he hands them his Coke as well and heads off in pursuit of his girl, *his girl* (at last he can say this!), the first girl in God-knows-how-many to offer him her mouth, who will never now be forgotten, not as long as he lives, a daydream in his old age should he ever reach it, a girl who will for ever be his sleeper hit, that low-budget romantic comedy not expected to do well but which explodes at his own personal box office, spawning a franchise: *Shelly*; *Shelly 2, The Sequel*; *Shelly 3, The Final Reckoning*; *Shelly 4, Resurrection*; *Shelly 5, 6, 7...* running for ever. Oh dear God let her run and run and run.

Int. Women's Toilet. Night.
Shelly enters but has taken only a couple of steps towards the mirror when the door opens and in comes a superhero.

SHELLY (*shocked*): What are you doing!? You can't come in here! Yuck! Get out! Weirdo!

Donald is taken by surprise and freezes, his mind hanging on a question of mathematics: six times seven... six times seven... six times seven... as he places his hand gently on her shoulder, ignoring her, working as fast as he can, before she can say "No". But he might as well have been puzzling the square root of a prime number, for she has effectively said no a dozen times already.

SHELLY: Get out, you creep! Weirdo! *Jesus*! *Get the hell out*! This is a women's toilet! Sicko! Get out!

As she knocks his hand away, Donald's mind ceases to scream forty-two! Forty-two! Forty-two! Shelly's expression is identical to that of Ann Darrow on the cover of his *King Kong* comic, screaming at the beast who molests her, a terrified voice bubble above her: **"AAAAAAHHHHHHHHH!!!"** He skedaddles from the women's toilet, feeling like a total rapist.

Int. Delpe Car. Night.
Donald's dad drives him home. Jim is in a jaunty mood and is even being quite restrained with the indicators. But not the windscreen-wipers. His father leaves the windscreen-wipers pumping for a good ten minutes after the last raindrop has fallen. If Don was to choose any two sounds to define his father they would be the *click-click-click* of indicators and the Delpe trademark *squeak-squeak-squeak* of dried-out wipers.

JIM: So, have a good time? That didn't take long. Go okay?

Don wants to reply: Sexual molestation doesn't take all that long, Dad. But he bottles this. Puts a lid on it.

JIM: I remember my first proper date. Ha! Went to kiss her goodnight at her gate. Was so dark I got her on the chin. Man! Heard back the next day she told everybody I was this terrible kisser. Ha! (*A warm smile plays on his face as he looks at* DON, *who sits in silence.*) I'm proud of you, son. We're beating this.

Donald feels like crying.

Int. Delpe House. Day.
Jeff fixes himself and Donald an ice-cream sundae as he works through a debriefing.

JEFF: Lesbian. Without a doubt. Don't worry about it, OK. Your time's gonna come. You're gonna get plenty.

DONALD: I know. I know.

JEFF: Don't worry about it. I'm gonna talk you through it.

DONALD: Like hell. You don't know shit.

JEFF: Oh, I don't know shit? Thanks a lot. I don't know shit? You know how many women I've had sex with? Wanna know? Honestly? (*He starts to count them on his fingers, appears to climb into the twenties.*) Two.

DONALD (*laughing*): Two?

JEFF: That's two more than you, numbnuts. And I've had my fingers in a lot more than that. So I'm telling you, the girl you had was either lesbian or… or I don't know what the hell she was.

Donald takes a mouthful of ice cream, then covers one eye with the palm of his hand. A shooting pain. Ouch.

JEFF: Uh oh. Brain freeze. Better take it slower, chief. Ice cream's dangerous at speed.

But then Donald covers over his other eye and seems puzzled by something.

JEFF: What? What's up?

DONALD (*goes back to eating*): It's fine. Totally fine. Bit… blurry, that's all.

Int. Examination Room / Hospital. Day.
An X-ray of a human brain glows on the screen.

DR SIPETKA: I'm afraid there's been a recurrence. I'm sorry.

Mangled dreams. Rockslides. Buried lives.

RENATA: Oh no. Oh please…

DR SIPETKA: We've found four tumours on his brain, I'm sorry. And more on the lungs. Ten in total. I'd like to recommend the strongest regime of chemotherapy we've got, in concert with more radiation.

RENATA (*through tears*): What? What are we meant to do?

Jim holds one of the encephalograms. He stares at it, can see nothing but a Stilton murk.

JIM: How long?

DR SIPETKA: With luck, I should think six months at least.

Renata hugs herself tightly, arms criss-crossed over her breasts, a shocked intake of breath, as if wading into an ice-cold river up to the waist.

DR SIPETKA: If the tumours shrink, much longer. We're not giving up. But this cancer is aggressive. I'm sorry.

Jim makes two efforts to speak. On the third try he gets beyond the word "how".

JIM: How long would he have, if we do nothing? How long?

DR SIPETKA: A similar period, but I think we should stay oriented to a medical solution. I want to do a bone-marrow harvest tomorrow. Marrow is the factory for the immune system. We can use this later on – when the going gets tough. He'll need it then.

Int. Cafeteria / Hospital. Day.
It's in moments like this that Adrian really earns his money. It's in moments like this that a well-chosen word or sentiment can really help someone get through. The only trouble is, Adrian can barely speak. And so they sit there, all three of them, at a central table in the large hospital cafeteria, just communing. They are holding hands, Renata holding Adrian's left hand, Adrian's right covering Jim's left, Jim's right around Renata's waist.

RENATA: Why is this happening? Why him? Why did cancer choose him?

ADRIAN: Nobody knows. Lot of theories. Genes. Environment. Animal fats in the modern diet. Inability to handle stress. Some psychologists think that those who find it hard to bond with others are more susceptible. The likely answer is that it's a combination. But it's on the rise. Ten million *new* cases worldwide every year. Will rise to twenty million by 2020. Staggering figures. You're now part of a fast-growing, unacknowledged global community. Actually, it's the thing we will soon have most in common, but it's hardly referred to. Would you like me to keep seeing Donald?

RENATA: Definitely. (*She consults* JIM *with a look, and he gives an of-course nod.*) Definitely.

ADRIAN: Because I've feel we've made a little progress.

RENATA: Definitely. We've seen that.

ADRIAN (*with sudden fire*): He needs to fight this. And he's the only one who can do it, of course.

Jim and Renata nod, heartened to feel that Adrian is their ally as they move yet deeper into the unknown.

Int. Hospital. Day.

Before going in to see their son, who has been allocated a bed in the oncology ward while he receives the first wave of new treatment, Renata dries her tears and gathers her strength as Jim supports her, arms around her shoulders.

JIM: Better out here than in front of him, eh?

RENATA: It's okay. I want to be strong. Just want to be... Last thing he needs is a weepy mother, right? (*She tries to smile.*)

JIM: We'll just try again. We'll just start all over and try again. We can do this. We can absolutely do this!

RENATA (*suddenly angry*): Yeah? Jim, listen. You do this, okay? Because I barely made it this far! Jim, I barely made it this far.

He didn't know. Thought her a bastion. Felt weak beside her. Now this news. He's been promoted. He's been offered the top job now, carrying his family.

RENATA (*her anger subsiding*): I'm sorry. But it's the truth.

JIM: Let's go.

And so, as thousands before them have done, they go to see their loved one.

Int. Oncology Ward. Day.

Donald lies in a bed two places away from the window as a machine at his side pumps piss-yellow toxins up the clear tubes fettered to his right arm. He looks wiped out, hardly like himself, a poor likeness by a mediocre artist, as he gazes around the room at the other wipeouts.

The bed closest to the window is occupied by a man who looks to be into his last days. Skinny as hell. Eyes shut. Skin the colour of old icing. Chest rising and falling, just a human breath-bag, air entering, having a sniff around and then exiting. A nurse has maintained the vanity of a comb-over hairdo to give him a semblance of dignity.

In the next bed down, between Comb-Over and Donald, lies Tracheotomy Man. What a sight. The flange in his neck gasps air like a whale's blowhole. The guy is in his fifties, by the looks. Big-bellied. An eater. Hasn't said no to too much on the menu, Don bubbles. While a nurse plumps his pillow the guy even smiles. A sunny personality.

TRACHEOTOMYMAN: Thaaannkk… yoouuu.

If this was a voice bubble, thinks Don, he'd surround it with a very jagged border indeed and choose a very jagged font, because this voice is rawer than raw. A chainsaw growl.

Jim and Renata enter, direct from the Orient, one king short of the Three Wise Men, carrying comics and flowers and fruit.

RENATA: Hel-lo!

JIM: How's it going, champ?

Their son, flanked by medical apparatus, held captive by cell-killing machines, a robot army.

DONALD: Terrific.

RENATA: Nice bright ward. Lovely. And remember, you'll be out again in three days.

DONALD: Touch wood?

RENATA: No. Not touch wood. I don't need to touch wood.

JIM: Three days, champ.

DONALD: Yeah. (*Silence*) Know what? They have a cute tradition here.

JIM: Yeah? What's that, Donny?

DONALD: The closer you get to the end, the closer they move you to the window. That's nice, isn't it? The men here have just been telling me about it.

JIM: That's not true.

DONALD: Just now.

JIM: Don, cut it out. They don't do that sort of thing.

DONALD: Wait and see.

RENATA: Don't, Donald, don't!

She rushes out of the ward. It's the only thing she can do.

JIM (*mildly reprimanding*): Come on, son.

Jim goes to fetch his wife. He starts out walking, but ends up running.

Ext. Hospital. Day.

Renata hits daylight at a gallop and implodes in tears of grief and rage. Jim catches up with her and holds her tight. They do a kind of tango, swaying back and forth, gripping each other for dear life.

RENATA: I just want to pick him up and carry him out of there! We can't leave him there. That's my baby!

The camera-of-human-decency slowly pulls away from them. Back and forth the Delpes sway. There are some things on which a camera ought not to dwell.

ACT TWO

Int. Oncology Ward / Hospital. Day.

It's one of those days for Donald when you feel like a piece of taxidermy; when the last thought you had has been frozen on your face since the moment you got shot. A jammed idea and a trophy expression now yours for evermore.

ADRIAN: Do you want to talk about anything?

DONALD: I'm not going to make it.

ADRIAN: We don't know that.

DONALD: I'm not going to make it.

ADRIAN (*after staring at him, waiting for more, to no avail*): What do you mean?

DONALD: I'm crapping out before I've even partied. (*Shakes his head at the raw injustice of it.*) And you know what the worst thing is? The worst thing? I'm gonna die a friggin' virgin. Pretty pathetic.

ADRIAN: You need to try and get sex in perspective.

DONALD: Hey, fuck you. I'm fourteen. Sex *is* my perspective.

ADRIAN: Okay. I know. I remember what it was like. Kids like you… you get a hard-on when you see a crack in the pavement.

Donald looks at Adrian with something like respect.

DONALD: I like that. Who said that? Oscar Wilde?

ADRIAN: Toilet wall.

DONALD: I like it. But it's wrong. A crack in the pavement would only give me a semi.

Adrian smiles.

DONALD: Now can I be left alone, please? I just want to be alone.

When Adrian is gone, a nurse checks Donald's chemo drip, then walks off.

Donald shifts in his bed, finds a less uncomfortable position (not easily done) and watches TracheotomyMan, who has smuggled in some cigarettes, the cause of his original undoing. TM lights up a fag and holds it to his – oh my God – to his neck hole, to his neck hole! – where he inhales. Hardcore, Donald bubbles. Extremely hardcore.

At this moment Trach catches Donald's eye and casts him a forlorn look – no triumph of guile there, just a sad recognition of a terrible addiction even now. Gonna take it with him, this habit. That's just the way of it.

Over the man's head Donald imagines a bubble that reads: "**!*^X?*^@!**"

TracheotomyMan starts to choke, splutter, the miserable flap dilating and contracting. He can take no more and extinguishes the fag as Donald turns away, revolted.

Int. Physiotherapy Ward. Day.

When Adrian first went to university he wanted to help people. This was his primary instinct. He wanted to be of use. Now, all these years later, Adrian wonders just how effective he has been. Standing at the entrance to the oncology ward, in between rounds and visits by out-patients to his office, he thinks how satisfying it would be to have a

job with finite goals and tangible results, rather than this
calling of his with its nebulous outcomes. Take a plumber
and a faulty washing machine – the plumber doesn't give
counselling once a week for six months, he fixes the damn
machine. But people aren't machines. Adrian's patients,
so indecipherable in their myriad complexity, merely drift
away when he's finished with them, either into their graves
or back into their lives, leaving him with little idea of how
useful he has been. For all he knows he is a failure, offering
nothing more than a couple of tools of magnification to
help patients see their turmoil more clearly, closer up. That
is all psychology is. A magnifying science. The problem
is… the problem is: the better the telescope the more stars
you see.

Standing in the wings, Adrian watches Roy working a
room full of patients. The maestro of mirth is in full flow,
getting the old, the infirm, even the irascible to throw a
mini-basketball into a rubbish basket clutched to his belly.
Soon they are all laughing, using their facial muscles again,
finding a way back into themselves. Roy is a natural. He
doesn't aim at cures. He's simply laughing, laughing no
matter what, as if there is nothing more absurd than
taking life seriously.

Adrian turns unseen and goes back to his office to get
on with some paperwork ahead of his next client.

Int. The Delpe's Dining Room. Night.
A dinner party. The Delpes, Adrian, plus another couple,
Larry and Louise, old friends of the Delpes. The red wine is
flowing. Veterans of such candlelit nights.
RENATA: What's the problem?
LARRY: She's not happy. Are you, hon?

LOUISE: I'm not. No. I'm not. But then – I've never been happy, so… It's not Larry's fault.

LARRY (*his hand on her shoulder*): Well that's good. It's not my fault.

The others smile.

LOUISE: It's just that… when I solve one problem, another one *always* appears. Always.

RENATA: Come on Adrian, you're the psychologist. Why is that?

ADRIAN: Well… (*wry smile*) solving problems has nothing to do with happiness.

LARRY: Here we go. Now we're getting down to it.

JIM: Solving problems has nothing to do with happiness?

RENATA: Explain. Explain. Explain!

ADRIAN (*smiling*): Okay, to put it simply…

LARRY: *Very* simply for me please.

ADRIAN: …it's impossible to experience all our problems simultaneously. We can't. Luckily for us. Our minds are pretty much preoccupied with one thing at a time. Our other problems just wait in line, in order of urgency, the greater obscuring the lesser. We don't even know they're there half the time, these less urgent ones, until we solve the first problem. So, there it is. You solve one, you reveal the next in line, solve that, the next one comes into view. To be alive is to have problems. Sadly, an infinite queue of them.

RENATA: Cheers. Great. (*Toasts*) To endless misery!

They laugh and clink glasses. Larry and Louise, married eighteen years, teenage sweethearts. Jim and Ren twelve-years-wed. But no one is more expert than anyone else. Adrian is the only one who has the moniker of professional in these matters and even he is only offering one possible model, a fresh metaphor to get by on.

LARRY: So – hang on – I shouldn't bother to solve problems then?

ADRIAN (*smiling*): Not if you expect it will make you happy, no. But there are many other reasons for solving problems.

JIM: Good God. How did we get onto this conversation?

ADRIAN (*swirling his wine, lazily liberating the flavours*): Personally, I like to hang onto a big ol' friendly problem if its doing a tremendous job of screening out God-knows-what behind it. But enough about my wife.

Big laughter. From everyone except Louise. Unhappy Louise. Her problems backlogged to infinity.

LOUISE: You're having problems with your wife?

ADRIAN: Was a joke.

JIM (*brightly*): And how is your beautiful wife?

ADRIAN: Still beautiful.

Int. The Delpe Kitchen. Later.

Adrian and Jim, one on one. Strauss from the next room. Murmured talk. The men's voices are lowered too.

ADRIAN: We may not have unlimited time. It could take weeks before he really opens up to me. And if the treatments aren't as successful as we all hope then... is this how you want him to spend his time? With me?

This is the kind of talk Jim wants. Craves now the uninflected truth. Needs a torrent of hard facts, now that it seems his solitary role to imagine the worst-case scenario.

JIM: Adrian – I don't want him to die angry.

Adrian puts his hand on Jim's shoulder, grips it tightly, steadying him, as if Jim is a companion climber on a sheerer part of the face.

JIM: Someone's got to think about it. Who knows, right? He could be on his way out. He probably is. But no one else will say it, except Donny.

Adrian can't reply. And if it is tough for Adrian to hear this, how much tougher must it be for Jim to say it?

Jim opens a high cupboard and pulls out Don's tatty journal.

JIM: He's been working on it again. He guards this more than his soul. This is my son in here. But I don't understand any of it. You're the professional. Maybe there's new clues. Somehow we've got to find a way into him.

Adrian holds the boy's old journal, its heavily doodled cover.

ADRIAN: Donald wasn't pleased to learn I've already looked at this.

JIM: Just… take another look. Please. The new stuff. Go on. Please. You have a father's permission.

Jim moves to the kitchen door and starts to push it open.

JIM: He draws this stuff more than ever. Garbage still, dark, disgusting, sexual storylines, semi-pornographic half of it. Check it out.

ADRIAN: Jim, I…

The door shuts. Jim is gone. Adrian is alone with the journal.

A NAKED MIRACLEMAN lies on his bed in the FOETAL POSITION, holding a whisky bottle – a picture of depression and self-loathing, as…

...the ANSWERPHONE on his side table replays MESSAGES.

MESSAGE ONE: Hello MiracleMan. This is the Mayor. On behalf of the city I'd like to thank you...

MIRACLEMAN reaches blindly and skips to the next MESSAGE.

MESSAGE TWO: MiracleMan. Hello. I am ringing from Sweden. We would like to nominate you for the Nobel Peace Pri...

MIRACLEMAN skips to next MESSAGE.

RACHEL'S VOICE: Hi. Just me. I uh... I'm performing today and... y'know... I just wondered if you'd like to come and hear me...

At the CLUB, RACHEL sings LEAD VOCALS flanked by FOUR GIRL DANCERS. She is great, athletic, playful, hot and raunchy in her DANCE ROUTINE. The AUDIENCE goes wild and, in the background, SMILING, is MIRACLEMAN.

LATER. STREET. NIGHT. MIRACLEMAN roars through the STREETS on a MOTORCYCLE, with RACHEL on the back, her hair streaming.

MEANWHILE... further down the street, THE GLOVE lowers his BINOCULARS and picks up a RIFLE. He and his NURSE have taken up a perfect position behind a LOW WALL.

THE GLOVE: Here he comes. Excellent.

NURSE: But darling, you said I could do it. You know how hard I've been practising. Pleaaseee let me kill him...

She's tough to resist, especially when she has her hand on his CROTCH. THE GLOVE gives up the RIFLE.

THE GLOVE: Okay. But don't fire until I say. (*Raises binoculars and once more sees* MIRACLEMAN *and* RACHEL *roaring closer, closer, closer.*) Wait till he comes within range… wait… we'll only get one chance… wait…

NURSE (*taking aim*): Can I ask you one question?

THE GLOVE: Shoot.

She FIRES! **BANGGGG!!!**

THE GLOVE: What are you?!!!!… I didn't mean – YOU IDIOT!!! – I just meant…

THE NURSE: What? You said SHOOT. You said shoot.

THE GLOVE slaps his head as MIRACLEMAN roars safely by on his MOTORBIKE.

THE GLOVE: Women! Aaarghh!

LATER, MIRACLEMAN stops the MOTORBIKE outside RACHEL's house.

RACHEL: Thanks.

When MIRACLEMAN takes off his helmet she touches his face.

MIRACLEMAN: You're welcome.

RACHEL: Will you… er… will you come in for a night-cap?

MIRACLEMAN: I think we both know that's a bad idea. I don't think we should see each other any more.

RACHEL (*disappointed*): When you told me you were immune to everything, you meant it, didn't you? You're immune to EVERYTHING.

MIRACLEMAN: It's a curse. Just forget me.

RACHEL: I'm seriously gonna try.

She CLOSES THE DOOR. MIRACLEMAN looks up at the full moon. A thought bubble appears over him:

"I can't take it any more. I LOATHE THIS LIFE!"

MIRACLEMAN heads slowly back to his MOTORCYCLE. As he crosses the street, an eighteen-WHEELER comes from out of NOWHERE. He hears it but doesn't even turn his head to see what kind of danger he is in. INSTEAD…

…MIRACLEMAN simply bends over and SLOWLY, DELIBERATELY, SUICIDALLY, TIES HIS SHOELACE!

A second later the TRUCK HITS HIM and FLINGS HIS BODY a GREAT DISTANCE. MIRACLEMAN lies MUTILATED on the pavement as the TRUCK comes to a stop further down the road. THE DRIVER in SILHOUETTE gets out and walks up to MIRACLEMAN's bloody body, standing over it. When his face catches the LIGHT we see that it is – THE GLOVE!

THE GLOVE: Now in most cases that oughta do it.

Int. Life-drawing Class. Night.

Jennifer is back on the cushions today. There is no life in Adrian's life-drawing. It's not that Adrian misses the younger model – heavy Jennifer is a more abundant challenge – it's more that he misses Donald drawing the younger model. He's also taken a seat at the rear of the class. He doesn't really understand why he has done this, and he doesn't want to psychoanalyse it. Sometimes his profession sickens him: this constant examination of human motives.

His thought are on Sophie. Before he married her, all those years ago, he believed in order. But with her he felt reckless, actually wanted her to give him no choice in what direction their lives took – he was bored with his own decision-making and intuition – and this is just what she did for him. She took over. But then her passion for him faded. *She* became bored, tired of providing all the excitement and stimulus. *She* began to look further afield. He had imagined all along that she would do this, that things would pan out this way, that *intrinsically* he wasn't vital enough for her and would have to regulate his feelings accordingly, to deal with the exit – stage left – of their physical relationship.

The years pass. His feelings are corralled for so long that they are tamed for good. A pattern is established. It is not a bad pact, as pacts go. They live apart. But maintain a bond too. He still feels unreasonably proud that she has never asked him for a divorce – her greatest compliment – and the idea of her beauty still humbles him at night when he lies in bed alone, the favoured left side of his face pushes into a soft pillow. Her physical beauty still immobilizes him. He was always a sucker for it. And when they make love, husband and wife, which occurs roughly once a year, he imagines himself the luckiest man in the world. For the rest of the time, he has his art: he too has his other loves, and they are much more durable than hers.

Returning from such thoughts, he looks again at his sketch pad. He takes stock of all he has not achieved. In sheer frustration at the disservice he has done Jennifer tonight, he gives her a tail: why not? He sketches a pointy little devil's tail on her butt and looks at it for a while.

Int. Hospital. Day.
Going about his rounds, Adrian notices instantly when the same nurse gives him the eye. It's more her smile that he notices. He stops, turns around and approaches her. Like Don in the burger bar, he is all nerves until he finds his voice. What will he say? He wants to get this just right. Finally he uses a word from a lost lexicon, centuries old.
ADRIAN: Hi.

Int. Don's Bedroom / Delpe House. Day.

Donald slides into bed while his father holds back the blankets for him. Jim then sets the blankets down again so carefully you'd think they could crush the boy. Don doesn't look good, but a little smile suggests he is pleased to be home from the hospital, the current round of treatment complete.

JIM: Attaboy.

RENATA: Take your Reglan, then some Benadryl. Come on.

DONALD: What's the point?

JIM: Come on buddy. (*Holds medication to* DONALD'*s lips but* DON *isn't interested.*) Come on, chief. (DONALD *reluctantly takes his medication.*) How do you feel?

DONALD: I feel like vomiting up my organs in alphabetical order.

JIM: That's good. Who said that?

DONALD: Nobody. Nobody did.

JIM: We love you.

Donald doesn't reply. He clearly has a rendezvous in another room of the multiplex and has slipped into that other movie already.

Int. Fancy Restaurant. Night.

Adrian looks up from the menu as...

...as ANGELA, with her nursey walk, devoid of sexy embellishments, just one foot in front of the other, crosses to the table from the powder room. Still, she looks fantastic in her elegant evening dress, a yellow rose at the apex of her décolletage. He takes a deep intake of air made fragrant by his own minty toothpaste as both she and the waiter arrive. No, Adrian thinks, she might not be the stunner his Sophie is, might not have the classic lines that always make him want to reach for a paintbrush (this impulse being a barometer of his desire), but she is real, and she is here; yes, she is here and is real.

ADRIAN: Perfect timing.

ADRIAN (*he raises his wine glass*): So. (*Smiles.*) Thanks for coming out. (*She glows.*) I uh... I haven't done this sort of thing in quite a while actually.

ANGELA: Oh, I find that hard to believe.

ADRIAN: Oh no. It's true. (*Pause*) I'm uh... y'see I'm married.

Her face falls.

ADRIAN: Sorry. I thought I should tell you early.

ANGELA: Early? Early is "Hi, my name is Adrian, I'm married". *That's* "early". (*Weary sigh*) Great. You're not wearing a wedding ring.

Adrian draws his gold band from his top pocket and puts it back on, mirroring the moment, fifteen years before, when Sophie and he had stood before an altar and her almost child-sized fingers worked the gold up his sausagey fourth digit, her eyes looking deeply into his at first but having eventually to go to the thwarted ring as she waggled, pushed and cajoled it into place.

ANGELA: Oh my God.

ADRIAN: Sorry.

ANGELA: You keep it in your pocket?!! Look, I don't go out with married men. I haven't got that much time to waste.

ADRIAN: My wife and I have an arrangement. Well she has her arrangement, I have her cat.

ANGELA: Is that, like, a joke?

ADRIAN: She's seeing another man. He's a vet. And she loves horses.

ANGELA: And you're okay with that?

ADRIAN: We spend a lot of time apart. I think I'm being realistic.

ANGELA: Have you heard of divorce? That sounds a lot more realistic.

ADRIAN: Oh no. We won't get divorced. I still love her. And the funny thing is, she says she still loves me. Even now. And you know what's completely crazy? I believe her. The thing is, I'm not physically desirable to her any more... She says she doesn't mind, that she isn't even a sexual person any more. And then Conrad comes along. So I'm wondering... if I should allow her Conrad. If I owe her that much. Or is that just crazy?

ANGELA: Who the hell's this Conrad guy?

ADRIAN: Oh, he's the stud. A randy vet. It's like a soap opera. Sorry.

The wine has stopped tasting so good.

ANGELA: Well – I think this date is going great. You really know how to show a girl a good time.

ADRIAN: I'm sorry. I shouldn't have told you all that. I shouldn't even be wasting your time. But I thought you were very nice. *Are* very nice.

Angela thinks about it. She doesn't move.

ANGELA: God, I hate being so desperate. Listen, I just wanna have some fun. I work hard. I just wanna have some fun. Can we just have some fun?

ADRIAN (*raising his glass, smiling again*): Then here's to that. To having fun. We deserve it.

ANGELA: I don't know about you but I sure do. (*Despondent*) The desert better be fucking good.

Then Angela, with her extra-special thirst, drains her glass in one.

Int. Don's Bedroom / Delpe House. Night.

It's a known side effect. The breathing patterns get disrupted because of the drugs, the brain thinks something physiological has gone wrong, the breathing arrests further, panic sets in, the chest constricts, as with the bends – what divers know as a dizzying and a crushing pressure on the chest.

When Renata arrives she knows already what's happening.

DONALD (*shouting, delirious*): No! No! Stop it! Stop it!

RENATA: It's okay. It's okay, sweetie. It's okay. Easy now.

DONALD: He's cutting me open!

RENATA: Who is? Who is, Donny?

DONALD (*coming out of it*): Oh God, oh God, oh God...

RENATA (*holding him, an accidental pietà*): Easy now, it's just an allergic reaction to the Reglan. The Benadryl isn't working. You're having a panic attack. But we're going to get you something stronger. Just wait. Just hold on. You're gonna be fine Donny. (*Clutching him tighter, angry determination arriving now.*) We're gonna beat this. We're gonna fight this together. I need you to fight, okay? I need you to fight and fight and fight.

Now Jim arrives. Baggy-eyed. Flapping pyjamas. Hair crazed. Hears the tail end of this, stares at this sudden pietà, his wife's appeal.

JIM: What is it, Ren? What is it?

RENATA: I think maybe a panic attack.

JIM: Okay. It's okay, buddy. Wait there, champ. Okay? I'll get you something.

Jim rushes out.

DONALD: I'm scared, I'm so fucken scared, Mum.

RENATA: I know, I know, I know. Sshhhh, shhhhh, shhhhh...

A sprinkler on parched grass.

Int. Hallway / Delpe House. Contin.
Jim beats on Jeff's bedroom door.

JIM: Jeff! Open this up! I told you not to lock this! Open up!

Jeff, naked but for a towel held around his middle, opens the door.

JEFF (*sleepy*): What is it?

JIM: Where's the dope? Where's your dope?

JEFF: The dope? What are you talking about? I haven't got any...

JIM: GIVE IT TO ME! GET IT AND GIVE IT TO ME NOW!

Int. Don's Bedroom / Delpe House. Contin.
Just two stoners. Father and son. Rest of the house in bed once more. Donald inhales a very long super-slim joint.

JIM: That's it. Hold it in. It's gonna take a minute or two. Feel better?

DONALD (*nods*): Yeah. Am I doing it right?

JIM: Have a little more. First time won't hurt you. We used to smoke this at high school. Ha! Never told your mother. The medical books say it's good against anxiety.

DONALD: You knew Jeff had some?

JIM: I know more than you guys think.

Donald passes the joint to his father, feigning inexperience.

JIM: No, no more for me. Oh, one more puff then.

Donald starts to giggle as Jim inhales. This sets Jim off giggling too.

JIM: Had enough? Okay, we'll put it out. (*He grinds the end of the joint out in a saucer.*) Jesus Christ, what's happening to this family?

DONALD: Oh, I dunno. It's just getting good if you ask me. Thanks for showing me how to smoke that stuff.

JIM: Don't say I never taught you anything. Can you sleep now?

DONALD: Might watch TV or something.

JIM: Okay. Keep the sound down. I'll leave this here, the rest of the joint, in case you need it later, okay?

DONALD: You're pretty cool.

JIM: I haven't had enough time for you. Haven't shown you very much of this world. I'm sorry.

DONALD: Go to bed.

When Donald hears his father's bedroom door close down the hallway, he gets out of bed, picks a DVD off the shelf, slips it in the player and then turns on his TV. There is no copyright warning on this particular DVD. The title comes up straight away: *Gina-Town*. The camera-work is shaky as hell on this bootleg reproduction (Raff is a shit cameraman), and the production values aren't helped by the occasional ice-cream-eating front-row cinema-goer drifting between camera and screen in silhouette, but it's an illegal gift of porn from close friends and it gains a lot in sentimental value as a result.

Int. Angela's Apartment. Night.
Adrian looks around at Angela's stuff – artwork, photos. Nice. Tasteful. She clearly has a vision of how she wants things to be. He then makes a decision, finishes his nightcap

in a single gulp and picks up his coat, just as Angela emerges from the bedroom in a wow frock of the "something a little more comfortable" variety.

ANGELA: Are you going?

ADRIAN: I thought so. Thanks for the drink though.

ANGELA: I don't know why I bother.

ADRIAN: I had a wonderful night, really.

ANGELA: Great. Fine. Yippee.

ADRIAN: I mean it. I'll see you at work.

ANGELA: No. I'm quitting. I'm joining a convent.

ADRIAN: Don't do that.

He stands before her. They look into each other's eyes. Close enough to kiss.

ADRIAN: Anyway…

ANGELA: Stay. (*Pause*) I don't normally beg.

He kisses her lightly on the lips. Her eyes close. His do not.

ADRIAN: Better go.

He goes to the door.

ANGELA: Hey, handsome.

He stops.

ANGELA: You're not bad.

For a second he just stands there, looking at her, doing a pretty good impression of a dog who's just been shown a card trick.

Ext. Angela's Apartment. Contin.

Adrian closes Angela's door, walks a few steps into the night and then stops, succumbing to self-loathing. Idiot, he thinks. Fool. And as if his self-contempt is linked to balance, he tumbles back against the nearest wall, drawing breath deeply, only now aware that he's been holding his breath since the kiss.

You're not bad... What did she mean? Is it an understated compliment? Is he not bad exactly, but not very good either? Which is it? All he can clearly remember is the look in her eyes. Here at least there is no need to analyse, to psychoanalyse, to fall into the trap of his profession, the habit of emotional vivisection. *They could have something*, this is what her eyes had told him: they could have something. If he wants it. If he wants it.

Does he want it? As ever, he is not sure. His morale fades slowly to black.

Int. Oncology Ward. Day.
Adrian needs to talk to Roy. It's urgent.

ADRIAN: How are things?

ROY: Not bad. Just got the results of my Aids test. Only positive news I've had in months.

ADRIAN (*slow to respond*): You're joking.

ROY (*shaking his head*): Ye-hess.

ADRIAN: You make a joke of everything, don't you.

ROY: Laughter through tears. One's sense of humour tends to become a little cloudy when you work around these poor buggers.

ADRIAN: Can I ask you something?

ROY: Shoot.

ADRIAN: When – well, actually, how did you first lose your virginity?

ROY: I love questions like that. Let me see, I've lost it so many times... Ummm, I think it was... look, can we discuss this over a beer or something? I feel funny discussing premature ejaculation while I'm on duty.

Int. Bar. Day.

The pub is mostly empty. A couple of thickset tradesman types are gathered around their pints at a standing table, and every now and again the *dot – dot – dot* of three darts searching for the bull is heard. Adrian and Roy are having a quiet drink at the bar.

ROY: ...So in the end, I don't think it matters how you lose your cherry, just as long as you lose it. You know? Past a certain age it's one hell of a monkey on your back, one hell of a monkey – especially when you're spanking the little fella as often as I used to. (*Sip of beer*) I presume there's a reason for this line of questioning?

ADRIAN: Oh sure. Well I think so. How old were you?

ROY: Old? 'Bout nineteen. A girl said she'd do it with me, but I got so nervous I ate a packet of dried nutmeg. Someone had told me it gives you a great high, so I ate an entire packet. I walked around for two weeks thinking I was a muffin. Swear to God. I was looking for one of those, y'know, one of those little cupcake trays to sleep in. Fuck-en wasted! Eventually I tripped over my girl again. She must have been drunk. Somehow by mutual consent my penis found entry. The rest is history. I recall very little. Am I allowed to know what this is all about, or is this, like, twenty questions?

ADRIAN: Donald. Donald Delpe.

ROY: Sure. Okay.

ADRIAN: He's a virgin.

ROY: Okay.

ADRIAN: I'm thinking... of helping him lose it. With a prostitute.

Roy's eyebrows climb up his forehead and stay there.

ROY: *You are?*

137

ADRIAN: He doesn't want to die a virgin. I might need your help.

ROY: Ohh-ho-kay. Um… isn't that kinda thing against the rules though?

Adrian rubs his brow. Even the thought of it is ludicrous.

ADRIAN: Somewhat.

ROY: Okay, let me reword. Isn't it like, completely fucking close to insanely out-of-bounds and kinda career-ending if you're caught, kind of shit?

No answer this time from Adrian. None at all.

Int. Don's Bedroom. Day.

Jim and Renata pack Don's suitcase. How many more times will they pack it? Today is D-Day for Don's new round of hospital treatments.

JIM: He needed it.

RENATA: I'm telling him to fight – and you're giving him dope.

Jim can no longer bite his tongue.

JIM: Ren – he's dying!

RENATA: Don't you say that! Don't you ever say that in this house! DON'T YOU EVER SAY THAT! HOW DARE YOU? HOW DARE YOU?

He is winded by this attack. He retreats. Returns to the packing of the bag.

JIM (*sulkily*): A little bit of dope won't hurt him.

RENATA: You left him a whole bag. Now if I take it away from him I'm the evil one again. I'm the one he pushes away, the one he draws pictures of, with horns and a bolt through my head.

JIM: It's harmless.

138

RENATA: Thank you, Bob Marley. Are you even aware of the latest research on pot? Are you? It robs people of motivation.

JIM: I don't read all the books you do.

RENATA: Well, try one. It won't kill you to learn what really going on inside your son.

JIM (*his own anger rising, unstoppable*): And you think a book from Amazon dot com is gonna tell you that? Look, at least I did something for him, okay? What have you done?

She pulls two pairs of shorts from Jim's hand and stuffs them in the case – angry, stunned by this latest betrayal in a numbing parade of betrayals.

JIM: ...Except fill him up with names in Latin that tell him he's gonna live for ever? Well, maybe he's not gonna live for ever, just like the rest of us. And maybe the order in which we go isn't gonna be chronological, oldest first! And maybe, just maybe, twenty boxes of books and ten thousand hours on the Internet isn't actually gonna change that!

Jim storms out. Renata can't even breathe.

Int. Oncology Ward. Day.
Fun morning. First a saline enema. Then a little vomiting. Mild panic attack, soothed by Benadryl. Then a jaunt down to Radiology around noon, akin to lunch on a nuclear test site, and afterwards, once suitably micro-, gamma-, x- and all-but-Mexican-waved, he is whisked back into the fun capital of the world, Ward One of Watford General, where he lies, churning with poisons, throbbing with half-lives.

How does he feel? Brill. Peachy. Like each part of his body has been operated on simultaneously and then sewn up again, but only after the surgeons have left every last one of their instruments inside him, a cutlery drawer full of oversights upturned and stitched inside his spatchcocked body. Every movement causes a terrible jangling, a pressing of sharp blades against super-tender organs. A scalpel against his spine holds him at knifepoint; a pair of scissors is ready to mug his innards; a small hacksaw behind his eyes is already at work, scraping, paring, sawing. It's like playing that children's game where you reach under a cloth and try to identify the hidden items. That's what he's doing now: running his hands under the sheet – over his body, his chest, his thighs – trying to make an inventory of the foreign bodies inside him.

Ward news? Comb-Over is gone. This has just happened, just this morning. Comb-Over went. Just like that. By the time Donald had returns from the Hiroshima that is Radiology, the bed by the window is occupied by Trachular. Donald, therefore, finds himself promoted, inching one bed closer to having the best view in the world, and one closer to the abyss.

Dozing under the sheer weight of medication, he is awoken by the sound of his bed curtains being swished aside like a matador's cape. It's Adrian and Roy. Adrian is slightly pale, looking nervous but excited too, as if he's done something extremely naughty that he's wanted to do for a long time and only just now got up the guts for. But Roy looks just how Roy always looks: mischievous, rubbing his hands gleefully. Adrian draws up a chair. Roy remains standing at the foot of the bed. Something is going on.

ADRIAN (*speaking rapidly but in a hushed voice*): Okay. You want to know what it's like? All right? What

I'm about to do is highly improper. It's illegal, immoral and it contravenes every oath I've ever taken, but there are times when… well, when you've just got to do as Roy says and burn some rubber.

Roy smiles, and gives the old Ebert and Roeper "two thumbs way up".

DONALD (*groggy, in pain*): Have you guys been smoking spliff?

ADRIAN: So… tell me… what do you want? I need specific instructions. Exact statistics. You're a teenager. I know you've thought about it.

DONALD (*confused*): About what?

ADRIAN: You're a smart kid, come on. If I'm going out there on a… on a shopping spree, I need to know what your tastes are. In girls.

DONALD (*even more confused*): What girls?

ADRIAN: I'm going to help you, Donald. Have an experience. But I need you to paint me a picture. Help me narrow down the field. (*Turning to Roy.*) This is a mistake, I know it.

DONALD: What's going on?

ROY (*taking sympathy on the kid*): Don? We're gonna help you get your rocks off. Take the German soldier on its maiden voyage. The cavalry has arrived.

DONALD: Me?

ROY: You. And a female. Together. In loving congress. The long wait is over my little *compadre*.

ADRIAN: What Roy is trying to say is we intend to assist you in losing your virginity. If that is still what you want.

There is a long silence. Donald's face doesn't brighten at all. His mouth hangs ajar.

DONALD: But… how?

ROY: Leave the details to us, young man. You just lie there and get thy mojo back.

ADRIAN: And think about what kind of woman you'd like.

ROY (*with mock seriousness*): It's a question which has occupied me my whole life.

Donald smiles at last.

DONALD: You guys are *serious*?

ROY: Poon Tang is not just the name of a small town in Korea.

As Adrian rises to go Donald sits up in bed.

DONALD: Wait.

He pulls open the drawer in his side table, takes out a comic and silently passes it to Adrian. It is called *Electra*, and its cover features a leather-clad warrior queen in shredded loincloth and with basketball breasts, a look of cold menace in her eyes. She's hungry for sex or violence, or both.

DONALD: Page three.

Adrian opens it. Roy leans in to see. Silence as the two men inspect the archetype. Roy gives a slow long whistle.

Int. Day Room. Day.

Donald sits in a room full of people knitting chickens: to be exact, chicken-shaped tea cosies. Donald would not have believed such a hospital scene could exist unless he'd seen it first-hand but here it is: a room full of sick and worse than sick people click-click-clicking, plain-and-purling their way towards a fabric poultry farm.

But woolly hens are not long on Don's mind. Adrian rescues him from the occupational therapy session, pushing his wheelchair into a far corner where it is presumed they indulge in a discussion of a highly professional nature.

DONALD: You can't tell my parents. No way they'd allow it.

ADRIAN: So. Here's what we've got. Your perfect-world scenario. Brunette. No tattoos. Twenty-two to twenty-four years of age, experienced...

DONALD: Definitely.

ADRIAN: White, between five-six and five-seven, if possible. Hourglass. Big eyes, C-cup or higher, silicon not a problem.

DONALD: Great arse.

ADRIAN (*sighs*): Great arse.

DONALD: I have a feeling I'm gonna be an arse man.

ADRIAN: This is mission impossible, you know that?

DONALD: I can pay.

ADRIAN: How can you pay?

DONALD: I can pay.

ADRIAN: I'll pay. You just finish your treatment and get your immune system going again. This only happens if you're strong enough.

A nice-looking nurse, the cutest one Donald has seen around here, passes behind Adrian's back. Donald's eyes stray. How sweetly she moves. What a twitch to her tush as she walks, walking right into his film library of fantasy gals.

ADRIAN: Donald? Donald? *Donald!*

DONALD (*snapping back*): Definitely. Yes. Definitely.

ADRIAN: One last matter. Do you know what to do... when you're alone with a woman?

DONALD: Why, are you gonna tell me?

Adrian decides to persevere, even at the risk of sounding like a government-produced textbook.

ADRIAN: What do you think making love is like?

DONALD (*with little hesitation*): Like stamp collecting – only stickier.

Donald is going to make nothing easy. But then, thinks Adrian, why should he? As the boy sees it, the world owes him everything and had better deliver it fast.

DONALD: What? Okay, I'll be serious. I promise. (*Assumes a look of studied concentration.*) Go ahead. Please.

ADRIAN: Are you serious?

DONALD: Yes. I want to hear this.

ADRIAN: Okay. Well, the first thing is… is respect.

DONALD: Uh-huh.

ADRIAN: When the time comes – when you finally have the pleasure of giving someone else the pleasure… of making love – when you both decide that the time is right to share this dual pleasure…

As Adrian's voice ebbs slowly away into the droning hinterlands of who-gives-a-damn, Donald finds himself unable to restrain his forty-frame-a-second imagination, and over the shrink's shoulder he pictures the hospital's most attractive nurse stop before a standing fan in front of the large window in order to cool herself, pulling open the lapels of her dress, fanning her large breasts, a full-bodied woman in her late twenties, succumbing suddenly to the terrible heat of the day and to the broken air-conditioning and perhaps also to her own pounding *inner heat*, yielding to an urge to lose a layer or two, throwing back her head as if offering her neck for execution or kisses, her right hand mopping that long neck, so hot, so hot, so hot today, cloth diving to dewy cleavage and soon moist with her musk, her left hand meanwhile undoing, undoing button by straining button, her trampoline-tight uniform, quick fingers seeking relief from the heat, the awful heat, peeling open the white layer of office and bursting out of that uniform to – to reveal – to reveal...

ADRIAN: ...and *that* is the joy of sex.

Donald adjusts his eyeline marginally back to the doctor, to the same degree that a newsreader looks back to camera from the autocue, reality restored.

DONALD: The... joy... of... uh... okay. Thanks. That's cool. I think I got it.

He looks back for his nurse, his vixen, his onanistic angel, expecting to see her in bra and panties, suspenders and stockings, but she is gone. Vanished. In the window stands an aspidistra.

ADRIAN: You're welcome. Well, I think that just about covers it for today.

Knitting a chicken: it doesn't seem the same after that.

Ext. Street. Day.

It's Adrian's day off. There is a lecture on cubism at the Tate Modern he'd like to hear. A world authority, a guy who'd interviewed Braque in Paris in '63 just before the painter's death, is going to speak. It's not the subject that really interests him – he feels that cubism's only achievement was the seeing of several sides of a subject at once (the task of all humanity) – but rather his desire to see the brilliant functioning of intellect.

But instead, what is he doing? With a couple of drinks inside him, he is looking for a hooker. He, a respected psychologist, easily recognized, is out with his wallet looking for a blue-light partner for a near-dying boy.

Technically, if it comes to anything, it's a crime. And the damage it would do to his career if word ever got out… What does he think he's up to? Is he having some sort of crisis? Is this an experiment in professional suicide?

He knows the answer. He knew it days ago when he made the decision. He is trying to save the boy's life. It is no exaggeration. Donald will die unless he cheers up. The equation may be this simple. The boy needs joy in his veins as well as cytotoxins, antimetabolites, alkylating agents, and certainly not the pollutants of thwarted ambitions. And if Don is not to survive, then how much better to die with his greatest earthly wish fulfilled, the big item at the forefront of his Problem Schedule solved. This strange solution is the only prescription that makes any sense to Adrian any more.

And something about the boy has got under his skin too. There is more than a little of Donald in his own actions now, which he welcomes. Sick of his own failed strategies he sees some genius in the way the boy does business. And so perhaps it is not just the boy's life he is trying to save here. What is the point of forever rearranging the deckchairs on the *Titanic*? Isn't that where his career is at? Morbidly throwing leaky life rings to those lost overboard? By helping the kid he will also be helping himself. This is fine too. Goodness is also self-serving. Whenever we reach out our hand in aid, doesn't our other hand always clasp a mirror?

And so he is out on the street with his credit cards, cash and chequebook. The kid has set the bar impossibly high. Brunette, no tattoos, twenty-two to twenty-four, experienced, between five-six and five-seven, hourglass figure, big eyes, C-cup or higher, great arse. Is there is such a woman in all the world, let alone in blustery Watford?

His first idea is to go from phone box to phone box, as coolly as possible, and take down the cards that hookers tuck behind payphones, wedge into cracks in the walls. He works quickly, moving from one fetid onion-smelling booth to another, taking every card he can find, little two-by-threes, either black-and-whites or full-colour jobs: *Friendly Knockout Needs Big Fun* or *Saddle up and Ride, Ring Jodi* – young girls, somebody's daughters from Woking or Colchester, presenting themselves rear-on to the camera like cows backing into a milking stall. He gets out of the booths with as many cards as he can pocket before some passer-by, perhaps a friend, some ex-client, acquaintance, whoever, sees what he's doing. He even takes the cards of blondes and black girls and Asian girls: he wants to be spoilt for choice at the end of all this. It may be a question of compromise.

He's got about twenty or thirty cards already in his pocket, but he's pretty sure he hasn't yet spotted his "Electra", as he's dubbed this impossible woman. Electra, who saved the life of her young brother, Orestes. In Greek, "bright one". A life-giver. And also the name used by Freud, father of his profession, to explain a mother's fixation on a young son. Salvation via illicit desire. Light. A warrior queen in a two-quid magazine. But where on earth will he find her?

About to exit the last booth, Adrian sees a single card stuck on the glass door at face height. The girl doesn't look bad. Pretty face, anyway. He plucks it down to check out later, only to expose, staring in at him from the other side of the glass, the close-up features of a disgruntled parking warden. She's seen what he's done! He rips up the picture, throws it down, feigning disgust, even shaking his head as he opens the door and brushes by the woman, whom he knows is watching him walk away, watching beyond courtesy, before she too goes into the booth, standing on the broken image of the working girl, grinding her into the road oil and grime and the last traces of dried urine and dog faeces, as her coins drop, clanking, into the payphone.

Int. Church. Day.
Jim on his knees. Praying to God. Hands meshed. Eyes sealed. Looking for magic. Miracles. Knees aching, thinking, *All life is suffering.* Gautama Buddha.

What the Lord giveth, the Lord taketh away. Dimly remembered sophistries drift through his head. He should be at work now, but he can't seem to leave this place. *Whatever thy hand findeth to do, do it with all thy might.* A line also from a Negro spiritual on an old Bessie Smith record: *I ain't got much but you can take it from me too.* Is that the deal? Non-attachment? A stripping to the bone that should not be contested? The strength to be robbed of everything?

And what are these pithy quotes anyway, he muses, but painkillers less long-lasting than paracetamol? Isn't the Bible just a pharmacy: shelf after shelf of short-term pain-relievers? God forbid this is true, that all we are doing is looking for better clichés to live by, spiritual novocaine to smooth the day out. On the other hand, find yourself with a headache and see how useful a little paracetamol suddenly becomes. Look at the cynic in a time of stress, Jim thinks, unable to get the tablets out of the fucking foil wrapper fast enough! Same with the Bible. Just when you count it out, it delivers consolation that can make you feel numbly good from the neck down. This is not to be dismissed lightly. Especially when life is hitting you with one hammer blow after another.

So, if God is a chemist, how best to present him with your prescription? In the old days you went on foot, you undertook pilgrimage, you went to Fatima, as far as Lourdes, to Guadalupe Hidalgo, to Mecca, wherever God had opened up a branch store. But Jim is a modern man with no time for such sorties. He's come to his corner church in the hope that a more contemporary method of contact will suffice. Today he just wants to send a text message, if that's acceptable, a time-saving little txt msg, and then wait for a reply to appear in his own message in-box – the heart – the next day. And what will it do for him, this reply? Take away his pain? That's his hope. Give him *the strength to carry on.* Bessie Smith.

Jim turns his head. His wife of twenty-odd years is lighting candles at a side altar like a little Benedictine. Little wands of smoke drift up into the apse but, in the manner of a sinner's prayer, meet the ceiling and can go no higher.

Salvation! Salvation! Salvation! Jim's heart wants to shout.

Int. Oncology Ward. Day.
Donald is smiling. It's been there for days now, this mysterious smile, and has become something of a talking point among the staff. The nurses have repeatedly offered him pennies for his thoughts but he's told them they'll need to have this amount decimalized and inflation-adjusted before he even thinks about bringing them into his confidence. Even TracheotomyMan is curious.

TRACHEOTOMYMAN: What's to smile at? You win the lotto or somethin'?

But Donald keeps his eyes on the ceiling. And keeps on smiling. Silence is a win-win situation.

TRACHEOTOMYMAN: The bastard's won lotto. Musta.

Int. Adrian's Apartment. Day.

Adrian opens his front door. A woman stands there. Doesn't smile. Short skirt. A little heavier than her photo, but she carries it well enough. Oozing luxuries. A sheer top lets her bra show through. Immediately he is hopeful – and then she opens her mouth. Game over.

This is Prostitute Day. Seven invitations in all. Half an hour apart. He will give each woman fifteen minutes, pay them for their time, then get them out, avoiding an embarrassing cross-over on the stairs. It is all organized.

The experience of phoning these girls had been mortifying. What to ask for? His criteria were ludicrous, and he had lowered his sights substantially after calling the first two. Also, thinking it useless to explain over the phone the delicacy of the situation – very low age of client, very high chance client is dying – he made it sound as if these interviews today are sexual appointments with him, the real thing. Is this a mistake? Well, it's too late to worry. The prostitutes are on their way, ready for action, dressed and psyched for flesh games, each believing they will be expected to provide, for a lonely soul, a feat of emergency love.

The first hooker. She stares at him from the doorway.

HOOKER 1 (*voice an acoustic nightmare, like a Lady-shave whining on stubble*): You wanna bit, innit?

You wanna bit, innit?... The first words out of her mouth. Adrian wastes no time. A pleasant voice was not originally a criterion, but it is now. He cannot get the door closed fast enough. He pays his money, makes his excuses, and breathes deeply with his back against the door after he has turned the lock.

But he has hardly sat down again – nervously shuffling through the six remaining pictures, psychologically analysing the desperate poses aimed at appealing to men's baser urges, urges to fuck, to take a woman from behind, to humiliate, to animalize, to fantasize that she wants it really, needs it, craves it, dreams only of male machinery, as well as the faux-friendly faces the girls put on, fake smiles, as if they want a job like this, gave up careers in broadcasting to showcase their butts like this – when he has to go to the door again.

This second lady is large. No, she is huge. The floor-boards beneath her ache. She is all ballast.

HOOKER 2: What's the matter?

ADRIAN: Uh... you don't look very much like your photo, that's all.

HOOKER 2 (*surprised*): Really?

More cash for nothing. Adrian makes a rapid apology. He is not feeling well, some kind of virus. He has to call it off. A disbelieving look from her, but no great protest – it's easy money in the end and so she calmly withdraws. Too calmly, Adrian thinks. He's been conned. No doubt this is how the woman makes all her money, relying on the client's reluctance to tell it how it is, too polite to say that she is too fat for him even to contemplate having sex with her, that she should be ashamed of her false advertising. A smart woman. Understands the human game. She has found her niche. Put out a sexy ad, a picture of herself at age seventeen, perhaps, and then show up looking like Godzilla, big enough to handle herself too if the client gets antsy.

Thirty minutes later, HOOKER 3. Too skinny this time. And much more aggressive. Plies her trade with the mentality of a guerrilla: storm the village, wreak havoc, then bugger off. She demands to know why, *why exactly*, why she is not what he wants. He prefers to fudge, but she is in no mood for wordplay. Finally, he is cornered.

ADRIAN: Well... I have strange criteria, I'm sorry. It's a very particular thing I'm looking for, and I'm afraid, if you want to know, your breasts are probably two sizes too small and – would you mind turning around? Please, yes, around. Yes, you see, I'm afraid we've got a problem at the back there as well.

So much for honesty. He is glad he put only one glass of white wine in her hand. The stains will come out. It would have been a shame to lose not just £60 (her charge for rejection, twenty quid more than compliance!) but a £200 shirt as well.

He is weary of this already. What a tawdry game. So mercenary. So loveless. And now hookers are throwing wine over him! He had thought these women would at least act as if they were pleased to be there, inject a little theatre into the proceedings, make it fun somehow, provide some sort of fantasy. How naive he is.

HOOKER 4 (*wearing dark glasses*): Hello.

At last, Adrian thinks. Hallelujah. If not Electra, then at least a distant country cousin.

ADRIAN: Thanks for coming over. Please. Come in. Please.

As the woman steps over his threshold, Adrian pops his head out into the hall to see if the coast is clear of inquisitive neighbours before he closes the door.

He shows the woman the couch. Stops her from disrobing beyond her coat as she seems about to do. Beneath her glasses she is, if not beautiful, then at least appealing, comely, passably pretty.

He tells her his story. He does not want sex. It is more complicated than that. The details flow. Donald's tragic situation. His age. The medical prognosis. The boy's terrible anger and frustration. Even the work they have done together, which has exposed Donald's own expressed wish to lose his virginity before he dies – if that is to be his fate – and to lose it with a perfect woman. This is Adrian's mission today. To find such a woman, one who will be a party to this last wish. But it's not easy. She is the fourth hooker he's talked to today.

She understands, understands perfectly. What's more, she is moved. Her eyes cloud. The story has touched her. She opens a handbag but cannot find a hankie. He brings her Kleenex from the bathroom instead. Now she is crying. She is quite lovely in fact. And Adrian is stirred by this display of heart, feels a little drawn to her himself, attracted by the compression of her features as she cries, the fact that she cares, signs of humanity. She finishes wiping her eyes and rescuing her mascara.

HOOKER 4: Honey, after a story like that, I'll do it for free. But there's something I want to be clear about first, okay?

ADRIAN: What's that?

HOOKER 4: I have a penis.

Adrian stares at her. It's all he can do. Where is the hand

lever that will open the trap-door under his seat? How naive can he be?

HOOKER 4: Oh dear. You didn't guess?

ADRIAN: I'm not very experienced at this.

HOOKER 4: I suppose that changes everything?

ADRIAN: Ohhh yeah.

HOOKER 4: I'm sorry. I really would have loved to help. He sounds a great kid.

ADRIAN: He is.

HOOKER 4 (*rising, taking up her coat*): And I think you're pretty cute too.

ADRIAN (*blushing*): Thanks.

HOOKER 4: Oh well. *Que será*. Anyway, I hope you find a real angel for him.

ADRIAN: So do I.

In taking her leave the transvestite places a surprise kiss on Adrian's cheek, causing him to blush. Even up close and personal the feminine disguise holds up. The perfume is strong. There is nothing draggy about her. She's almost someone you could take home to meet the parents, seriously. It's just a shame about her dick, thinks Adrian.

When they reach the door, Adrian opens it for her with a flourish, only to reveal...

HOOKER 4: Talk about abracadabra! Think you just got lucky, sweetheart.

...to reveal, standing there, Sophie, his wife. Sophie looks at the transvestite, then back at Adrian.

SOPHIE: *Sweetheart?* Do I... get an introduction?

How long has it been since Sophie has paid him a call in town? No, it's impossible. It can't be happening. Three months since she has visited his apartment, and she chooses *now* to arrive, looking sensational as well, dressed for seduction herself, as if she too had been on his phone list. But she's everything the other girls he has seen today are not, trailing a classic beauty that no amount of cosmetics or hoicked-up mini-skirts can approximate. Yes, thinks Adrian, here is his Electra. Donald's search for perfection is very close to his own.

SOPHIE (*to* HOOKER 4): Hello. (*To* ADRIAN) Some woman, some neighbour is down there with a digicam having a blue fit, filming everything, all the comings and goings – she's about to call the police. She's counted three women today already.

ADRIAN: Really? Three? She can't count. There's been more than that. I'll… I'll talk to her later.

SOPHIE: Amazing.

The transvestite follows the conversation with interest from the sidelines.

ADRIAN (*turning to* HOOKER 4): You can go now. Thank you.

He takes out his wallet, gives her £50.

HOOKER 4 (*tucking cash into her bra*): I'm gone already, honey-child. And good luck.

Now it's the hooker's turn to be surprised as Adrian drops a quick kiss on her cheek. She goes, with a twinkle. Her heels can be heard clattering down the hall as Adrian confronts his wife with a "What?" expression.

Int. Adrian's Kitchen. Day
Adrian wears rubber gloves. Sophie watches him at the sink. She holds her forsaken cat, strokes it. The cat is in bliss. All creatures respond gratefully to her touch.

ADRIAN: His name's Donald Delpe. You weren't listening. Mind on other things, perhaps.

SOPHIE: Are you?... I don't understand. Surely you're not allowed to do such things?

ADRIAN: It's not normal practice, no.

SOPHIE: Do his parents know?

ADRIAN: No. They don't.

SOPHIE: Well, I'm sure you know what you're doing. You always do. Can we talk?

ADRIAN: A first time for everything.

SOPHIE: I want to talk about Conrad.

ADRIAN: I thought so. And how is our virile vet?

SOPHIE: He likes you, you know. A lot.

ADRIAN: I'm flattered. I'm actually quite likeable. Not lovable, but likeable.

SOPHIE: Nothing has happened. If that's what you're thinking.

ADRIAN: I really don't want to know.

SOPHIE: As you know, he's married.

ADRIAN: All the best people are.

SOPHIE: And he doesn't want to leave his kids. He's happy being married.

ADRIAN: How symmetrical of you both.

SOPHIE: But we have developed certain... certain...

ADRIAN: I think the word is "feelings".

SOPHIE: But he's worried about hurting you.

ADRIAN: Really? Well gee – I'm starting to like him too.

SOPHIE: Please don't be sarcastic. He's... he wants to know, well, he wants to know... that we have your consent.

ADRIAN: What? He wants!... Jesus Christ! Ha! Does he want it in writing? Does he need a contract before he humps you?

SOPHIE: He'd like to call you. He'd like to speak with you. Man to man.

ADRIAN: *Rat* to man, you mean. You want a divorce?

SOPHIE: No. I always want to be married to you. Do you know why? I still love you, Adrian. This doesn't have to jeopardize anything. But I feel... there is something going on with me right now. And I have no choice but to explore it if I am going to move on. This is the next big thing in my path. Or am I wrong? Should I just deny these feelings?

ADRIAN: You tell me.

SOPHIE: And I'm sure you're seeing people. (*Silence*) So... can I tell him it's okay for him to call you?

ADRIAN: How did we get here, Sophie? At what point did we turn off the highway and end up here, up to our waists in... in shit?

SOPHIE: I will always feel the same way about you, Adrian. You know that. (*She steps forwards, takes his hand.*) That won't change. You don't have to worry. Nothing will change how I feel for you. (*Adrian has begun to shake, to tremble slightly.*) But our destinies are different. Our journeys are different. We both know that. Oh, and I need some more money. I need a cheque.

ADRIAN: Don't tell me... veterinary bills.

SOPHIE: Adrian. Are you okay? No wonder I don't come and visit you more often, if this is the reception I get. Stop this. I love you. You're just being silly.

Int. Oncology Ward / Hospital. Day.
Adrian's visit to the cancer ward is a truncated one today. He doesn't dare to approach Donald with news of his failure, so walks past him and merely waves.

And Donald, desperate for news, unable to escape the gaze of the monitors that keep him in his bed, is left in a troubled and confused state. He turns to Trachman, lying there, eyes closed, on the window bed. The guy's having a bad day; the very act of breathing has become a full-time job. A nurse comes and pulls the curtains around his bed.

Donald, by contrast, is feeling better each day. And if they would let him out of here, he'd take to a basketball court this second and start draining buckets from every point on the goddamn court. If they'd let him. Which they won't. And why? Small matter of being only two days free of the most corrosive medical treatment known to man.

Thus he lies there, sunrise to set, a student of clouds.

Int. Roy's Flat. Day.

Roy needs a cleaner. Dust upon dirt upon unshiftable grime. Layered like substrata. Like lasagne. And that's just the bottom of the "clean" coffee cup Roy picks off the dish rack and hands to Adrian before filling it with piping-hot coffee.

Adrian notes the lethal electrics in the flat. Every appliance in sight is wired to a single snarl of six or seven double plugs, each impossibly piggy-backed upon the other, all of them powered by a single extension cord that snakes out of the kitchen window and off the property. A death trap.

Roy explains that he has something of a running dispute with the landlord over two years' unpaid rent. Despairing of "closure", the landlord finally cut the power three months ago, thus setting in motion a siege, an attempt to drive Roy from the address, but Roy has foiled the man and has been drawing an electrical feed from the sympathetic next-door neighbour via a chain of four linked extension cords. Adrian winces as he hears this, and winces even harder as Roy removes the coffee machine's plug with wet hands and without a second's precaution.

Adrian notes a snapshot of an African boy in grey school clothes. An open grinning face. Bridgeless nose, high-swelling lips, grinning, happy, a world away. In the background a building with a raised cross, a Christian mission school, no doubt.

ROY: Oh, that's Tito. World aid scheme I'm signed up to. We have a little financial support thing going, him and me. Hands across the water, that sort of thing. It's working out okay, but he doesn't always send me as much as I need.

They clear some room on the couch, sit down and are immediately rocked together by the broken springs, their legs rubbing like lovers'.

ROY: So, you were saying?

ADRIAN: Well, then my wife walks in.

ROY: You're kidding! Your wife? Motherfucker.

ADRIAN: I need your help. Like I say.

ROY: Hey, you've come to the right man. Cometh the hour, cometh the man.

ADRIAN: But she has to be right. (*Passes* ROY *a manila folder.*) The hooker. I'm serious.

ROY: I know, I know, I know, I know. Leave it to me. No skank. I'm your man in Manila. Won't let you down. I love this kind of assignment. Can we synchronize our watches? Oh, do we have an upper limit to the money? Let's talk fiscal envelopes.

ADRIAN: Money no object.

ROY: Beautiful. Perfect. Excellent. I'm on to it.

Int. Cafeteria / Hospital. Day.

Roy slaps a business card down on the Formica tabletop.

ROY: Bingo.

ADRIAN: But... there's no picture on it.

ROY (*looks to be in love*): She's discreet. Classy. Ask for Tanya. (*Sighs, lovelorn.*)

ADRIAN: Tanya? What's her real name?

ROY: Tanya. Talk to her, you'll understand. She's happy to meet with you. And that's when you can tell her...

ADRIAN: Tell her what?

ROY: Tell her what a great guy I am, and that if she needs a man who can take her away from her sordid life...

ADRIAN: Okay, Roy. Thanks. Tanya? Is she Russian or something? She speaks English, I expect?

ROY: Will you relax? Look, she's everything on that list and then some.

Int. Roller-skating Rink. Day.

Shelly and her pals take a breather. They spot an older boy showing off, speed-skating past them, pirouetting and trying desperately to impress *everyone*.

SHELLY: Oh my God. What is that?

PAL 1: That's Jeff Delpe. (*Watching his antics.*) God what a jizzbrain.

SHELLY: Okay, I know.

PAL 2: Did you hear his brother's, like, dying of cancer and stuff?

SHELLY (*reacting with shock*): Cancer?! His brother?!

PAL 1: Yeah. Oh right, you know him. Didn't he make, like, some gross move on you or something?

SHELLY: Yeah. (*Drifting into thought.*) Jesus.

PAL 1: You didn't fancy him, did you?

Shelly doesn't reply. Jeff races at them from the far side and swishes right through the middle of them, showboating offensively, then cross-steps away again, generating speed once more, sometimes leaning forwards, sometimes skating backwards, his hair blowing over his face.

PAL 2: He is like so disgusting.

In the background we see Raff and Michael. They are filming Shelly as she sets off. She skates slowly around the edge of the rink, all by herself, unaware that her every gesture is being captured.

Int. Oncology Ward / Hospital. Day.

Don presses Playback on Michael's digicam and watches stony-faced.

DONALD: You filmed my dickwit brother dicking about on skates?

RAFF: Keep watching mate… Okay, here she is… Awesome.

MICHAEL: We got her roller-skating too… See? Damn she's good, this chick could roller-skate in a field of wheat… And then check this out, there's this stellar bit we got, where she's like…

RAFF: …before her dog found us…

MICHAEL: …and barked its frikkin' head off…

RAFF: …yeah…

MICHAEL: …like, doing aerobics in her front room at her house… so you got a whole library of leotard stuff there to jerk off to now.

DONALD: You guys are so grunge. Seriously. You staked out her house? Don't do this ever again. God. Leave her alone you arseholes.

MICHAEL: How's that for gratitude, eh? Unbelievable. You're really turning into a sorry-assed motherfucker. (*To* RAFF) Let's get out of here. (*To* DON) Let me know when you're on your last breath.

They go. Donald thinks. Rewinds. Then starts to watch Shelly again.

This girl sure is balletic. Whooa. Young beauty. Fluid, swirling, lovely, soaring three inches above the ground, or so it seems to Don, who can see no wheels beneath those white-booted feet of hers.

Ext. Tanya's Apartment. Day.

Adrian pulls up in front of a brand new upmarket Italianate apartment complex. He crosses the road. A valet takes his keys. A doorman opens the door for him. A doorman? This must be the only private apartment building in the city with such a service. He wonders if it houses attachés, legation staff, local dignitaries. How could it also house the kind of girl he's looking for? He double-checks the address. No mistake.

Int. Lobby / Tanya's Apartment. Day.

Inside the foyer there's a fountain and an arbour of climbing plants and flowers – he has walked into a Monet. There's an iron elevator, stolen right out of an old Parisian hotel. He pulls on the handle; the webbed steel concertinas smoothly. He clanks the gates shut, pushes a button. His cage rises. Slowly, slowly it bears the big man upwards. The fountain falls away as he smells oleander gathered in the upper atmosphere of the hall. Adrian King is going to heaven, ascending bodily.

Int. Tanya's Apartment. Day.

She gives him milkless tea in an elegant glass cup like a Persian, and sits very near to him. A stunning brunette. Beautifully spoken, super-smart. This is clear after her first comments about America. She has just spent six months in Dallas.

TANYA: The difference between the British and Americans is that in Britain people are ashamed of success, wealth and fame... whereas in America people celebrate being ashamed of success, wealth and fame.

He laughs, and not falsely. What a woman. He's instantly attracted to her, and knows it, but then he reminds himself he is not here to play the enamoured old man, falling into her eyes, succumbing like a fool. He does his best to suppress unactable urges and tries hard not to look her in the eyes at all, those black-water lagoons. And until they get on to Donald he's all fingers and thumbs.

She tells him only the barest details about herself, retaining her mystique, whilst he hardly stops talking, behaving as if he's on *Jerry Springer.* The episode? *Men Whose Wives Are Unfaithful but Who Don't Have the Balls to Kick Them out.*

TANYA, mid-twenties, father Russian, from Georgia's steppes, mother English; comes here at nineteen on a holiday, never leaves. Hourglass figure, C-cup, Taurus, a voice to calm oceans. She conducts her business less like a prostitute than a corporate headhunter, filling positions on merit. Sex isn't what she charges for by the hour, it's her beauty. Few can afford it. She writes the fee on a slip of paper, slides it face down across the coffee table.

ADRIAN (*reading it*): No. That's fine. (*Then folding it, putting it in his breast pocket.*) Now I don't know how much Roy has told you...

TANYA: You have a young friend. That's all I know.

ADRIAN: But he's not just any young man. Let me explain. Do we have much time? I mean, am I paying now?

TANYA (*smiles*): No. You are not paying now.

Adrian's polar ice caps melt; New York, London and Amsterdam are flooded, and his wits run for high ground as the tide pours in.

Int. Restaurant. Day.

Just the two of them over lunch. Tanya listening attentively. Adrian introducing Donald, in all his dimensions, even coming up with a few new ideas about the boy he has never formulated before. By the end, he has the impression he's learnt more than he's imparted.

He orders a main course, she only a starter. She has a figure to watch. This is just as well for him. His bills are mounting up. He's nearly £400 down (the price of lunch and the prior interviews) and Tanya hasn't even done anything yet.

While he drinks wine (she Evian), he describes a boy of fourteen, astonishingly mature in some ways, just a boy in others, a super-talented young cartoonist, but who lacks the will to fight his terminal illness, ready to leave this life, even suicidal at times. Tumours have had their secret way with him. Then he meets a young girl. Signs of life. A simple experience, a first date: it brings him back. Remission, and the beginnings of a rally. But too late. The tumours have migrated and down he is dragged again. But now that it's hopeless, the boy can't extinguish his own life force. He has a last wish. Donald seems to be telling him that he will postpone his departure for one last experience. But it must not be ordinary. This is the implied stipulation. It must be – the word is – *unreal*.

Unreal? Adrian tries to explain this shadowy concept.

ADRIAN: He intends this to be the first and last big experience of his life, I think. Its… quintessence. He feels cheated and wants something out of this world before he says goodbye to it all. Hence, all of life, everything, must be condensed into a single event. The night of his life. After this, there may only be resignation and release. I'm sorry. This puts impossible pressure on you.

Tanya nods. Does not flinch. She understands perfectly what he is saying.

TANYA: No. I think I understand. And, actually, I think what you are doing is very…

ADRIAN: Please, I'd love to know what word you were going to use.

TANYA: …good. Nice. And as for the last bit, I am no stranger to my clients wanting "everything". You should hear some of the "special requests" men ask for…

It is at this point that Adrian thinks her fee is cheap: £500. He even flirts with the idea of retaining her phone number in his sock drawer, calling up this girl himself. Five hundred, for the night of one's life? To taste the quintessence? A bargain. But then he strikes the thought. He must resist this metastasizing of Donald's fortunes into his own.

TANYA: You are doing a good thing for this boy.

ADRIAN: Funny, I don't think my superiors would see it that way.

TANYA: Forget them. Let him embrace life.

And what an embrace that would be, thinks Adrian. Yes, embrace it. And for a teenage boy, what better symbol of life to embrace than this marvellous woman?

ADRIAN: He's a wonderful, wonderful kid.

He takes out his wallet, but he is being gauche. She shakes her head, raises her palm, so he puts the wallet away. She is, in his eyes and in that instant, a painting by Hogarth, the mistress in the first panel of the painter's *Before* and *After* sequence, feigning an improper advance. This picture, that Adrian saw at the V&A with Donald, is one of art's great early comic strips: the damsel with her right hand raised, resisting a suitor, but only until the second panel, when she is seen lying ravaged and red-faced and skirt hoisted, and this rejection is revealed to be what it really was: a tease, a vital aspect of the tryst, only a necessary preliminary to enhance the excitement.

Int. Oncology Ward / Hospital. Day.

Donald's curtains have been drawn shut since his hand-wash half an hour before. He has been drawing and filling in the voice bubbles for a new MiracleMan episode while waiting for the curtains to be pulled back. But when they are finally drawn wide he is not emotionally ready to see...

Shelly.

SHELLY: Hi.

Shelly is standing there.

SHELLY: How's the karate kid?

Shelly is standing there, in the flesh.

SHELLY: Is "hello" too much too ask?

Shelly is standing there, in the flesh, in her yellow cardigan.

Whooa. Way too surreal. Way!

SHELLY: Is "hello" too much to ask? (*Nothing*) So... is this like a martial arts code of silence? (*Nothing*) Anyway,

I've been to the bathroom a few times lately and I didn't see you once. I was getting worried.

Donald gawks at her, stripped of the ability to say a single word, even the filthy ones for expressing surprise. Nothing for Shelly, nada. And so, feeling embarrassed, rejected, out of rehearsed lines, her smile starts to fade.

SHELLY: Okay, so, um… anyway… so maybe um… I'm gonna go now. Just wanted to… anyway… bye. I should have… have… (*She rushes away.*)

DONALD (*recovers the power of speech far too late, only has his decrepit self to talk to*): You… big… *dick*… HEAD.

He closes his eyes. Stupid, stupid, stupid… what a monumental fucking dope! He needs putting down, eradicating or something. How big a chance has he just blown? The girl came all the way too his bed to talk, to see him, him, him, him, him, only to run away thinking – what? – he dreads to know. Christ knows. Shelly, Shelly, Shelly. Arrgghhh! Please come back!

At this moment he hears the curtains being quickly drawn open around Trach's bed, and the bed by the window is empty. Where's Trach? The guy is nowhere to be seen. He's gone! The man's things have even been cleared away. No *Turf Digest*. No token flowers donated by a nurse because no one else was coming in to see him. Only a tightly made bed of crisp folds (the hospital tuck) lies empty under the big-skied window.

Don had not guessed. Sure, he'd seen the wheels of gurneys come and go beneath his drawn curtains, heard a commotion and known something was going on, but he'd thought it just the usual soundtrack of someone being wheeled away to Radiology. And there hadn't been even a murmur from Trach himself. A nurse must have found him and drawn all the curtains quickly. That old voice box had had nothing more to add.

A lump as big as a golf ball forms in Don's throat. Shelly has gone. And Trach is dead. Gone. Dead. **Biff - Boff!** A one-two jab combination to the solar plexus. But he arrests his feelings, steadies himself, breathes, keeps his shock at bay and picks up his pen in a reflex gesture, suspending it above a blank frame of his cartoon. Life is shit. He begins to draw, going in for the kill this time for Trach's sake now, swooping ink-wise from the mega-wide panorama of the last frame to a super-close-up in this new one, modern style (Stan Lee or later), taking a suddenly tough line with his comic narrative. Life is shit. No last-second rescue or unexpected reversal of fortune here boy. No frickin' way. And while thinking, "I'll ram the damn story right home right here and now, end it with a kind of *deus ex machina*," as Brother Max, his old English teacher, would have said, he draws a frame he hadn't predicted, sketching a human hand, a right hand with its third, fourth and fifth digits curled so that only the index finger and thumb stay cocked, forming a perfect cradle for a…

…handgun, a gun that, as he draws it in extremely accurate detail (how does a fourteen-year-old know such things?), penetrates at its tip a human mouth, lips enclosing the steel, before adding, in a final touch, two world-weary eyes above, the liquid eyes of someone whose fantastic gifts of rejuvenation cannot save him now, and whose mortal end, by his own hand, is but a frame away.

And then Adrian appears. Spangle-eyed at the foot end of the bed. Real life restored.

DONALD: Where have you been?

ADRIAN: Busy.

DONALD: I've been going crazy here. So?

ADRIAN: How are you feeling?

DONALD: Perfect. Last hour has been amazing, you never saw so much fun. I need to get out of here.

ADRIAN: Tomorrow night.

DONALD: You're kidding.

ADRIAN: If you still want to go ahead with it.

DONALD: Are you serious?

ADRIAN: You sure?

Donald stares at Adrian. Adrian at Donald. Yes, thinks Donald. This is the perfect prescription for what ails him. And if he blows this one, hesitates like he just did with Shelly, then he might as well go join Trach right now.

DONALD: Count me in.

ADRIAN: If you're sure.

DONALD: I'm sure.

ADRIAN: You seem a little... nervous. We should take some time to think about this.

DONALD: No. I just didn't think... you'd really go through with it, that's all.

ADRIAN: Donald. We don't have to do this. If you're not ready.

DONALD: Have you got a picture?

Adrian takes a photo out of his breast pocket and passes it over. Donald looks at it, then at Adrian, then back at the photo, at Adrian, at the photo.

DONALD: No way. This is *her*?

ADRIAN: Yes.

Donald studies the photo in a reverential trance.

DONALD: This is her.

ADRIAN: I know.
DONALD: You found her.
ADRIAN: I know.

Int. Oncology Ward / Hospital. Day.
Michael and Raff slouch all over Donald's bed, showing no mercy, no respect at all for the sick. In their defence, Donald hasn't looked less sick in months.

RAFF: You're gonna… what?!!

DONALD (*lowered voice*): Tomorrow night. Here. Look.

Donald hands the photo to Michael. Raff looks over his shoulder. The boys' jaws drop as they look at it.

MICHAEL (*almost a gasp*): Holy shit…

RAFF: No way!

MICHAEL: Don, you're gonna fuck Lara Croft.

DONALD (*lowered voice*): I know. I know. Boom Shalaka.

Donald's eyes stray to the bed by the window, but they don't stay there. He doesn't want to let anything spoil the high he's feeling right now.

RAFF (*examining the photo*): More like Lara Croft's older sister. She's gotta be twenty-five.

MICHAEL: Who fucking cares. Angelina Jolie was twenty-five when she played Lara in *Tomb Raider*, okay? Anyway, who gives a shit. So who is she?

DON: She's a hooker.

Michael and Raff practically haemorrhage.

MICHAEL: Ex-*cuse* me?

RAFF: How did you?…

DONALD: Ssshhh! You can't tell anyone. One of the shrinks here set it up for me, and it's totally zip, OK?

MICHAEL (*staring at the photo, not listening*): This girl is a...

RAFF: I want to be next. Man, I'm so overdue it's killing me.

DONALD: Overdue? I thought you... you said you'd...

Raff looks at Donald, then Michael, then Donald.

MICHAEL: He has so much sex with himself, the girls don't get a chance.

DONALD (*looking at* MICHAEL): And how about you?

MICHAEL: Yeah, well... I'm real close with a girl right now. Another couple of weeks – booom! Swear to God. I can taste it I'm so close.

DONALD: Give me my photo back, losers. What a couple of dorks.

RAFF: No way. I'm keeping this. You get the arse, we at least get to keep the photo.

After a silence...

MICHAEL (*wistful*): Man, I wanna be a patient of this hospital.

Int. Adrian's Office. Day.

When Adrian arrives this morning, a little late – some outpatient has hijacked his reserved parking space – he is surprised to hear that his "nine o'clock" is here. He doesn't have a nine o'clock. At least, doesn't think so. It's Donald. Sitting in Adrian's chair, reclined at full tilt with Vanettes up on the desk, a dressing gown over his pyjamas. He is holding Adrian's framed photo of Sophie.

DONALD (*grins*): The big day.

ADRIAN: You should be resting.

As Adrian takes off his coat and hangs it up, Donald returns to his inspection of the photo.

DONALD: She's a babe. I'd be with her every second of every day.

ADRIAN: It's more complicated than that.

DONALD: Why is it? She's a nine or a ten. You should be rashing her. (*Sees incomprehension.*) All over her. What's with this living-apart thing?

ADRIAN: It's just better that way.

DONALD: Oh, I get it. You're banging someone else. Right?

ADRIAN: No. No. (*Pause*) I'm not.

Donald's eyes widen.

DONALD: Oh... oh, I see, wow – okay – so you mean she's... okay, I get it... Man, shit... Kick the bitch out. Seriously.

Adrian sits down in the stiff, upright patient's chair.

ADRIAN: Life isn't a cartoon, Donald. It's not always black and white.

DONALD: Isn't it? Man, for a psychologist you're pretty fucked up. I'm serious. Life is short, mate. Take it from me. Kick. The. Bitch. Out. Unless, y'know, you're getting off on it or something, she's gotta go.

Adrian presses back in his chair, feeling an urgent need to tilt, to full tilt back – a feature denied him here – and he has no choice but to sit up and confront the encephalogram the boy has just taken of his private life, the hard diagnosis arising from hard evidence, a serious malignancy photographed at the centre of him, a cloudy area that is sadly inoperable. The surprise finding freezes his blood. And for a change it's he who is on the receiving end of terminal news. For once it's he who is being told – and not very sympathetically, courtesy of one of Donald F. Delpe – *I'm sorry, but it looks very bad.* Donald's verdict seems impossible and possible. Both absurd and too obvious to doubt. But in the end it's probably one hundred per cent right. There's too little reason to hope that it could be wrong.

Int. Hospital. Night.
The respectful silence. The lemon-scented floor polish. The corridors empty. The ward's lighting at a minimum for sleep. The night staff reduced to skeleton. No one around. Time to roll.

This is insane, of course. And yet their shared insanity has a momentum that is irresistible to all analyses and second thoughts. Sometimes people are tired of being ruled by fear; they simply want to set the clock running on the explosives, to see what they, personally, are made of as that timer ticks down.

The clock is ticking.

Donald is about to get laid. He emerges from a ward cloakroom wearing sunglasses and an old Italian coat that Adrian no longer wears. He looks ridiculous, he knows. Roy brings around a wheelchair, Donald sits, and Roy pushes him down the hall and ultimately out of bounds.

Int. Adrian's Car. Night.
In the car Donald plays rap on his iPod; Adrian can hear the bass even over the noise of the traffic. As the boy nods along to the booom-shick-boom-boom-shick drone, he's clearly getting pumped.

Don's thought bubble as he sits silent in the passenger seat is close to a movie-trailer voice-over, the stock male voice dripping with buttery baritone over every blockbuster storyline: "*Two men... a race against time...*

in a hunt for one woman." Cue orchestra: *dumm dumm dumm…* the bombastic symphony swells… "*Will he get his penis… inside her love box… before uncontrollable forces… destroy them both?*" Music crescendos as the title finally explodes on-screen in two installments, first the triple detonation: *Hooker Fucker 2*; and then, **KOOOSH** (the sound of imploding TVs): *Return of the Stud.*

And as if this too is audible, the senior psychologist looks over at him. The boy appears ready for anything, as though he's been seeing hookers for years. Don returns the look. Excited, expectant, nervous.

DONALD (*suddenly pulling out his earbuds*): Oh, hey. Can I pick up a rose?

ADRIAN: A rose? Okay.

DONALD: Yeah. A single rose. Be cool, wouldn't it?

ADRIAN: Yes. It would actually. Nice idea.

A pro, a real pro, this kid.

Int. Lobby / Tanya's Apartment. Night.

DONALD: Will you come in with me?

ADRIAN: Would you like me to?

DONALD: Yeah. I think so.

ADRIAN: Okay.

Int. Tanya's Apartment. Night.

Adrian (the coach) and Donald (the star player) wait for Tanya (the opposition). There is the basic game plan. Adrian will wait in here while Donald goes into the bedroom with Tanya. Don and she will have about an hour to an hour and a half. That's about as long as they can reasonably expect to conceal Don's absence from the ward. *Tick… tick… tick… tick…*

ADRIAN (*in a low voice*): Just… be yourself. Take your time.

He does sound like a coach.

DONALD: Right. Right.

ADRIAN: Think of it like heavyweight boxing. There are twelve rounds. So, you know, pace yourself. You don't have to go for a knockout in the first round.

DONALD: What does that mean?

ADRIAN: I have no idea.

Adrian is aware of his own nervousness now, feels butterflies in his own stomach, so God knows what Don feels like.

DONALD: Cos I was just planning on jumping her bones and screwing the lights out of her.

ADRIAN: Well, you obviously have the idea. It's your night. And I hope that it's… I hope that… all you've imagined… that it…

Then Donald sees something over Adrian's shoulder.

DONALD (*his eyes widening*): Whoah.

Tanya is finally making her appearance. Both men stare at her. A silk gown. Hair unfurled. In silhouette in the doorway. Gloriously backlit. Frosted outer edges. Impossibly hourglass. Unreal. Yes, unreal. She has managed it. Brilliant woman. Post-Stan Lee, maybe even Frank Miller, like the latter's work on Daredevil in the early '80s, bubbles Donald.

DONALD (*whispered, to* ADRIAN): Art.

ADRIAN (*inadvertently*): Semi City.

DONALD: Not a pitchfork in sight.

Tanya advances, finding more light. And all of it, every single photon, flatters. Her advance is a swoon-making footless-ghost-style glissando, a special effect. She arrives at Donald as if flown by invisible wires.

175

TANYA: And you must be Donald. Hello.

She shakes Donald's hand, but it has been de-boned, and it waggles filleted in her palm. Donald, Lilliputian, relegated by her stilettos to miniature, gawps up at this poster babe come to full, vivid, luxurious life.

TANYA: I'm Tanya. You're very handsome. Adrian didn't tell me you would be so good-looking. Shall we sit, get to know each other a little bit?

Donald nods, head on a spring, *boing boing boing.*

DONALD: Okay.

As he follows her to the couch, at last getting to grips with her sheer dimensionality – her image popped from 2-D billboard and cartoon dreams – he gives Adrian an excited glance, then a wink.

Adrian takes a chair in the corner and does his best to pretend to read a magazine while Tanya and Donald begin to chat – Tanya the ultimate geisha, earning her dough right away, able to animate a sphinx, Donald soon uncrossing his arms and putting his trainers up on the coffee table. Adrian limits his glances and feigns invisibility, allowing himself to look over only when he hears Tanya laughing. Don the comedian is grinning a smile normally the preserve of cats in Cheshire.

TANYA: So. Are you ready? Yes? (*Nod from* DONALD) Come on.

DONALD (*eagerly*): Let's rock 'n' roll.

TANYA (*to* ADRIAN): I think we might go next door now. Make yourself at home.

ADRIAN: Oh sure. Great. Fantastic.

Tanya turns up the music (a silky jazz) by remote control, and leads Donald by the hand towards the bedroom. At the door, that threshold, Donald turns, raises a triumphant fist to Adrian, grins, and then retires inside. The door makes no noise as it closes.

With a hummingbird's heart rate Adrian tries to settle in for a wait of uncertain duration. He feels a shot of envy at this moment, a stirring in his own loins, a sympathetic reflex. He is fourteen himself right now, a kid again at heart, way back when having beauty to hold in his arms was still a mirage: it should be him in there, reacquainting himself with pleasure. He is only fifty-two-years old, for God's sake! He might live to be 104. Why does he think everything is over for him? He deserves to desire and be desired; doesn't he? Why can't joy be imminent? But then again, the old voices of caution reassert themselves: You are fifty-two! Stop, think, your career, your encumbrances, your arrangements, the deep love you still bear for your wife and that she, even now, bears for you. Don't imperil all that. No, he cannot afford to be alone at his age. His true talent is acceptance, the acceptance of his lot: this is the proud quality in which Dr Adrian King is clothed. And yet, yet – as he glances at his watch his mind flips back and forth, shedding and gaining forty-odd years – every soul has the power to imagine, and with such imaginings comes desire, and with that desire, youthful hope. So then, which is it? Fourteen, or fifty-two? He is both and neither. He is doctor and patient, the wise man and the naïf as he turns to look towards a certain bedroom door and thinks: What have I done? What have I done? What have I done?

Int. Adrian's Car. Night.
Adrian drives the boy home. They cruise along Waterfields. Street lamps pulse rhythmically into the car, strobing a middle-aged driver, silent, reflective, giddy with unused

adrenaline, and a young man, silent also, glowing, and not because of the sodium lamps but because of a new secret he seems in no hurry whatsoever to disclose.

Donald leans forwards and picks something off the floor. A rose.

DONALD: Oh. I forgot to give her the flower! Shit!

ADRIAN: So did I.

Donald unzips the backpack in his lap and gently slips the single stem inside so as not to bruise it or lose a petal. Finally, Adrian's curiosity can take no more.

ADRIAN: Are you happy, Donald?

DONALD: Happy? Happy? Are you kidding? Happy? That was the best moment of my life.

ADRIAN: Really? It was everything you expected?

DONALD (*emotional*): It was... man, it was... awesome.

ADRIAN: Really? That's... well that's...

DONALD (*dreamy*): Awesome.

ADRIAN: ...fantastic. I'm so... well, I couldn't be more pleased for you. It was worth it, then?

DONALD: Are you kidding?

Int. Tanya's Bedroom. Night.

The world through wavy glass. A time somersault, a backflip, a flashback, a spinning psychedelic pinwheel of returning to Tanya's bedroom, to the moment when Tanya, having led Don into her bedroom and closed the door, lets drop her gown and steps towards him. Don's mouth falls open. Game on. Fade to black. End of story. Or at least the U-certificate version of it.

No, start again. This will not do. Why not R15? Don is led into her boudoir. She steps away from him almost at once. She pulls aside her shoulder straps. Her gown glides to the floor, revealing her body in bra and panties and high heels in the half-light. She is a whole lot of woman. Donald smiles. Fade to black. End of story.

Start again. There is no way around it. In Donald's X-certificate mind, there can never now be a fade to black upon his wistful smile. This film cliché would be a lie. The *truth* is X-rated and he will not censor it. Every beat of the action is a frame in his mind, and he will not let a single one die on the cutting-room floor. It's a sequence he has mentally broken down into twenty-four shots, the length of each shot calculated in seconds, the entire sequence divisible into three major movements or shifts in mood and thematic values. Here is Donald's personally story-boarded movie trilogy.

Part One

Shot 1. Tanya releases Donald's hand as she moves away from him, taking some six paces in all. The bedroom is a large triple room. It is lit only by standing lamps and is bathed in soft red half-tones. Medium long shot, this. The shot lasts five seconds.

Shot 2. Donald's eyes only, showing his true emotions. His gaze is reverential, awed, permitting us to contemplate his rapture in the face of so much beauty. His eyes wander all over her. Four seconds.

Shot 3. Cut from Donald gazing to what he actually sees. A full appreciation of this angel's body in its totality, a waterfall of hair down to a pinched waist, wide slender shoulders, a shimmering dress of satin that floats about her like a purple gas. Her walk that of a lugubrious catwalk model but with less swing. Four seconds.

Shot 4. Tanya's arse as she moves, those oscillating, indented and deeply radiused orbs. Four seconds.

Shot 5. Her heels rise and fall, in slo-mo, from her high-heeled slingbacks; above, her calves, harp-shaped, muscular, flexing alternately. Two seconds.

Shot 6. Three gold bracelets dance on her right wrist as the arm swings and brushes the satin on each pass. Two seconds.

Shot 7. Then wide once more. A repeat of the Shot 1 master. She turns. Her shoulders lead the rotation, her hair follows after a delay, also in slo-mo.

Everything settles, slowly: shoulders and expression slowly, dress, arms slowly. She faces him. The composition underlines the consciously iconic quality of her appearance: goddess, divine, oozing her luxuries. Six seconds.

Shot 8. A mid-shot, showing the effect of all this on Donald. The young man blinks slowly, breathes deeply. Prepares himself. A small smile begins to form then it fades, as if this is no time for humour, as if he finally comprehends the seriousness that is required. Five seconds.

Shot 9. Tanya's face, empathetic, focusing on Donald, slight smile to free him from the burden of his tensions. Five seconds.

Shot 10. A repeat of Shot 8. Donald is now the embodiment of anxiety, internally preparing himself for the task at hand. Two seconds.

Shot 11. Tanya full frame. Her thumbs go to the shoulder straps of her dress and hook themselves under, hold for four long seconds before she releases the garment. It falls in a single waft. A gust. The purple gas is exhausted, revealing cloudless topography beneath, mountains capped with filigrees of black lacy snow, valleys deep. Two thin black rivulets cross the plains of her hips and conjoin at the delta of her vee, a thong. Seven seconds.

Shot 12. The impact of this act on Donald. He has stopped breathing. Face immobile. A kind of system error, crashed program, data loss, screen frozen. Three seconds.

This concludes Part One. Title for this forty-nine-second epic: *Young Man for First Time Experiences Love with a Capital S.*

Part Two

Shot 13. Tanya advances on Donald, slow rolling hips, her heels on the polished wooden floor the only sound punctuating the soundtrack (soft jazz). His mind's camera pans with her, until she draws into a mid-shot as she reaches her client. The two of them, for the first time, inhabit the same frame, less than a metre apart. The curtains in the open French door billow behind her. In her heels, she towers over him. He looks suddenly very small and very young. She kicks off her shoes, then expertly flicks them aside with a toe, coming down to his level. As she reaches back with both hands to unfasten her strapless bra, elbows akimbo, she acquires two wings: winged Fallen Angel. Thirteen seconds.

Shot 14. Cut to rear shot of Tanya, and Don's face a-tremble over her shoulder. Her soft-focus fingers close on a bra clasp as the camera sharp-focuses on Donald, his eyes falling to digest, account for, cope with, read, fathom, comprehend, interpret, reckon with this woman's chest. His eyes register mounting emotion. When the bra is released with a twang, Donald gulps. His eyes lock onto those unseen boy-dream-wonders. *Thirty-seven seconds.*

Shot 15. Sustaining that tension, still shooting Tanya from behind, cut wide as Tanya's hands now fall, fall, fall down her guitar body until they find – find the elastic of the thong measuring her hips. Donald's eyeline drops with her hands, regarding those hips as her thumbs loop under and begin to wriggle her panties down. At this moment, Tanya turns, rotates fetchingly, feigning modesty or else saving on the power bill, goes and turns off the strongest lamp, and then, with her back to him, lowers the elastic at last. Oh temptress. Twenty-two seconds in all. A miracle of chiaroscuro, of less being more, of the unseen saying much more than the seen.

Shot 16. Donald's eyes widen. He is so intently shaken up that tears form in his eyes. Four seconds.

Shot 17. We see again what Donald sees, but now in a series of close-ups – a thong strap travelling south, elastic straining as it traverses the double domes. Three seconds.

Shot 18. Donald blinks slowly. Two seconds.

Shot 19. The thong strap still travelling down, down athletic thighs, then calves, until it reaches the floor and Tanya, naked, steps out of her hip-holster. She turns and faces Donald. She lifts her left hand, inviting him forwards. Enchantress. Seven seconds.

Shot 20. Donald moves towards the naked woman. She recedes from him as he advances: she is a mirage. She stops only when she reaches her bed, waiting for him there. He appears to undergo minor cardiac arrest as he finally closes on her, doing as he's bidden, advancing on the large canopied love nest, dollying forwards, transported on rails it feels like, drawn by the tractor beam of her eyes. Don on autopilot now. A miracle of preprogramming. The only sound, the faint chirrup of his Vanettes. (*Cringe!*) At the bed's edge he stops. She is sitting there now, and smiles gently at him before she slowly, luxuriantly lies back, the act a sigh. Her fingernails, sporting a hundred quid of lacquer, drift up her body as if applying balm to every hill and dale, anointing an erotic body, lean, tanned, full-blown womanhood awaiting him, offering herself to the apprentice at last, her legs parting, parting, a tiny parting in perfection. Thirty-three seconds. The film then clicks to hardcore, drifts into another certificate rating altogether, as he is allowed his first ever view of – of – of...

Shot 21. Don stares, an X-rated stare, and cannot move. His head is too busily flooding with the 101 sacramental names for the promised land, the massed, toilet-wall phrases that he and his friends have used to try to describe nirvana: pussy – loveboat – Brazilian landing strip – minge – floss-bordered paper cut – cunt – mickey – snatch – clam – Disney World – rug – box – twat – fanny – muff – poon – womb room – beaver – phrases streaming across his face like stock prices on CNBC, as we cut to what he is staring at...

Shot 22. Close up on her vee, the fine-ball, artist's-quality cross-hatchings of pubic hair, the clefted and bisected separations and deeper inner challenges of her opening genitalia: reality.

Shot 23. Extreme close-up. Lips opening: but it's Donald's mouth, where a word is being breach-born: "Tiaw." He has to invert it on the tip of his tongue to make it live.

DONALD: Wait.

Wait? *Wait?* Stop the camera. "Cut!" wails the director. What's going on? Did the lead male porn star just say "Wait?"

The grandmother's fall is arrested 5 cm from the ground. The hero defuses the bomb by cutting the green wire. The clock is stopped with only two seconds remaining. Title of Part Two: *Last-Second Reversal of Fortune.*

DONALD: Uh… I've uh… got an idea.

Int. Adrian's Car. Night.

The most beautiful hooker in the world, fizzes Donald (in a hectic trail of bubbles), and I go and say "Wait" like a dork. Call him a coward, squeamish, a child still, but it is an issue of proper narrative sequence for a cartoonist. He is fourteen, after all. And this was his first live-action X-rated film. It's not as if he is a cigar-smoking, snatch-weary director, used to every corporeal reality and hole. One has to get *used* to certain women wonders. A woman is a lot to handle, he has learnt. A major woman is not to be rushed. You have to grow into it. Naturally. Bit by bit. Fold by delirious fold. Well, go figure, he bubbles. So much for the movies: turns out the only thing they prepare you for is other movies. Go figure.

Int. Tanya's Apartment. Night.

Part Three

Shot 24. The style of filming has changed for ever now. There are no cuts any more. There'll be no stylized magnification of moments. The action is played wide, *mise en scène,* single-shot, hand-held documentary style, *le cinéma-vérité,* without artifice. The aim: reality.

DONALD: I'm sorry. I'm… I think you might be… that I'm just… Do you mind if we?…

TANYA: What is it?

DONALD: …do something a bit different?

TANYA: Different?

DONALD: Yeah.

TANYA: Okay. Different? Okay. What did you have in mind, young sir? What would you like to do?

DONALD: A special request. Do you mind?

TANYA: Um, I guess not. What is it?

She is a little curious now as to what new sophistication this young gentleman wishes to add to normal proceedings. She smiles. She is so lovely. And already Donald half-wonders if he shouldn't just stick to the original script, launch a reshoot, pull the crew back together and shout, "We're going again!" rather than set up a kinky new scenario.

As she watches him closely for his next move, he pulls from a seam in the hem of his jacket… a backup artist-quality fine-ball, sliding it out of its secret chamber.

TANYA: And what do you want to do with *that*?

DONALD: Draw you. Do you mind?

TANYA: Draw me?

DONALD: Yeah. It'd be cool. You look so hot. It'd be… y'know… just… I'd like to draw you. Do you mind?

Thrust into surprising new territory here herself, she takes a few seconds to respond. Yes, she will be his model, of course, if that is what he wants. And Don *is* sure. He knows exactly what pose he wants her to assume as well. Reclined. Of course. On the bed. On her side, one knee slightly raised, an arching hip, her head rested on her outstretched arm, her hair a fall of tresses: his billboard broad. She goes to the bed, follows his suddenly forceful orders. When he is happy with her pose (and he is picky, it has to be just right) this little Toulouse-Lautrec opens a small notepad, this one also concealed in the jacket's lining for such moments of epiphany. He makes a start: six feet from the side of her bed he marks the first tentative lines. Right away he is a study in concentration. His eye travels to her body, then back to his work, back and forth. But slowly. This is not the scribbled blitzkrieg of the life-drawing class. This time his pen moves no faster than a nervous caress. The nib doesn't squeak at all now. In fact, the nib hardly leaves the paper, tracing a long sinuous line in and out, defining the outer swerves and then the inner contours unbrokenly, as if not wanting to quit contact for a second in case it should break the spell, as Don frowns all the while, deeply concentrating, wanting to get it right: a version better than a photograph, perhaps in the end better than the real thing.

Int. Living Room / Tanya's Apartment. Night.
Adrian is waiting for the young Romeo to finish losing his virginity with the hooker. He looks up from his magazine when he hears crashing noises and squeals of female delight coming from the bedroom. What the hell is Donald doing in there? The sounds summon up images of a rumpus. Experienced gymnastics. Real sexual fireworks. He hopes that the boxing analogy he chose was not a mistake. But then, it is probably Tanya who is in control, setting the agenda and giving Don – as ordered – the time of his life. Lucky kid. Yes, Adrian is not a little envious as he listens to...

Int. Tanya's Bedroom. Night.

In a controversial scene cut from the final film (but available under "Additional Material" on Donald's own personal Director's Cut of the Redux DVD), Donald and Tanya stifle laughter as they rattle the furniture and dupe Adrian next door, making the filthiest noises they possibly can, a groanathon of orgiastic pumping, first she – a total hands-down genius at convincing men that her body is in ecstasy when it's not – then he, sounding like a poor imitation of Jeff from the secret tape he made in their parents' bedroom. But he makes a fair stab at it, for an ignoramus, for a complete amateur, and the two of them end up on the bed laughing, tumbling into one another. She wins this contest easy. Big surprise. Crying and bucking her hips, tossing herself about, *loving it, loving it, oh, oh, oh,* she rolls into Don, hand over her mouth to stop herself from peeling with giggles as he feeds her the odd line – *this is so sexy, so sexy* (© **Jeff's Bitch, 2006**) – so that Donald doesn't even have to touch this goddess to make her peak, to give her the best goddamn time she has ever had, whereupon he, too, very easily reaches his own make-believe nirvana.

Finally, they lie on the bed, flank to flank, panting, smiling, and Tanya delivers upon Donald's lips the lightest, sweetest most honey-dew kiss in a fast-expanding universe.

DONALD: Can I ask you something?

TANYA (*pulling a sarong around her, knotting it above the breast*): Of course.

DONALD: What's sex like?

TANYA: Like?

DONALD: Yeah. For real. Just… I dunno.

TANYA: Well... what do you think it's going to be like?

DONALD: I don't know, do I?

It deserves an honest reply. More than that, under the circumstances, it deserves the best reply she's ever given. She crafts her answer.

TANYA: Well... when you are with the right person... you could say it's like... I guess, like a competition. Where you're both trying to let the other side win.

He reflects on this, stares at the ceiling for a few moments, then turns back to her.

DONALD: Thanks.

TANYA: You're welcome.

Looking into that unthinkably pretty face, reflecting upon this, music seems to swell all about him. Part Three ends. Working title? *Death of a Pornographer*.

Int. Adrian's Car. Night.

As Adrian's car gets closer to the hospital the problem of smuggling the kid back into his ward begins to trouble him. They are over the hour and a half mark now, but there hasn't been a warning call from Roy so, fingers crossed, they have got away with it.

He glances to his left. Don, in the passenger seat, shining with secret knowledge, is contemplating... what? Processing a million impressions, certainly. The insights of the flesh. The kid looks happy. And why shouldn't he, from what Adrian has heard through the halls? Good God, he wonders, when has he ever made such noises himself, or caused them to be made? Never. Not even when he and his wife had been at their most boisterous. Drifting into his own thoughts about Sophie, unfaithful Sophie, and his own fading memory of such excitements, they hit a red light.

DONALD: Adrian?

ADRIAN: What is it?

DONALD: Just – thanks man.

And the passenger door flaps open and Don is gone.

ADRIAN: Donald!

Cars behind blare their horns as the lights go green. Adrian jumps from his car but vital moments have gone by. He looks around but already Donald is nowhere to be seen. Adrian runs up and down the pavement a few yards in both directions but soon realizes, over the bleating of car horns, that Don has slipped his custody and has escaped. And unless he can find the kid, and fairly rapidly, this plan, so perfectly executed thus far, will turn into a nightmare scenario. All hell will break loose and Adrian's crisis, up till now an inner one, will soon have no end of external manifestations.

Int. Oncology Ward. Night.

The charge nurse is outraged. Her arms are folded intransigently. Fault lines criss-cross her face; that is to say, a lifetime of fault-finding has left its marks on her. Adrian knows such a face is but a foretaste of the hospital and community-wide outrage that will flow once the whole story of what he's done gets out, which it seems destined to. One thing's for sure, he must delete the bit about the prostitute.

CHARGE NURSE: What do you mean, he's gone?

ADRIAN: I took him out for a walk. But he disappeared. We need to... we need to notify his parents, in case he's heading home. And perhaps the police.

CHARGE NURSE: For a walk? (*Pause*) You took a fourteen-year-old *boy*, a *tumour* patient, out for a *walk*, in the middle of the *night*, and he *disappeared*? Is that what you're telling me?

It isn't a good story. *Boy* plus *tumour* plus *walk* plus *night* plus *disappeared* doesn't sound great.

ADRIAN: I know. You don't have to tell me. But please, if we can focus on Donald. I need to enlist your help. So please. Let's just see what we can do.

Sabotaging further enquiry, he turns, his head low, his large body with its superfluous strength a study in distress as he hurries down the long corridor.

Int. Hospital Staff Room. Night.

ROY: Oh man!

ADRIAN: I want you to help me find him. Here's his number. Keep calling him, texting him.

ROY: This is so fucked up. Someone's gonna lose their job over this.

ADRIAN: Let's just try and find Donald, shall we? Can we just focus on *that*?

Int. Delpe House. Night.

Jim Delpe takes the call.

JIM (*into phone*): Yeah, I'm still here. Okay. Okay. Mmkay. Well, thanks for... All right, thanks for telling us. I dunno, I'd better go. Better make some calls. Yep. (*Hangs up.*)

RENATA (*O.S.*): What is it?

JIM: It's Raff's father.

Renata appears in the doorway, stapler in hand, in its jaws a sheath of papers too thick for the staples to penetrate – another heft of cancer articles to collate, digest, circulate, evaluate, respond to, dismiss or enact, perhaps to try to get Jim to read, hopefully without argument, hopefully without another fight which always makes her think she can't go on, not without support, not alone, not any more.

Conservatively, they've had five arguments today already. In her bedroom Renata has one article detailing the stats for marriage break-ups caused by the inveterate sickness of a child. Terminal illness is an assassin of love as well as life. Such articles qualify as light bedtime reading now.

RENATA: What?

JIM: Don – it turns out that Don's... Don has been bragging to Raff and Michael about... about seeing... about seeing some kind of hooker.

RENATA: A what? Who...

A good proportion of the unpinned papers cascade.

JIM: He's been talking to them about seeing a prostitute, apparently. I don't know! Okay, I don't know! It could be nothing. It sounds – it's so far-fetched, anyway, that's just what Paul Bennett said. The boys told him Don was getting help to do such a thing, from someone at the hospital. But it's probably nothing.

RENATA: *At the hospital*?!

The remaining cancer articles fall to Renata's feet.

Ext. Hospital. Night.

A couple of hours later, removed from all the panic, a cab decorated with phone numbers draws up at the hospital kerb. The back door opens and a young man gets out. He pays the driver, chooses coins from his palm, then as the cab pulls away turns to regard the hospital building before him, his eyes counting the floors up to the oncology ward. It's like the Seven Ages of Man, this process, starting with the prenatal ward on the ground floor, the maternity ward over it, the children's wards with their cartoon characters painted on the windows a floor higher up; then the young persons' ward above, a few superheroes painted there, alternative saviours; above that the general adult wards on five, six and seven, flowers of mature sympathy and the heart-shaped balloons of love on their sills. And then his ward, on the eighth floor, the top floor, the taking-off point, the end of the ride. The odd crucifix in the window. Above that, there is only night sky. Cooling stars. The open, freezing heavens. Beyond this, the unknowable.

A dozen security cameras pick up Donald as he stands there, recording his presence on the steps in slow sweeps. He's no threat. He has a legitimate right to be here. He has advanced disorders of the brain. Numerous other organs aren't right either, and so there's an elevator ride waiting for him inside, the ride of his life, one that skips out all the intermediate stops, express all the way to the top. He climbs the steps and enters under the Admissions sign, as ready as he'll ever be.

Int. Hospital. Night.
Donald slips into his bed, the bed by the window, the ultimate bed, what old Trach once called "the last Station of the Cross". Two clipboards dangle on the bed's tailboard, reports bull-clipped to them, pages full of ticks and crosses in columns, measuring results, improvements, deterioration. He doesn't bother finding his pyjamas. His underwear and T-shirt are what he wants to wear, because they smell of *her*.

He rests his head on the triple pillows of his moon-white bed. At this hour the ward is stony-quiet save for the low rasp of human breathing. Donald lies amid monitors and masks, wires and pumps, and a new contentment creeps over him, passing across axons and motor neurons and synapses, effecting changes that will not register on the clipboards at the foot of the bed after the doctor's morning rounds. No endocrinic responses these, nor thoracic or lymphatic, but changes all the same, undifferentiated stirrings, gaugeless, undetectable, extra-cellular. A hallucinatory calm passes over him in the manner of morphine. Couldn't good health metastasize as well? Why not? Why was it not possible to contract an acute case of Feeling-Great, a disease that will take the World Health Organization by surprise, a strain of virulence that will tear aggressively through bodies, respecting no one, leaving all who catch it feeling... *terrific*? Fucking hell, if he could only catch that!

He closes his eyes. He is ready to sleep, wondering for the first time about miracles. A smile plays on his lips. It took a visit to a hooker to begin his age of innocence. Go figure. What would Brother Max call it? *Irony*. He should've paid those classes more attention. In the dark he finds his earbuds and pushes them into place: no music to be played, just out of habit, and he goes to sleep like that: attached. Attached to something.

ACT THREE

Int. Oncology Ward. Day

Donald, standing at the window which has the best view in the world, and watching clouds, and *just* clouds today, clouds no longer suggestive of lady parts or anything crazy other than clouds, just standing there thinking how cool they are and how continually "almost-becoming" they are, so that they keep you fascinated with their clusterings, hypnotized, hopeful... he turns when he hears footsteps coming towards his bed.

His parents. Grim-faced. Pissed off. Uh oh. Carrying flowers and fruit and stuff, but clearly outraged too, looking for answers fast, answers to questions such as what has happened to their sweet little boy, their second-born, what the hell has happened to turn him into a... into a goddamn sex fiend! Wanting confirmation also, that Dr Adrian King, their trusted friend, had gone and done what the hospital authorities now believed he had gone and done. Could their son really have been taken, without their say-so, to visit a hooker? A *hooker*? Well, they won't get any answers from me, Donald decides – he's claiming the cancer patient's right of silence. He's pleading the fifth.

Damn, are these two walking anxiety sponges really his parents, one in flapping corduroy pants and a pale-blue button-collar shirt, the other in jeans and clackety shoes and a white-flecked jumper with cherries or some shit woven into it? Are these two the actual X and Y chromosome donors who decided one night, nearly fifteen years ago, to bring him into existence? They have once or twice alluded to that long-gone ski weekend in the Dolomites, their excitement over finding a spa bath in their room by dint of a complimentary upgrade plus a bottle of Asti Spumante which they promptly drank at altitude. His own personal big bang ensued. *Their* idea. *Their* plan. *Their* dizzy collaboration. His whole life, their spur-of-the-moment idea of a good time. Jumpin' Jesus. No wonder they look worried right now. No wonder anything bad that happens to him lies on their conscience like lead.

But he has news for them. He's okay. And more than that. He feels ecstatic, like he owes them some kind of cornball thank you or some shit for, y'know, *being here*, a *gracias* to say that their sozzled idea hadn't entirely been a bad one. And so he smiles at his two pale, tired and worried-looking co-creators with the kind of easy, cheesy grin that could sell a 4 x 4 to an environmentalist.

It stops them in their tracks. Man, it's like some tractor beam arresting them. And his mother is so amazed that she seems to need confirmation of his identity.

RENATA: Donny?

Int. Delpe House. Day.
All they can think to do when they get home is make a cup of coffee. Ren gets down two Ikea mugs from the Ikea cupboard, and Jim looks out the window at Jeff, who is

lobbing a ball at the backboard and missing time and again, not caring. Miss, miss, miss...

Jeff ought to be at school but he wasn't feeling good at breakfast, and didn't look too great either: pale, drained, dark under the eyes as if from a forty-eight-hour jag of TV watching. By noon, the kid is restored. What a faker, Jim thinks. The guy can manufacture a temperature at will. But then, this has all been very tough on him too. So, he's calling a few of his own time-outs, good for him. And even if he refuses to lower his guard and admit it, he is missing Donny already. They all are. For it's probably true to say that at some point this week, one never ascribed to any single moment or event, they each in their own way have realized that Donny isn't coming home again. The final stage has begun. Jim knows it and has said as much. Ren feels it but has said nothing as usual, determined to the last to set cosmic store in the powers of Hope. And Jeff worked up a 40 °C temperature.

Jim remembers that he and Ren had mainly wanted another baby to give Jeff a brother or sister. There was an aspect of missing the way new babies are – the smell, the look, that innocence – but mainly it was to make sure Jeff didn't grow up alone, locked in his head, cut off and self-sufficient. And giving him Donald, a brother three years younger, had worked out pretty well for Jeff, taming him the way only a sibling can, forcing him to be less ego-driven, providing a companion in the hermetic hours, a captive audience also, and a whetstone upon which to sharpen his act. And now, it was teaching Jeff something new: something traumatic.

RENATA: Oh, and you've got to remember, the car insurance is due. Always forget.

JIM: Okay. I'll take care of it. It's okay.

Jim stares at his wife. The midday light makes her blotchy. The skin above her breasts is wrinkled, a darker pink. Her good looks are leaving her. She stares back at him. And he suddenly "SEES" what she's thinking. How long has he had this skill? Not long.

RENATA: What? (*Nervous laugh*) What?

JIM: Yes. I do. I always have. And I always will.

RENATA: Sorry?

JIM: That's one thing you don't have to worry about.

RENATA (*impressed*): How did you know... what I was?...

JIM: Little superpower of mine I've picked up some-where.

Int. Oncology Ward. Day

Donald comes out of his intense concentration on MiracleMan's penultimate adventures when a Mont Blanc pen is dangled in front of his nose. He takes the lid off and touches the gold nib.

ADRIAN: It's yours.

DONALD: I can't take it. I mean, I can't take it again...

ADRIAN: I want you to have it. It's yours.

As Adrian starts to go he gives a wink. He refuses to let the boy know what pressure he is under.

DONALD: Is everything gonna be okay? About last night?

ADRIAN: Under control. It's going to be fine.

DONALD: It's fine then.

ADRIAN: Yes. It's fine.

DONALD: Sorry...

Yes, Donald had changed the plan without warning. Jumping out of the car like that and disappearing for hours had exploded the situation badly. And Adrian would have to pay the price, whatever it ended up being.

ADRIAN: Where did you go anyway? After you got out of my car? I wish you'd tell me.

DONALD: I just needed… to do it my way.

Adrian nods, no point in telling the kid off, or pursuing this. How should a kid be expected to behave on such a night, after losing his cherry to a goddess? And at least Don had a smile on his face. This was no small thing either.

DONALD: Hey, when it's all over, like, when I'm gone – I want you to have this, okay? (*Lifts the graphic novel.*)

Adrian is speechless as Donald returns to his precious work. *When I'm gone?* Such lightness in the delivery of this heaviest of lines. Adrian stands and watches and listens to the feverish scratching of the boy's pen on paper, rapid strokes now – as if there's no time to lose.

THE GLOVE's HOTEL ROOM, now a makeshift SURGERY. MIRACLEMAN lies strapped to the bed. His hand clenches. He groans and revives.

THE GLOVE: Vital signs, surprise, surprise. (*Explosively snaps on a GLOVE!* MIRACLEMAN's *eyes flicker.*) Wakey, wakey, wonderful one. How's my best patient feeling today? Don't tell me – alive. Well, don't worry, the symptoms won't last, not this time.

MIRACLEMAN (*groggy*): How long have you had me here?

THE GLOVE: You've been under sedation for three weeks while I've slowly conducted my operation.

MIRACLEMAN: Uh… urr… ughh… what operation?

THE GLOVE: Oh, nothing much. I've just been harvesting your bone marrow, you freak of modern science. Yes, the factory of your incredible immune system is what I've been after, all those lovely white blood cells – though I like the red ones the most – and all those yummy platelets. Yum, yum. Then we'll see how immune you are.

MIRACLEMAN: Fine. Go ahead. You're doing me a favour. I don't want to be immune any more anyway. Take it all.

THE GLOVE: Thank you, I have. Your bones are now as hollow as flutes.

MIRACLEMAN: Maybe now you'll find out how much fun it is to go through life cold, indestructible, alone.

THE GLOVE: Stop it, I'll be too excited to hold my scalpel! And you've got the wrong idea anyway. Your marrow isn't for me. Much too unprofessional. Nurse? Throw the lever!

NURSE: Yes, my surgical sweetheart.

The NURSE throws a LEVER on the WALL and a compartment REVOLVES, revealing A DOZEN UNCONSCIOUS BODIES on LIFE SUPPORT. Each wears a SURGICAL MASK and ROBES like The GLOVE's.

THE GLOVE: Your marrow is for them! Meet the staff of my all-new Immunology Department, you doner kebab.

MIRACLEMAN: What the…

THE GLOVE: Like any country doctor, I simply want to create a master race! One no hospital can possibly kill. I'll hold the world's medical insurers to ransom. Basically, I'm after a pay rise.

MIRACLEMAN: I… I can't let this happen. You'll unleash a plague of immunity. DEATH WILL DIE OUT. Life will be pointless!

He struggles to free himself.

THE GLOVE: Bet you wish you were Superman right now, huh? Well, no escape this time.

The NURSE passes him a LOADED SYRINGE. THE GLOVE inspects it.

THE GLOVE: Good. Dirty needle? No wonder I'm losing my patients.

THE GLOVE SQUIRTS a LOADED SYRINGE of liquid into the air, and is just about to INJECT it into MIRACLEMAN when...

...he SMELLS something. SOMETHING AWFUL. He GRIMACES.

THE GLOVE: Oooohhhh man! Wow! (*To* NURSE) Did you... That is DISGUSTING!

NURSE: What? (*Smells it too.*) Ooooohhhh! It's him.

THE GLOVE: Sure it is. Here. (*Passes* NURSE *the syringe.*) You do the dishonours. It's anthrax. Be careful. I'm heading for higher ground. (*Turns.*) And make sure he's dead.

THE GLOVE leaves the SURGERY. THE NURSE advances on the barely conscious body of MIRACLEMAN, who is NAKED to the waist. He OPENS HIS EYES. They look at each other. Her eyes glance over his body.

NURSE: What a waste. (*Sighs.*) Before I do this, I'm granting you a last wish.

MIRACLEMAN: My last wish... or yours?

She STARES at him, lays the syringe in a kidney tray with a CLUNK, and then begins to UNFASTEN the leather straps that bind him. As he SITS UP, shakily, weak, she stands back and unzips her WHITE UNIFORM, revealing herself in BRA and PANTIES, a knock-out body with KNOCK-OUT KNOCKERS.

NURSE: You're very weak. You have no immunity left at all, prey to any bacteria or virus – so that even (*seductive*) A KISS COULD KILL YOU.

She releases her bra, then turns as she lowers her panties. When she begins to BEND OVER, and as he glimpses, backlit, for one split second, PARADISE...

MIRACLEMAN: Wait!

She stops.

MIRACLEMAN: You're a nice girl, you just fell in with the wrong crowd. My heart belongs to someone else. No hard feelings, huh?

NURSE: So what? Don't you want to... to taste the sweetness of this life just one more time before you go? (*She licks her lips.*)

MIRACLEMAN: You're right, sure. Why not.

NURSE: Attaboy.

They EMBRACE, hold each other. THEIR LIPS come together. THEY KISS.

MIRACLEMAN: Killed by a kiss.

They look into each other's eyes, and the NURSE suddenly FLINCHES...

NURSE (*in pain*): Ouch.

MIRACLEMAN: I'm sorry.

NURSE: You bastard.

ANGLE ON... The SYRINGE implanted into her THIGH!!!

MIRACLEMAN: Good luck with finding an antidote.

MIRACLEMAN escapes. THOUGHT BUBBLES appear over NURSE's head: "**I loved him so**." She pulls out the SYRINGE from her thigh and throws it away.

A comic-book title card spins into prominence: **"THE DEATH OF MIRACLEMAN"**.

CUT TO: The HOTEL CORRIDOR. MiracleMan staggers down the hallway. He pauses to marshal his non-existent strength and glances at his CUT HAND, which DRIPS BLOOD. His THOUGHT BUBBLE reads:

"It doesn't heal…"

He sinks to one knee and closes his eyes. At this point he hears…

A woman's voice interrupts the COMIC-BOOK WORLD…

RENATA (*frantic*): Darling, darling, oh my darling…

MIRACLEMAN: It's alright. I'm okay now.

With this, MIRACLEMAN rises, rejuvenated, and walks off into the darkness out of sight.

Int. Private Room / Intensive Care Unit. Night.

RENATA: Ssshhh… Ssshhh… Ssshhh.

Renata stands over Donald, stroking his face. His eyes are shut. They haven't been open for three weeks, except for when the nurse prises them open thrice daily to apply saline drops. For twenty-one days he has been in this coma, beyond anybody's reach, even his parents', who have been living in that private room since he slipped into twilight.

Nor does Donald's body look much like it did at its best. The art department's model-makers, if they're the ones who are now in control of him, have done a lousy job here – an underweight prosthetic, a fragile dummy: his head is crenellated, veined, his limbs those of a Gollum, emaciated. This is a horror-movie stand-in. Only the rise and fall of the chest look life-like. The sound of breathing is lousy too: like a saw through wet wood.

Occasionally the patient's face distorts in pain. Donald winces again, fingers contort, legs flinch, a pain that expresses itself even through the thick veils of his coma, registering even on a disenfranchised body. It's always then that Renata and Jim draw closer to him, and nurse him through such moments by stroking his hand or brow, glancing at the IV bottle to make sure the morphine hasn't run dry. Skin and bone now, their beloved hand-reared son.

The charge nurse appears then, tweaks the IV flow and stands over their shoulders.

CHARGE NURSE: He's amazing. His systems have shut down but he doesn't want to go. He doesn't want to leave you.

This is the last thing Jim and Renata want to hear.

JIM: Going on like this for three weeks now.

The woman nods.

CHARGE NURSE: He must have had a great life.

Jim stares at her. Was this true?

JIM: He thinks he can beat it. He still thinks he can win. That's why he's fighting. He doesn't know it's too late.

No protests from Renata to such a statement. But no acknowledgement either, no endorsement.

CHARGE NURSE: Have you thought of… have you thought of telling him… that it's okay… to go now? He may still be able to hear you. A lot goes in, you know.

JIM: Three weeks. I've been telling him that for three weeks. Just that. That's all I've been doing. But he still thinks… (*His voice breaks.*) He's coming back.

Renata's hand goes slowly to her mouth: her husband is crying. She hasn't seen this for years. It's the first time in this whole ordeal that he has broken down like this, and it punches a hole in her. She regards him as though he's a stranger. But then, recalled to action by Donald's body flinching involuntarily, she leans close to Don's ear.

RENATA: It's okay, honey. Listen, my darling... Listen to me now. You can let go now. We love you.

Jim turns, looks at his wife. Holds his breath. Ren's face is resting on Don's, cheek to cheek, like a couple of old-time ballroom dancers. She is waltzing his son out of this world.

RENATA: You can stop fighting, sweetheart... It's okay to go now. We love you. You can stop now, my darling. We love you so much. Relax and go now. Oh my lovely boy. Relax, just relax now.

After all these months telling him never to give up, not to surrender, and now these words to her deep-sleeping boy, words addressed also to her own grip on him – Jim can see this – a grip which is just as firm yet gentle and certain, he remembers, as the first moment when the pink newborn was set triumphantly into her arms, while he stood grinning at the side of the bed, his heart somersaulting with the news: A son! A son! My God, a son!

Int. Corridor / Hospital. Day.

Jim has two instant coffees burning his hands as he hurries from the machine to Renata. They sit beside each other on metal chairs and sip their coffees, passing the piping-hot plastic cups from one hand to another, as a TV set without sound runs pictures surreally disconnected from their lives. Regardless, their reality-stung eyes fall on the screen and can't break away. Hypnotized, ensnared, they blow the steam off the coffee's surface and welcome the distraction. It's a kind of coma of its own.

Int. Private Room / Intensive Care Unit. Day.
Donald's hand, so long lifeless on the mattress, flinches.

The coma breaks. His eyes snap open. Drenched with sweat, in something of a panic, he revives, taking in the room, seeing he is alone and that no one else is there to see it – that he has managed a miracle and returned.

The cardiograph beeps intermittently at his side. His eyes take in the window; the clouds drift in the sky. A greenhouse's worth of flowers sit in vases on the sill. An entire gift shop of Get Well balloons buoy against the glass. Someone has attached some of his cartoons to the walls: superheroes, arch-enemies, bad defeating the good mostly. The old battles. A thing of the past. He settles back; his attention is coming and going like a radio losing its signal. He closes his eyes, ready for the last round, letting all the air in the world go out of his body.

What a breath: so strong it thrashes the curtains, forces every petal from every rose, blows every picture from the walls, shreds all his old illustrations and even through the glass gusts the sky clear of gauzy clouds. It's the wind of the cosmos, the last breath leaving him. Only then does he subside. His breathing becomes shallow and, almost by willing it, stops. No more thought bubbles from Donald.

Seconds pass without another stir. After twenty more seconds without a vital sign, his right hand, the one he always drew with, gives one more twitch, then lies still. No more miracles. There is no last-second rescue. The alarm on the cardiograph gives out a shrill cry, followed, shortly after, by the sound of footsteps skittering towards the room, running towards an emergency that has already passed.

Ext. Hospital Corridor. Day.

Jim needs to stretch his legs. He traipses down the corridor with cooled coffee in hand. It takes him past a dozen private rooms in which loved ones are gathered around railed beds, each enduring a story no doubt as tough as his own. But what he is thinking right now is how the lino under his feet looks very shiny today. Especially shiny. How do the staff get it so reflective? It must be some kind of silicone-based product, or a sort of bee's wax. He even *prefers* to think about the floor, its refreshing lustre, and puzzles only on the wonderful effect of the shiny floor and the foolish human pleasure it creates in him.

At this second the sound of running shoes grows in his ears until he feels a hand on his shoulder. He turns. He knows. A nurse, short of breath. Telling him to come. To come now. He knows. His legs feel wobbly but he runs. He runs, over the floor, over the wonderful shiny surface – such a mirror that everybody here should be on ice skates.

Int. Private Room / Intensive Care Unit. Day.

JIM (*at* DONALD's *side*): Oh Ren. We're too late.

RENATA (*to* DON): It's okay…

JIM (*breaking down*): We missed it.

Renata, in tears, strokes Donald's face.

RENATA: It's okay. Good boy. He's gone. Oh God, Jim, he's gone. He's gone, my sweetheart. My beautiful boy…

Jim's heart gives out too then. No defences left against his wife's song of surrender and late acceptance. Nothing to stop the tears from coming again, and nothing to stop them either from this day forwards. His body starts to shake violently. He cannot stop shaking. But Renata is calm.

RENATA: It's okay, sshhh, shhhh, shhhh. He's gone

now. (*Stroking, stroking the boy's face.*) Goodbye, my love. Sshhh, shhhh, shhhh.

Ext. Delpe House. Night.
Twelve hours later – a lifetime later – on the day their world stops revolving, Jim Delpe is out in the backyard with the porch lights on, shooting some baskets. Nothing much is falling. Moths swirl around the porch light. Jim stops often and just holds the ball, taking in night air, looking up at the stars or else idly at the paintwork on the Saab. Then he takes another shot, rims it, and chases the fleeing ball into the darkness before bringing it back to where he can see what he's doing, gripping it with two hands and trying his best to make the damn thing go in.
Int. Delpe House. Night.
Renata can hear the sound of Jim's ball hitting the backboard as she writes – writes even at this hour, even on a day like this (but perhaps *especially* on a day like this), an email to a perfect stranger who has requested a cancer reading list. The list is longer than she expected but it's something to do, at least. She's going to need a lot of things to do in the next few weeks, months, years, she realizes, as she reaches for another Kleenex from a box that is almost empty now, the used tissues lying in balls on the carpet. *Tok, tok, tok, tok* go her fingers on the keyboard.

Int. Adrian's Flat. Night.
Adrian sits on the couch, steel-combing his wife's cat, not so much for fleas – he's too consistent in his flea checks for the critter to be crawling – but more for the comfort it brings him. Every four or five passes of the comb he stops and examines its teeth under the anglepoise light. Nothing.

He's waiting to feel tired enough to go to bed. The combing is equivalent to counting sheep. He wipes his eyes with the cuff of one hand and continues, waiting for sleep to come.

Maudite à jamais soit la race.
Amour! Viens aider ma faiblesse.

Int. Donald's Bedroom. Night.
Jeff lies on Donald's bed listening to Donald's iPod at near full volume, staring at the ceiling, scrolling through the storehouse of his brother's 2,000-odd songs, looking for that one track in the whole bunch that will arrest his own scrolling emotions and express perfectly all that he is unable to express. What that song might be he has no idea. It's a case of searching. He's been through about half the catalogue already. The track he wants has yet to appear.

Int. Funeral Chapel. Day.
Single roses are the flowers of choice. Rose after rose is laid on the casket of the superhero until they topple onto the floor and rise around it in a tide of crimson. The mourners file past, paying their last respects, a queue that runs out the front doors of the church, down the steps and across four blocks of Megalopolis in a single thread of grief and gratitude…

This is how Donald had imagined his hero's end. His own funeral lacks such overblown numbers but is no less moving. The eulogies focus on the way he fought in the end, when it was in vain, surprising everyone who knew him. The priest mentions this "last defining battle". Jim also points it out in his small, broken address, which he reads from a single sheet of paper that quivers in his hands. The disclosure of Don's fight, news to many, has the intended effect throughout the congregation. Hands tighten on wooden pews, handkerchiefs rise to faces, neatly applied mascara becomes clownish. The will to live. The will to live.

Donald, prone in the open coffin, is covered with the heavy lid. Next stop for his body, the fire. Gold wing nuts are wound down and then, at the push of a concealed button, the mortal remains are drawn on a conveyor belt towards velvet curtains. Jim and Renata and Jeff, and Michael and Raff behind them, even Adrian King inconspicuous at the back of the chapel, watch as the curtains part to receive the coffin, then close again automatically, leaving the main congregation to file outside and talk about the weather, the chance of a squall coming in.

Int. Furnace Room / Crematorium. Day.

The heat in the furnace room, where the coffin stands on a roller deck before the furnace, is intense. It's even a little hard to breathe. Just the immediate family and the priest are here for this final farewell. Handkerchiefs formerly used to mop liquid eyes now wipe brows as the priest anoints the casket with water one last time. The furnace doors open: a raging world. The coffin is pushed by hand inside. It slides into place in the belly of the fire where it bursts into flame. It's shocking. So sudden. So much heat. Was the coffin doused, the timber impregnated? The heat is immediate and immense. Jim and Renata and Jeff feel it on their faces, the backs of their hands. Donald's body – the one that won him a third place in the 200-metre relay in 2nd Form but that had yet to develop the follicles for a beard, the one that was a perfect fusion of parental features, a little of both, and that in the next three years would have grown another six inches – is consumed.

The furnace door shuts with a deep clang, shutting him in.

The mourners stumble, stricken, away from the insufferable heat, heading for daylight.

Ext. Cemetery. Day.

And so… even his ARCH-ENEMIES bow their heads in respect as MIRACLEMAN's COFFIN is lowered into the ground. The cemetery has never seen such a crowd. Two friendly cops, JIM and RENATA, stand in the shade of some trees, watching, whispering to each other, his arms folded over his chest, her thumbs tucked under her gun belt.

JIM: How many y'think here today?

RENATA: Ten, fifteen thousand.

JIM: That many?

RENATA: Sure. (*Noticing something.*) Say – who's that guy?

They look at a man standing under another grove of trees, a SILHOUETTED FIGURE.

JIM: I've been watching him. He's not the man we're looking for.

RENATA: Sure?

JIM: Yeah. Let him go.

ANGLE ON… The dark figure, as he turns and walks away from the service, heading back towards a waiting TAXI, and gets in.

TAXI DRIVER: Is anyone else coming, Doctor?

DOCTOR: No. (*Pause*) I'm alone. We can go.

THE END

MiracleMan™, registered trademark of the late, great Donald F. Delpe, 2006

OUT-TAKES

AND

DELETED SCENES

Montage of land, sky, silver seas like photo negatives, sweeping aerial shots of geology and elements, scarped headlands, undrained moors, forests and firths and fields, roads impossible to drive, bays and boats locked in ice, lending a sense of the cathedral majesty of nature, culminating in the words (superimposed, of course): *Six Weeks Later*.

Int. Disciplinary Hearing Boardroom. Day.
Adrian sits down in front of a tribunal of eight men and women and sees that their professional faces are as icy as air conditioning, frosting everything in the room: cool expressions, cold medical hands palm-down on the tabletop, glasses of chilled water set at regular intervals, a chill symmetry to everything. Art direction by Albert Speer, he reflects with zero-degree irony, as he awaits his interrogation.

How had he reached freezing point? His professional qualifications (his BA, MA Psych, his PhD, numerous other diplomas and accreditations) should disincline him from viewing what he did in a religious context. It would be nonsense to think – wouldn't it? – that fate compelled him to do something as lunatic as break a kid out of hospital unseen, unsanctioned, and whisk him across town to an assignation with a *demi-mondaine*; nonsense to think that a divine destiny had sent Donald Delpe to his door in the first place, making their partnership a pact blessed by the will of the universe. He can speculate, but – he gives his head a little shake – no, he's a senior psychologist with his career on the line, and what he must face instead is a harsher analysis, forcing him to wonder if he's made the biggest mistake of his life. And for what? For vanity, perhaps? To show that he was special when he did not feel special any more? To prove that his own moral judgement and understanding of the *real* Donald was better than other people's, Donald's parents included? All those certificates, all his qualifications, whole alphabets of letters after his name, and he was so desperate to prove himself *to himself*, to flex his muscles, that he pimped for a hooker and a boy?...

Unforgivable. If it's true – and he hasn't yet accepted this self-verdict – then, unforgivable!

CHAIRMAN: Dr King?

The voice pierces his reflections. He looks up and into the faces of those men and women of the tribunal who sit in judgement upon him.

Int. Oncology Ward / Hospital. Day.

Roy, keeping spirits up as usual on the cancer ward, showing Gunga Din a classic trick (places a coin on the table top with a *click*, concealing it under one hand, a hand that rubs it until it disappears, only to reveal that it has passed through the table and reappeared on the underside). He even has the largesse, lost on professional magicians, to show how it's done, which is, naturally, to have *two coins* all along.

ROY: Okay. One last time. But this is the last time, okay? Watch me get rid of the top coin. Watch the top coin. Okay. Watch. (*Thumps it down. Click!*) I rub it away… and here it is… it's gone through the table. Did you see me get rid of the top coin? I'm dropping it here, in my lap, when it looks like I'm putting it down on the table.

The dying man stares glumly at the table, the coin, the table, the coin, back and forth, on the edge of fury.

GUNGA DIN: Do it again.

ROY (*laughs*): No way. We're gonna be here all day. I've shown you how it's done!

GUNGA DIN: Do it again.

ROY: Okay. One more time, but this is the last…

Gunga Din watches this trick a further sixteen times until, none the wiser, he allows himself to be returned to his bed, two away from the window.

The bed by the window is empty.

Int. Adrian's Office. Day.

Adrian is clearing out his desk when there is a knock on the door.

ROY (*entering*): Hey boss.

ADRIAN: How are you, Roy?

ROY: Just wanted to thank you for not mentioning my name. No way they can deregister you, man.

ADRIAN: Oh yes they can.

ROY: I feel like, in some way, I put you up to this. Awoke the sleeping public enemy inside. I'm sorry if I did. Mea culpa, mate.

ADRIAN: There's really no need.

ROY: When do they reach a decision?

ADRIAN: A few days. A week. I'm suspended until then.

ROY: Maybe you'll be okay.

ADRIAN: I know what's going to happen.

ROY: This is a fucking miscarriage of justice. This place will riot. Seriously. The guys (*points to the wards*) are ready to burn mattresses. Everyone I speak to is on your team. Well, almost everyone. Okay, there are a few who think you should be imprisoned for life without parole for taking a dying kid to see a hooker, but the vast majority want you knighted, man. Sir Adrian King. Has a ring to it.

ADRIAN: Thanks, Roy.

ROY: And as for me, chief, you're my superhero, okay? Spiderman, Daredevil and Scooby-Doo all rolled into one. No way they can fire you. This place will riot. Everybody's rooting for you. The guys are ready to burn mattresses.

ADRIAN: Thanks, Roy.

ROY: Okay. Well…

The two men embrace clumsily. Sweat is soaking through Roy's regulation shirt. He is adhesive. Adrian can feel it as he grips him. Chest to chest, their two fat-taxed hearts beneath, beating out of rhythm, communicating somehow. The guy is one in a million, Adrian thinks.

Roy leaves. Adrian clears out the rest of his desk, putting into boxes the props of his trade. He pauses only when he picks up Donald's comic journal, at the last bequeathed to him. He has been carrying this about with him for weeks now, dipping in and out of it most days, as much as he can bear, never reading much, always meaning to post it to the Delpes. Once he had tried to hand-deliver it, and got the door slammed in his face. It seems they aren't ready for it yet, or him. And so, still in possession of the young man's masterpiece, he opens the journal again, flicking through the episodes randomly, feeling grief take him over. He would like to finish it today, find out what Donald ultimately did with his alter ego. And his eyes narrow in concentration and curiosity almost at once as he encounters scenes near the end that are entirely unexpected. A love story?

MIRACLEMAN sneaks through the bushes and SPIES into a SUBURBAN house, where he sees…

…a YOUNG WOMAN going about her business. It's RACHEL. He cries.

Later, when RACHEL opens her door, she is surprised to find MIRACLEMAN standing there. He looks at DEATH'S DOOR.

MIRACLEMAN: Can I come in?…

Adrian reads the last line and closes the journal. He is still at his desk. Oh my God! Now he gets it! Why did it take him this long? Donald has run rings around them all. And kept it all a secret, too, disclosing the truth only in code, locked inside the pictograms of a superhero diary. And if Adrian's reading of this encrypted message is correct, then… what a character, what a class act. No wonder Don had a smile on his face, carrying this with him to the end. He'd managed to end his life as he had lived it, rich with secrets. A mystery man. Foiling all attempts to understand him. A millionaire in the deception stakes. Adrian has to grin, and then to laugh. Can't help himself.

ADRIAN: Well, what do you know… You little…

And his thoughts go back to that moment when Donald bailed out of his car and dropped him in whole heap of trouble – a moment which, when he thinks about it, makes him realize where Donald must have gone, and what he got up to…

Int. Adrian's Car. Night.

…His car is getting closer to the hospital, and the problem of smuggling the kid back into his ward is beginning to trouble Adrian. He and Donald are over the hour and a half mark now, but there hasn't been a warning call from Roy so, fingers crossed, they have got away with it…

ADRIAN: Awesome, you say?

DONALD: Oh yeah.

ADRIAN: I'm glad you hit it off. Certainly sounded like you did. From where I was sitting.

DONALD: Hey, thanks for spending all that money. Was worth it.

ADRIAN: No. Thank you. (*Limpid-eyed*) I'm serious.

DONALD: How come?

Just at this moment Donald's mobile phone spews out four very loud bars of Mozart's Fourth Piano Concerto, or as he prefers to think of it, Motorola Ringtone No. 6.

DONALD: Text.

Donald reads it, then turns off his phone as Adrian stops at a red light.

DONALD: Women. You know how it is.

ADRIAN (*surprised*): Are we talking… girlfriend?

Don doesn't reply, just taps his mobile on his knee instead.

They hit a red light…

DONALD: Adrian?

ADRIAN: What is it?

DONALD: Just – thanks man.

And the passenger door flaps open and Don is gone.

ADRIAN: Donald!

Ext. Cemetery. Day.

Adrian visits the area of the cemetery reserved for the cremated. No tombstones. Brass plaques are set into the bowling-green-quality grass. These carry the basics: name, dates, a little dictum. But Donald's has no epitaph. He is described only as a beloved son and brother.

Adrian considers a few possibilities. *Life is a Sexually Transmitted Disease.* No, Donald did not go out on that. Of this he is almost certain. *I want my money back, I didn't understand a thing.* Not that either, for there had been some late understanding. *Squeak, squeak, squeak*, perhaps, his trademark, but very obscure. *Swish.* Maybe. *Gone*, this would say, *all net.* It would work. But even better: *Here Lies Donald F. Delpe. Go Figure.* He smiles. Why not? Don, this mystery man, would look for a joke to go out on, one tinged with blackness, but funny nonetheless. And oh boy, did he achieve it…

Adrian has brought along a few roses. A perforated planter sits beside the plaque and can accommodate a dozen stems. On his knees, he inserts the flowers one at a time. When he's done the wind immediately sets about stripping them bare.

Int. Coffee Shop. Day.

Looking like one of the nighthawks in Edward Hopper's famous *Diner* painting, Adrian sits on a stool at the end of the long counter and puzzles over, not the swirl of cream in his coffee, but the riddles locked inside Donald's comic-book masterpiece one more time, as…

…as he is joined by his wife. Sophie is late, perhaps by twenty minutes, but he feels sudden resentment at her arrival. He could use more time alone in the company of this 2-D alternate version of Donald. Sophie leans in to kiss him, but he's distant, emotional, cool in the way he deflects the kiss, demotes it to a peck on the cheek. He closes the precious book and looks at her, sizes her up. She is different today. Jumpy. There's a pinch in her face, deeper parenthetical grooves around the mouth, watery eyes as she tries to smile. Hints of strain, sudden urgency. Something's going on. And yet he doesn't really care. Not today. He wants to cry for a dead boy.

SOPHIE: Sorry I'm late.

ADRIAN: How was traffic?

SOPHIE: A lorry and a car. Terrible mess. I came off the M1 at Milton Keynes. Anyway. Doesn't matter.

ADRIAN: You said it was urgent.

SOPHIE: Not urgent. Not really. But you work so hard I feel I need to make up an excuse to see you.

Adrian raises his eyebrows. He has never heard this complaint before.

ADRIAN: What is it, Sophie? Do you need money?

SOPHIE: It's over. Completely. Last night. I wanted you to know. I didn't fall in love with him. And he didn't fall in love with me.

ADRIAN (*pauses*): I almost feel I should offer my sympathies.

SOPHIE: I suddenly decided I didn't want to hurt you any more. I cried all last night – I've never cried so much. I've been so stupid. But I've learnt something from this. I don't want to be alone. I *do* need a lover. (*Reaches for his hand.*) And I want that person to be the person I love.

ADRIAN (*a wry smile emerging*): He dumped you.

SOPHIE: It was… it was… a mutual…

ADRIAN: Ha! Well what do you know…

SOPHIE: Please don't be like this.

ADRIAN: You know, I suddenly have a whole new respect for your veterinary surgeon. But I guess you become quite adept at learning when to put things out of their misery when you're in his profession. In mine we try to keep everything ticking over for as long as possible. Who's got the better idea?

SOPHIE: Adrian – I want us to be how we were at the beginning. Remember? Let's try again. Can't we? That's what I've come here to ask.

ADRIAN: At the beginning? We are at the beginning. That's exactly where we are. At that lovely point where I'm looking at this beautiful stranger I'd very much like to know. When will I ever stop hoping that I'll get to know you, Sophie? Anyway… we have returned to the beginning. It's all a bell curve, you see. You go up, you go down.

SOPHIE: Please don't say that. Just let me show you. I'm going to prove it to you. I am! Just wait and see.

Her cheeks are flushed. Adrian can see she is barely keeping herself together, this Sophie who is before him. Then, a second thought strikes him: Is it possible that she really fell in love with Conrad, is in love with the guy still? He does not want to imagine the scenes those two have shared.

ADRIAN: Look, I've got to go. Call me. From the farm, okay? We'll talk. (*Moves to go.*) You know, you're still the most beautiful thing I've ever seen, Sophie Colet, a work of art, but I sometimes wonder… I wonder if you're real. Are you?

At this, Adrian reaches around her and lifts the back flap of her jacket.

SOPHIE (*confused*): What are you doing?

ADRIAN: Looking for a tail.

Sophie can say nothing as Adrian rises, takes his coat and walks with composure out of the door, then back past the window where she sits, watching him go, trying to work out the cross-cultural subtleties of what has just happened. A tail? Then the tears come.

Int. Law Offices. Day.
JIM: What do you want?

ADRIAN: To return this.

JIM: Leave it on the desk and go.

ADRIAN: Okay.

JIM: Then get out.

ADRIAN: Some day I'd like to expl…

JIM: You lied to us!

ADRIAN: No. I did not lie.

JIM: We trusted you. Then in secret… in SECRET you…

ADRIAN: I know. I'm sorry.

JIM: With some… some filthy little pox-riddled low-life tart? How old was she? Fifty? Stinking of, of… (*Face contorts.*) …of other men's… This was what you thought my boy should experience before he died? You thought this might be… what?… a good idea?

ADRIAN: Jim, look, please, it wasn't like that.

JIM: I ought to smack you in the mouth.

ADRIAN: She was nice-looking.

JIM: Fuck you!

ADRIAN: Please! Listen to this at least. Before I go. For your own good. The woman was…

Jim's right hand had closed into a fist way back when Adrian denied lying, but it takes till this moment for Jim, a non-violent man, one of subtle argument and dialectics, to muster the steam to take a swing. He catches Adrian dead. Adrian wobbles, staggers back. Jim has not hit anyone since his schooldays, but Adrian has never been hit in his life. His body doesn't know what to do and soon takes refuge in a chair. To be punched, he is learning, is incredibly disorientating. Foggy shapes dance. His vision is flecked by darting fireflies of light. He touches his pulsing eyebrow, then looks at his fingertips. No blood. Shouldn't there be blood? He looks up at Jim. The man is standing at his open office door.

JIM: Get out.

Ext. Tanya's Apartment. Day.
It is always a mistake to think you will never return somewhere. Adrian sees this now. The fact is, no sooner do you decide this than you lay the groundwork for a return, taunting fate to prove its circularity.

And so, here he is, at the doorstep of this woman who has yet to give him an hour's mental peace since he last saw her, figuring in his daytime thoughts almost as much as in his night-time dreams. Added to which, she can now resolve for him a few questions posed by the comic journal. Only this woman can confirm what he already suspects. And so he stands on the street looking up to her floor. Do the curtains twitch? Has she seen him, and is she peering down even now through a hairline crack in the drapery?

He crosses the road and enters the lobby, finds the golden cage waiting for him. He enters, heaves closed the trellis of the door and lets the whirring motors bear him upwards as the bruise on his head throbs in time like the punctuating colon between minute and second on a digital clock.

227

Int. Tanya's Apartment. Day.

ADRIAN: I know you want to respect his confidence but – he left me his graphic novel. I know what happened.

TANYA: You think so?

ADRIAN: Nothing. Nothing happened. He didn't sleep with you, did he?

TANYA: Did he tell you that himself?

ADRIAN: Indirectly, yes. That's exactly what he's done. I've just worked it out. I must have been losing my touch.

TANYA: Maybe he wanted to fool you.

ADRIAN: Maybe. Knowing Donald – or test me. It's possible. Can you tell me what happened? Would you mind? Between the two of you?

Tanya pauses, closes her eyes for a few moments, thinks over her position carefully.

TANYA: He drew my foot…

ADRIAN: He drew your… foot…

TANYA: I modelled for him. Nude. He drew my foot. That's all. And then he asked me what sex was like. He was very sweet and shy.

ADRIAN: Do you remember what you said to him?

Tanya repeats the description she had given Donald, more or less word for word.

ADRIAN: And the sketch. The one he drew of you? Do you know what happened to it?

TANYA: He gave it to me. A gift.

ADRIAN: Do you still have it?

TANYA: Of course.

ADRIAN: Do you mind if I see it?

He watches her go sashaying away to get it, his Electra. When innocence ends, what follows? A lifetime of thinking you are working it all out.

Ext. Delpe House. Day.

Jim Delpe opens the front door to find…

…to find her standing there. Stunning. Holding flowers and a card. He removes his half-moon glasses and says nothing, can say nothing for a moment.

TANYA: Hi. I knew Donald. Hello.

Int. Delpe House. Day.

Jim and Renata Delpe sit on the couch, side by side.

TANYA: I only met him once. He was wonderful. I'll never forget him.

RENATA: He never mentioned you.

TANYA: I modelled for him, you see. But only once, so… Adrian brought him to see me.

JIM: Oh. Him.

RENATA: Oh! I see! You're a model at the Arts Centre, are you?

TANYA: Not the Arts Centre, no. No. And not a model. I'm an escort.

JIM: How do you mean… an "escort"?

Jim and Renata have been charmed by this cultivated, young beauty so far, albeit puzzled as to what the visit is about. Now all the lines go dead. Their brainwaves become a dreadful dial tone of astonishment. *Ommmmmmm…*

TANYA: You see, I know it must seem shocking to you, at the moment, when you don't know what… but… Adrian hired me to spend some time with your son. I believe you know about this?

JIM: *You?*…

TANYA: Yes. I will leave, if you like. But there's something I'd like to show you first. Please. It's why I came. I know you'd like to see it. It is a drawing, one that Donald drew of me.

JIM: It's *you*?...

RENATA: A drawing? What do you mean... you *posed* for him?

TANYA: Yes. I posed for him.

JIM (*uptight, breathing getting quicker, not really wanting to know the answer*): And what else did you do for him?

TANYA: Nothing.

RENATA: Nothing?

TANYA: He chose not to do anything else. Donald. He chose not to.

The Delpes try to... attempt to... somehow absorb this news, their suspicion vying with relief, their relief vying with their confusion, their confusion vying with their residual anger, this anger vying with their disbelief. Fatigue is on their faces. Strife. Pain. How to process yet more data, on top of the awful fate of their son? The strain is already intolerable. Beside the couch, almost hidden, are a stack of two sheets, a blanket and a pillow: someone is sleeping on the couch.

RENATA: And why should we believe that?

TANYA: Because you know Donald. (*Pause*) You can sense that it's true.

The Delpes gape. They really wish... what they really wish is... is to elicit from this woman an entire world of details, to furnish for ever their understanding of this crucial but missing episode in their son's life, one which seemed to have helped him – this much they will concede – turn a corner for the better. But what can you ask a hooker in circumstances like these?

JIM: Did Adrian ask you to come here? To save his skin...

TANYA: No. He asked me not to come here. He couldn't care less about saving his skin. But I told him I was coming anyway.

An image has been torturing Jim and Renata for weeks: Donald losing his virginity to a bored hooker, the third man inside her since lunch... and now here is a new storyline from this well-spoken glamour puss, who has leapt straight from the cover of Paris Vogue to conjure up the even more far-fetched image of Donald passing up intimacy with this gorgeous specimen in order to doodle her nude? Their son, at this moment, has never seemed more mysterious to them.

Jeff goes wandering past the living-room windows, clutching a Coke and giving an extremely poor performance of a disinterested party, casting an extended look indoors. Jim waves his son away, but no one can blame the kid for trying. Jeff had copped a load of the leggy brunette when she came in, and his jaw had dropped – *clang* – like an overhead locker in a 747. It isn't every day that chez Delpe plays host to eye-poppers like Tanya.

TANYA: Adrian told me you disapproved of what he did. I'm hoping this news might bring you some peace.

RENATA: Peace?

Is there such a thing? Renata's expression asks. Peace? Well, if there is, she doubts she will ever feel it again. The loss of a child is not something to recover from after three months or three years. No, as Renata now understands it, her life from now on will be that of a seagull in an oil slick, struggling in the sludge, trying as hard as she might to break away but only ever a pathetic, trapped creature who will end her days that way: flapping, tarred and feathered.

Tanya takes a folder from her bag, and carefully extracts Donald's drawing, handing it to Renata.

Close-up on… The drawing – of her foot – as immaculately observed as a Michelangelo, a brilliant distillation of beauty. A foot, only.

TANYA: He was very talented. And his cartoon book – you have it now? You've read it?

Jim spreads his hands out helplessly.

JIM: What do you know about that? You don't understand. It's just smutty teenage filth.

TANYA: You should read it. Both of you.

Int. Roller-skating Rink. Day.

Another pure distillation of beauty… Shelly performing a ballet on wheels. Free. Uninhibited. Expressive. Operatic. Eyes closed as if in a dream. She swirls. She swoops. Glides. In a world of her own. Others skate around her but she is really alone in the centre of the rink. Eventually she stops on a dime, then opens her eyes and catches her breath. She finds herself looking right at…

…at Jeff Delpe, sitting in the stands, listening to music on an iPod, and looking extremely down. She watches him some more, skates away, does a circuit, then skates over to him finally. He looks up only when she's standing right in front of him.

SHELLY: Hi.

JEFF: Hi.

SHELLY: I knew your brother.

JEFF: So?

SHELLY: What are you listening to?

JEFF: Every single fucking track of his life.

SHELLY: Try 'My Heart Trembles at the Sound of Your Voice'. That's Donald. It's on there. Dalila's Aria.

JEFF: How do you know what the hell I'm looking for?

SHELLY: Try that one.

JEFF (*remembering*): Shelly. Right? Your name's Shelly or something.

SHELLY: Right.

JEFF: Forty-two. You're forty-two.

SHELLY: What?

JEFF: Six times seven.

She shrugs, then skates away, as...

...as Jeff scrolls the menus for this unlikely track. And finds it. She's right. 'My Heart Trembles'... No artist name listed. How weird is that? How does this ditz, who gave his bro the brush-off, know this? He presses Play and puts the buds back in his ears as he watches Shelly, number forty-two, probable dyke and tormentor of Don, sweep around on wheels, giving a performance that would seem to indicate she too is listening to, and lost in, the same track...

...which she is. Precisely that one. Gliding round in slow circles that get bigger, bigger, bigger, skating to her own bootleg soundtrack ripped and burned into her own Random Access Memory...

Int. Burger King. Night.

...Shelly. Shelly Driscoll. Waiting for Don in a booth on her own. No girlfriends anywhere to be seen. And to Donald she suddenly looks not at all the intimidating fortress of sexuality she had formerly seemed. Rather, she's a kid like him, pretending to have experience of a game that neither of them knows how to play.

SHELLY: Thanks for texting me.

DONALD: Thanks for replying. After your visit, the hospital thing… well. (*Awkward*) I wanted… I just wanted…

She stares at him. He gazes back. The floodgates break.

DONALD: Fuck it. I love you. I mean, I don't even know you, but I love you. And the bathroom thing, I was just nervous and I went a bit spastic, I mean I never do that sort of thing, I'm not like this bathroom fiend or anything, but I just wanted to get through to you and I couldn't talk to you out here, so many people, and I had this crazy idea that maybe you wanted me to follow you, which obviously you *didn't*, judging by your King Kong Ann Darrow impersonation, which was pretty convincing, so I blew it, but I just wanted to say sorry, because I'd give anything not to have blown it. (*A breath*) Basically.

SHELLY (*impressed*): You learnt to talk.

DONALD: Yeah. Kinda.

SHELLY: That's sweet. That's really… sweet. And the bathroom thing, I thought that was cool.

DONALD: Eh?

SHELLY: Yeah.

DONALD: You thought it was *cool*?

SHELLY: Yeah.

She stares at him with new intensity. He shifts under her gaze. Maybe she knows the rules of the game after all, Donald bubbles.

SHELLY: I heard about you being sick. So I thought I'd visit you. In hospital. It's a real bummer. Cancer, right?

DONALD: So they tell me. I don't want to talk about it.

SHELLY: Okay. Anyway…

DONALD: Anyway, that's all. I better be going. So… see ya round, and ah (*trembling visibly*)… you're gonna be beautiful. You are already, but… you're going to be mind-altering in a couple of years. Anyway, have a great life, okay? I bet you it's gonna be great. And, uh… if I don't see you again… (*He cannot finish the sentence – he's tearing up badly.*)

SHELLY: You'll see me again.

She grabs his hand. An electric shock.

Int. Shelly's Parents' House. Night.

Shelly enters with a key, followed by a nervous Donald. Two burglars minus a torch. The house is dark. Shelly turns on lights and then disarms the security alarm with four jabs at the keypad.

SHELLY: Come on in. It's okay. My folks are away for the week. We can just hang out for a couple of hours. I'm meant to be staying with friends, but I can sneak in late.

DONALD: Cool.

Donald, the escapee, stealing moments. That's what these are: stolen moments. Moments stolen from someone else's screenplay.

SHELLY: Do you want a gin and tonic, or something? Or – a martini or something? Are you allowed a drink?

DONALD: Probably not. Water'd be good.

Shelly unzips her rayon jacket with the words J'AIME PARIS on the back and drops it on the couch. She advances on him in jeans and a little pink T-shirt with a rhinestone ♥ over her chest.

SHELLY: Just water? Is that all you want?

She leans in and kisses him on the lips. A short one. He's blown away.

SHELLY: What are you thinking?

DONALD: This is my lucky night. Sometime I'd like to tell you the whole story.

As Shelly goes into the kitchen for the water, Donald's mobile plays Mozart again. Don pulls it out, takes a look and quickly kills the call. He turns off the phone and repockets it.

SHELLY (*from kitchen*): Who is it?

DONALD: Just my… my karate teacher.

SHELLY: They call you at this hour?

DONALD: Yeah. It's a… a discipline thing.

Donald sits waiting on the edge of the couch. He's shaking a little. He looks at his right hand, holds it out. A slight tremor. But who cares, right? So long as he doesn't bow to these nerves. What a night! That's all he can think. What a night. The night is exuding pheromones like a nebula spits stars.

Int. Shelly's Parents' House. Twenty Minutes Later.

On the couch, in very dim light, Donald and Shelly break from a tentative kiss. Their eyes open. At a distance of a few inches their parted lips draw on the same admixture of air and carbon dioxide and spearmint chewing gum. Shelly is wearing Don's iPod earbuds and only now takes them out.

SHELLY: Cool. Wow.

DONALD: You like it?

SHELLY: Yeah.

It's wonderfully unclear whether they are talking about the track, the kiss, or both.

SHELLY: Do you want to undo my blouse?

DONALD: Whoah. Phew. Yeah. Course. I just…

SHELLY: Go on then.

DONALD: Why are you doing this? I'm not a charity case.

SHELLY: I'm not thinking about that. I wanna do it. You're cute. I like you. And that's it.

DONALD: You're doing this out of pity?

She shakes her head.

DONALD: Then what is it? What's changed all of a sudden?

SHELLY: You have. You have. You're different. And I have too. Big time.

DONALD: How have you changed?

Shelly smiles, perfect teeth brushed twice daily since teething, a bright healthy girl who will live till she's ninety. She points to the sideboard and its display of birthday cards, most of them clearly bearing, in bas-relief foil of either red or gold, a number to light the universe: "16". Shelly Driscoll is sixteen. And this sixteen-year-old grins mischievously at her ageless boy.

SHELLY: *That's* how. I'm a woman now. Just means I know what I want. And now I'm a woman, I don't want to waste a second of it. See?

DONALD: Yeah.

Slowly he begins to fumble with the buttons on her blouse. His fingers are suddenly bratwurst, her mother-of-pearl buttons like confetti to be picked out of the carpet. And he is bubbling with more thoughts than there are bubbles in a super-sized Pepsi.

DONALD: One of us is shaking. I'm pretty sure it's me.

SHELLY: No, it's me. I'm a virgin. I know you're probably not – right?

Donald inserts the tip of his tongue into the vestibule between his front teeth and his lips.

DONALD: It's okay. Don't worry about it. I'll take care of you.

SHELLY: It's good that one of us knows what to do.

DONALD: Oh yeah.

She leans in and kisses him again while he makes heavy work of the blouse…

MIRACLEMAN pulls out a CD, and puts it on her player. But it's not gangsta rap. It's opera. He turns.

MIRACLEMAN: 'My Heart Trembles at the Sound of Your Voice'. I know, corny title.

RACHEL: With true love (*smiles*) everything's corny.

MIRACLEMAN walks naked towards his DELILAH/ RACHEL, who waits on the bed, covered by a sheet. He slides in beside her. Her body is way hotter than he expects. WAY!

MIRACLEMAN (*thought bubble*): **She's so… warm. But of course, every necrophiliac must think this when they finally get a live one**.

It helps him to stop shaking. Lying on their sides, their hands begin to explore. They TOUCH. Hands trace the living shapes. The breathing shapes. The panting and short-of-breath shapes. The hardnesses and softnesses. The ins and outs. The dry and wet and wetter plus the cool and warm and warmer. So many places. So many sensations. He is inside her. She is enveloping him. He, her, he, her. So this is it: this is what they call making love. Geronimo. MEGA. Off the Richter scale. It's like… it's like Hallelujah and Hosanna in the Highest and *Gloria In Excelsis Deo* and Heaven On Earth and *Swiissh!* all rolled into one big Egg McLovin. MiracleMan ain't ever had nuthin like this, boy.

MIRACLEMAN: It's like a contest. Where both sides are trying to let the other side win.

RACHEL: That's nice.

MONTAGE of the two of them making love – slowly, nervously, coyly, where every mistake is a perfect memory, one that will outlast the non-mistakes.

LATER, post-coital, while she sleeps, he rises from bed and goes to stand at the WINDOW.

MOONLIGHT floods in. A beautiful night to be ALIVE. He closes his eyes, more content than he has ever been, and opens wide his arms in surrender, as a SHOT RINGS OUT! The glass in the WINDOW cracks, there is a HOLE in the middle of it. MIRACLEMAN looks down. A HYPODERMIC DART sits over his HEART. He pulls out the dart without emotion. The long needle withdraws. His mood does not change. He is ready to accept whatever happens. He sighs and SMILES as he throws the dart aside.

Outside, THE GLOVE lowers a RIFLE, and looks at the silhouette of MIRACLEMAN in the high window. The figure stands there for several more moments and then... CRUMPLES and FALLS. THE GLOVE, surprisingly, shows no joy.

Inside, RACHEL hears something and rises from the bed.

RACHEL: What is it? What is it?

She sees MIRACLEMAN lying on the floor.

RACHEL (*in panic*): Oh no! Oh no!

She rushes to him and holds him in her arms, a PIETÀ of a dying man in the arms of a BARE-BREASTED WOMAN.

RACHEL: What's happened? What's the matter?!! Talk to me.

MIRACLEMAN opens his eyes and looks into hers, then smiles, content.

MIRACLEMAN: I've seen a lifetime tonight. I can go now.

She cries. His eyes drift towards the window and fix on the brightening sky.

MIRACLEMAN: The sun's comin' up. (*Pause*) It's gonna be beautiful again.

He closes his eyes then – FOR EVER – as SUNLIGHT breaks into the room.

Int. Living Room / Shelly's Parents' House. Night.
Shelly wakes on her parents' couch to find herself alone. The mantel clock says 5 a.m. Someone has chivalrously draped a rug over her. She raises it and looks down at her body, her camisole hiked up to her armpits, her young breasts exposed. A few beach towels cover the couch underneath her. She stands and bunches them up. There are traces of her on them. She remembers why, earlier, she went and got the towels to protect her parents' Scotchgarded upholstery. She remembers also why her blouse is hanging off the japanned standing lamp some five metres away. Sleepily she fixes herself up, remembering all the events and emotions of the night just gone. She remembers further that she is no longer a kid. And a smile comes to her face.

But where is her boy, boyfriend, *lover*? Yes, her lover is missing. Perhaps those are the hoof beats of his horse she hears fading away? No, it's the beating of her own carnally aware heart. Her virginity is gone. The anxiety can end. The ancient questions are answered. She can lead discussions now with her friends, not just listen as she used to, silently furious. She can watch the love scenes in the movies now and *know* when they lie. She is jubilant. She is *of* the world now. For better or worse. But where did her lover go? It's morning almost. She rises, goes to get her blouse, and then turns to find, on the carpet in front of her, a rose. A single stem.

She picks it up, smells it, holds it against her pumping heart, then wistfully looks out the window, replicating the age-old gesture of women who have lost their men...

Int. Roller-skating Rink. Day

...Jeff rolls up to Shelly, who is about to leave the rink. Stops her.

JEFF: How did you know? About that music? The name of it and everything?

She looks at him hard, evaluating him for risk, reliability, trustworthiness, and seems none too convinced he is sound on any front.

JEFF: What?

Finally, she reaches inside her knapsack and takes out a diary. Opens it. A dried and pressed head of a rose. He stares at it. Her. The rose. Her. The rose.

Ext. Street. Day.

Jeff rollerblades down the street, slowly at first. Subdued, deep in thought, kind of stunned by all he's just heard, he eventually picks up speed, working the blades, and is soon travelling faster and faster as a smile can't help but creep over his face. Six times seven, baby. That's all he can think as he overtakes his first slow-moving car, speeding right up the centre lane on an otherwise empty street. Six times seven. Boom. All net. And the lesson? Man, Donald learnt

241

that lesson good: when you get your chance, make your move. And make it *fast*.

Int. Lounge / Delpe House. Day.
Alone on the couch, Renata Delpe closes her son's comic-book journal, shaking her head half in wonder and half in confusion. Grips the book in her lap. Her husband comes into the room, has pulled out some faulty fairy lights from under the stairs and has been isolating the burnt-out bulb. He wants to string the thing around the love seat in the back garden for some reason. To Renata's mind he's clearly just finding things to do.

JIM: So? Did you finish it?

RENATA: I don't know whether to laugh or cry.

An uneasy silence.

JIM: I think we should talk to Adrian. What do you think? Get to the bottom of this.

RENATA: I'm so glad you said that.

JIM: I'll do it then. I'll call him tomorrow.

RENATA: Do it.

Jim plugs in the Christmas lights, testing them. All the lights fire at once. He stands again, pushing off one knee. His back isn't what it once was. He's pleased.

JIM: Found it. Took some doing to find the dud. Bastard of a thing.

RENATA: Okay.

JIM: Stupid invention. One goes out, they all do. What a terrible system.

The couple regard this interdependent skein of electrical circuitry and say nothing for a while. It is. It's a terrible system.

Int. Hotel Lobby. Day.

It is an outfit calculated to make Adrian swoon. First, the short-sleeved blouse that leaves her arms exposed. Conservative by most standards, Adrian has a weakness for a slender woman's upper arm. Tanned, lean female arms. So pervasive in summer. Also, a woman's wrists, with their raised veins like the wiring inside an electric blanket. He loves these too. Therefore, if it's bare arms that work for him, then of course her arms are bare today, for Sophie is on a mission.

She has driven through the usual hell to get here, three and a half hours bumper to bumper, trapped between what Adrian once called the id and superego of the common British motorist. The slow lane proved the most benign. But she is exhausted. At a hotel near Adrian's hospital she has ordered a room for one night only. It will hopefully be all she requires. She waits as the manager taps her details into his computer, saying "Only one L" as he enters her maiden name. Her mouth tastes of metal. Her body has absorbed emissions.

This little hotel is perfectly suited for what she has planned. Into this parlour she will lure her damaged, bitter, wounded, insulted, rejected husband and make amends. She has hurt him tremendously, monumentally, but today she will begin to put things right.

As well as the short sleeves she wears a dun-brown and knee-length tight woollen skirt, also very conservative, like a 1940s secretary. But what Adrian will love here is the extra-long zip running down the back, right over the derrière. He is old fashioned in his tastes, but when she is dressed like this, wearing also her Palestinian medal, attesting to her good works, her global sympathies, her courageous heart, then he always imagines her as one of those war-time heroines who went undercover for the French Resistance.

MANAGER: One night?

SOPHIE: Yes, just one night. But two keys. We'll need a key each.

Once inside the room she sits on the tightly made-up bed, holding her mobile phone in her right hand, and waits, a picture of astonishing elegance.

Int. Hallway / Final Disciplinary Hearing. Day.

What makes us behave, conform, be (in fact) who we are? wonders Adrian. Is it because we fear the worst? Do we simply construct our entire lives as a defence against the worst thing that could happen to us?

Problem: if most of us have little or no experience of what the worst thing is, then why should we let our fears steer everything we do?

Imagine for a second – thinks Adrian as he crosses the marble floor, fresh from the hearing, fresh from that final harsh judgement, and still reeling, but not shocked by the panel's decision – imagine, yes imagine that when the worst actually happens it's not nearly as bad as we think it will be. Then go one step further. Imagine the worst thing turning out to be in fact *the best thing* that could happen. What a shocking indictment this would be of our precautionary lives.

In the middle of the hall he wonders what he will do with the rest of the day. Such words: *with the rest of his life*! He turns on his mobile phone. It loads with a half-dozen new messages from Sophie, six more to go with the four from yesterday. The inbox is clogged with dispatches.

"I LOVE U. PLEASE CALL." "WHERE R U? GOOD LUCK TODAY. AM COMING TO TOWN. MUST MEET." "AM IN TOWN. WHERE R U? WHAT HAPPENED? HAVE SURPRISE. MEET ME THISTLE HOTEL. I LOVE YOU. URGENT. YOUR WIFE." And lastly, "A PICTURE FOR YOU, MY LOVE."

Lovely Sophie. An erotic assignation. He can imagine her waiting, even now, drinking from the mini-bar. Dutch courage. Ready to beckon him to the bed. Her body making many promises. He looks at the photo she has sent. She is atop Regency, her steed. Shiny knee-high boots. Screen-siren smile. Working her old spells on him again. Good old Soph. Her beauty spellbinding him, or trying to. A tyrant of love. Oh yes, in sending him such a picture she is showing him again who is the boss. She knows how to control him, just when to dig the spurs in deep. And no art has ever moved him so much as Sophie. She has always been his most prized piece. His most cherished "still life".

He snaps shut the clamshell phone. At a trash bin, he stops. There is something he needs to do right now, before he falls back into illusion. From his finger he prises free his wedding band. He does it feverishly, tugging at it. Almost the climactic scene from *The Wizard's Apprentice*. On the edge of the volcano. And, like in a B-movie, this talismanic item won't come off easily. Why should it? Hard to put on, hard to pull off. Then finally, off it comes. And he knows what to do. It hits the bottom of the steel bin. A marriage over. *Clang*. The sound you hear when you finally fall off the end of love's bell curve. *Clang*. So that's it. He wants to cry. All the years. All the feelings. But he also wants to laugh. What high comedy. And how disappointingly banal. Far from opera or film, this ending. *Clang*. But at least it isn't corny. People put out different amounts of love. That's just how it is. Different amounts, different kinds. Nothing can be done about it. Donald had a simpler way of viewing it. *Kick. The. Bitch. Out*. Well, Adrian is following such orders at last.

He sees a figure walking towards him. The chairman from the tribunal. A dozen paces away, an extended hand, gestures of sincere sympathy.

CHAIRMAN: Adrian. Now that formal side of things is over, can't say how sorry I am personally. Honestly. And remember, you could appeal this decision. But I think I speak for everyone when I say that… what we all felt… well, as I said in my closing remarks… was that… in striking your name from the register… and rescinding your licence…

But steadily the voice trails off in volume. Soon, the chairman is just a talking mouth, no sound at all. Then, using another Donald technique, Adrian imagines doodling over the man's face with a felt pen… actually scribbling a moustache, an arrow through the head even, blacking out some teeth. Only at the end of the reverie does the chairman's voice breaks back in…

CHAIRMAN: So, have you had time to think? What will you do now?

ADRIAN: Now? Oh, maybe paint the Sistine Chapel. Try some crack cocaine, I always wanted to know what that was like.

Adrian smiles, shakes the deboned hand, and turns away, emitting a bubble of his own as he makes for the stairs: "WHAT WILL I DO NOW? HOW ABOUT CUT YOUR BRAKE CABLES. ARSEHOLE!"

At the top of the staircase he stops. Professionals flow up and down in great numbers, models of certainty, all possessors of the certainty that he has lost. But Adrian feels he can see through everybody today. And here he sees it again: *fear*. Fear of the worst thing happening. Fear everywhere guiding lives. Steering multitudes along the approved paths. And having a wild idea he slides his rump on to the stairway's broad handrail. Why not? What's to lose? One for Donald then. And ignoring a few disapproving looks from strangers, he lifts the anchoring foot and takes off down the balustrade, takes the fast route to the bottom, picking up speed very quickly, his bulk propelling him, hands locked on the rail behind him for control, his legs out, his hair blowing back, his tie flapping over his shoulder, doing one for Donald, that crazy kid always at odds with the world but always, always out there fighting, even when it seemed he wasn't, and never more so than at the end, when there was no point in fighting at all.

Faster and faster the big man goes, a human monorail, until it looks as if nothing is ever going to stop him. People at the bottom scatter in advance. They see him coming, pull each other out of the way. No one wants to get hurt after all. People want a long, happy life. Nobody wants to be crushed by a flying executive. Freeze frame. Fade to black. The End. Go figure.